The
Dragon's Banner

The Dragon's Banner is a work of fiction. All names, characters, incidents, and locations are fictitious. Any resemblance to actual persons, living or dead, events or places is entirely coincidental.

ISBN: 978-0615738130

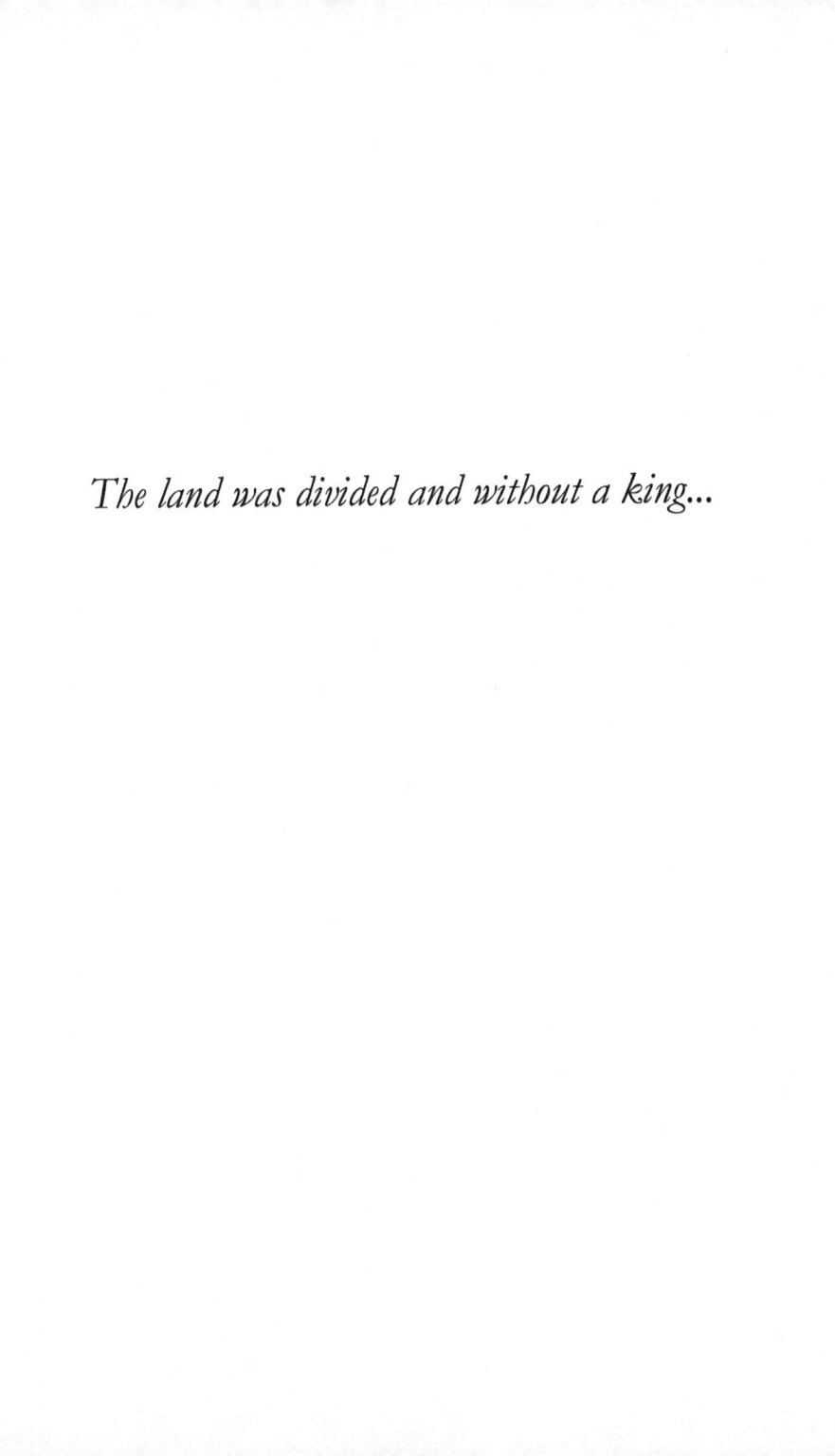

The land was divided and without a king...

Prologue

495 AD
East of the Ruins of Londinium

"God, why hast thou forsaken us so?"

Elwin looked heavenward, tears streaming from his raw, reddened eyes as wrinkled hands grasped the crude wooden cross of the altar. He grieved not for himself, for he had seen sixty winters and was tired in body and soul, ready to depart the world and its endless pains. His tears were for his flock; for the babies impaled on spikes in the village green; for the maids, whose wretched cries filled his ears as the filthy, blonde-haired invaders took them one after another to satisfy their lust; for the mothers driven to madness as they clung to the blood-soaked bodies of their murdered children, before they too were dragged off to be ravaged and slain.

For three decades Elwin had served the village, and he had found contentment in caring for these people and joy in a simple life. He had often thought to retreat to the monastery to live his final years in solitude and reflection. But he could never bring himself to leave his children, and now, if this was to be their bitter fate, he would share it with them.

The invaders had come before, savage and terrifying like God's own wrath, but never in such numbers. Always they had raided along the coast, killing and robbing, then sailing back to their homeland with their slaves and booty. Even when they stayed, they claimed only lands far to the east. Now they had crossed the narrow sea in many of their dragon-prowed boats, and they cut like a scythe deep through the unresisting countryside. They had come this time to stay, and blood and tears were their legacy for the conquered.

The village was small, not worth conquering, so torment and death became the villagers' fate. A ragged cluster of cottages grouped around a small, muddy green, the village itself was dying too. Thatched roofs were ablaze, filling the air with thick, acrid smoke. The enemy's first charge had scattered the small force of townsfolk who'd stood in defense, and the flimsy wooden stockade that had been the village's only protection was dashed and broken, its splintered remains strewn all around.

Elwin prayed softly, beseeching God Almighty to welcome his children. "Forsake them not, Lord, if their faith deserts them in their final torments. For they are simple folk and cannot grasp thy purposes. To thy wisdom and mercy I commit my body and soul, and I pray that my faith protect them if theirs should fail."

The invaders ran through the tortured village, shouting their war cries, and with torches alight they put to fire every house, every hut, every barn. They were angered, driven to rage by the fruitlessness of their expedition. For they had plunged further inland than ever before, determined to sack Londinium. But instead of a rich Roman capital they found an abandoned ruin, with nary but a handful of families living a poor existence in the old villas. Denied their plunder, they focused their wrath on the villagers for no other reason than these unfortunates were the ones standing in their path.

Those of the townsfolk who were able to reach the chapel had sought refuge inside, barring the door with wooden benches. Perhaps they thought the attackers would respect the sanctuary of God's house, or possibly it was just blind fear that drove them to the one place of comfort in their hard and bitter lives.

Elwin knew better, and he could smell the smoke, heavier, closer than before. He knew that this sanctuary would soon be little more than the charnel house of the village, burned remains of the townsfolk buried under blackened beams and ash. The invaders were not here for slaves, and the village had little of value. They would let the miserable peasants burn in their house of worship, sending them to their god with fire.

Some of the village folk had escaped and fled to the old Roman fort on the bluff. Elwin prayed silently that they find the strength to hold out against the invader, though in his heart he knew it to be hopeless. They were too few to man the crumbling stone walls of the fortress, and the villagers were herders and farmers, not soldiers.

The warriors were gone, dead or off fighting each other. Since the Breaking of the Council and the death of the High King, the land was at war with itself. Brother spilled brother's blood at the behest of petty lords striving for power, while the barbarians from across the sea ravaged the land unopposed and enslaved the people.

A group of invaders was roasting villagers one at a time over a fire, demanding to know where the town's treasures were hidden. The tortured, dying peasants screamed out what few locations contained anything of value, but it availed them little. They were left to the heat and fire and cheated of the promised rewards of their confessions.

Elwin knew it would soon be over, for he felt the heat, then the flames as they began to engulf his body. The pain was great, but he cared little and endured in silence. In just a moment he would stand before God, to whose grace he had remained faithful through a life of trial and testing. His only real torments were the cries of the villagers as the flames took them. Be merciful, heavenly father, he thought, both to your faithful servant and to your people who lived in this place and now die here.

He could see the blazing section of thatch from the roof begin to fall toward him. With his last breaths he spoke softly, his regretful words barely audible, "I have failed thee, Merlin, for I have no strength to protect the child. I have done all I could, little though it was. Alone I placed him, on the last horse in the village, and sent him westward, though for protection he has only the grace of God and the amulet he wears bearing his name...Arthur."

Chapter One
The Council of Kings

475 AD - Twenty Years Before
Caer Guricon, Capital of the Kingdom of Powys

Uther Pendragon stood in the center of the fighting circle, alone and unbeaten, long hanks of dark hair framing his sun-baked face, moist with perspiration.   Around him, prostrate upon the ground, were his bruised and battered adversaries, those of the local warriors who would dare fight him in the tournament. Five he had faced, and all he had bested. Now he extended a hand to each to help them to their feet, for Uther respected courage above all things, and these men had matched with him when others had feared to do so. The metallic taste of blood was on his lips, for Cowen of Celtiborne had landed a blow before Uther took him down with a strong strike to the shoulder. With a smile, Uther pulled Cowen to his feet and gave him a hearty slap on the back.

Uther took his leave of his opponents and walked from the fighting circle across the castle courtyard. At the well he stopped and poured the bucket of icy water over his head. Thus refreshed, he stood and looked out over the town below, and the rolling, green hills of his homeland.

Tall was Uther, and strong, though he had seen only sixteen winters. It was said he could lift a bull, though such were only tales shared in the villages and the inns of his father's kingdom, where legends of the young prince were told and retold over flagons of ale. Proud he was too, haughty and noble, with the arrogance of a warrior who had never been bested. His first man he'd slain at thirteen, when he had hid himself among the host and followed his father and brothers to war.

He was old enough to be married and, as would be expected for the son of a king, there were many high noblemen ready to offer daughters and dowries, though for different reasons both father and son had shown little interest.

For Uther there was only the call of battle, cold steel in his hand, and the brotherhood of comrades in arms. Already he was the sword of his people, and it was on the bloody field that he served them, where he had already slain a score of foes in Powys' wars. He had normal desires, strong ones indeed, but willing village girls and tavern wenches were enough to satisfy his lusts, and he had no stomach for romantic dalliances or the distractions of hearth and home.

His father Constantine, King of Powys, had his own plans for the boy. The youngest of his father's sons, Uther was originally destined for the church, where a bishop's robes awaited him when his theological education was complete. But Uther would have none of it. Four times he had fled the monastery, and each time he was brought back he silently endured the Father's beating while planning his next escape.

Finally, after the thirteen year-old boy plunged from his hiding place among the camp followers into the thick of melee and slew three of the Saxon invaders, his father relented. Henceforth, Uther joined his brothers on the field of battle, and he grew into the scourge of the enemies of Powys. Still though, Constantine clung to the hope that Uther would find his way back to the clergy, and with three older sons, all married, he could indulge the thought that Uther's wife might yet be the mother church.

The enemies of Powys were many, and war was continuous. The land was divided and without a true king. It had been a man's life since the legions departed, and Britannia had bled, savaging itself as local noblemen styled themselves petty kings and fought their neighbors for hegemony. Fields lay fallow, or crops were trampled under warriors' feet, and hunger and pestilence frequently ravaged the land. To the east, invaders from across the Narrow Sea, tall blond savages with blood-chilling war cries and terrible battleaxes, plundered and conquered, enslaving the peasants and driving the local lords from their lands.

The Pendragon had the greatest claim to high kingship. Son and namesake of a governor of Britannia who had become an emperor of Rome, King Constantine had fought in Gaul in the army of Flavius Aetius and returned to wrest control of the largest of the Britannic kingdoms from the usurper Vortigern.

Vortigern, with help from the Saxon invaders to whom he had offered large swaths of the Britannic coast, had slain the old king, Brochwel and forced the king's daughter to marry him. But the slain king had been ward and friend to Constantine, who returned from the Battle of Chalons with a band of veteran warriors and swore to unseat the usurper. Rallying the old king's retainers with a cry for vengeance, Constantine marched on Powys. At Pengwern, in a battle that lasted from dawn to darkness, his army routed Vortigern's host, giving quarter to none who fell into their grasp.

Ariene, King Brochwel's daughter and only child, he was too late to save, for she had been murdered by Vortigern soon after he'd taken the throne. True vengeance also evaded Constantine, as the usurper escaped the field and fled into exile and the protection of his Saxon allies.

Constantine's victory, lineage, and years of wise and noble kingship gave him great renown and respect among the petty kings, but not suzerainty. Though all knew Britannia bled because of its fragmentation and that the invaders could only be repelled by a single strong king, none would yield their power or bend the knee to another. Unity would not come free, it would be bought with blood, and the Pendragon would bring their adversaries one by one to heel. Such was their creed and battle cry, and to this quest, Constantine and his sons had committed all.

Allies they had as well as enemies, and many of these were even now guests at Caer Guricon, come for the council called by King Constantine. All about the castle and town were the tents of their retinues, and from the battlements of the stronghold flew a row of seven banners - the coats of arms of the kings here assembled. Alone, above all the others was hung the great silver and blue standard of the Pendragon, flapping furiously in the wind.

All about, there was a whirlwind of activity, for the morrow was Easter, and King Constantine had declared a great celebration to inaugurate the council. All, it was said, would be feasted, from the kings to the lowliest camp follower, and on this holiest of days all would pray to God that Britannia's wounds be healed.

Come for the council was another man, old and stooped with age, yet agile of mind and spirit. Not a king, not a warrior, yet all assembled would hear and respect his words, and those who did not respect would fear. Uther had many companions, but the old man was his closest friend. He would come in his own time, sometimes not for several years, though usually every few months. No man held dominion over Merlin, who had helped many lords but bended his knee to none. Some called him a wizard who could summon great devilry and that no good would come from his visits. But most regarded him as a wise and learned counselor. There were even those who believed he came from far off Rome itself, to guide its lost people back into the Empire's embrace and bring back the days of happiness and plenty.

Long into the night would his father and Merlin sit in counsel, discussing what Uther could only guess, for Constantine met with Merlin alone. Grave tidings Merlin usually brought, and his warnings were heeded by the wise. Whether one thought him wizard or advisor or kingmaker, only the foolish ignored his counsel.

Merlin was fond of Uther, and he had always had time to sit with the boy, telling him tales of battles and great deeds from long ago. Uther was excited to see Merlin again, for it had been nigh on a year since the traveler had last visited Caer Guricon. But Merlin was deep in conference with his father and, his tournament battles over, Uther was bored. He wandered through the camps, seeking out comrades from past battles, for the Pendragon had been allies with all of these kings at one time or another. His great friend, Leodegrance, he found, just arrived in the company of his father, the king of Cameliard. Leodegrance had fought alongside Uther on the field of battle and had struggled against him in the tournament circle, for he was one of the few warriors who could match the young prince of Powys.

"Welcome, prince of Cameliard." Uther bellowed cheerfully to his friend. "For Powys shall ever be for you a second home."

Leodegrance turned, and his face erupted into a broad smile. "Uther Pendragon! Ah, 'tis good to see you, old friend."

Uther warmly embraced his old companion. "Come, my friend, for you must be ravenous. Begone with this camp food, for heaping plates of mutton and casks of good ale await. I pray thee, let thy servants fight with tent poles and stakes, for when you and I war, it is against different foes than these."

Leodegrance laughed deeply, and put his hand on his friend's shoulder. "Uther, my comrade, I daresay I could eat a whole sheep myself, so I will accept your invitation with joy."

The two of them made their way to the castle, talking and laughing as they walked up the winding path. Together they raided the kitchens, devouring slabs of mutton, two large geese, and loaves of bread, washed down with cups of strong wine.

Uther and Leodegrance had known each other for many years, and Powys and Cameliard were close allies. They had been born within a few days of each other, though Leodegrance was his father's only son and destined for kingship, while Uther had three elder brothers.

Though they had sworn to eat the kitchens bare, finally they had to admit defeat, for not another morsel could either of them manage, though the larders were still bursting. The two sat long, talking of many things, until a messenger came to Leodegrance, delivering him his father's bidding that he return to the camp. With regret but a full stomach, he took leave of his friend and trod back down the hill to answer his father's summons.

Uther sat long in the kitchen, silently thinking of all that was taking place. He longed to join his own father in counsel with Merlin, but he had fought this battle before and lost. He walked past the heavy oak door, which he knew would be bolted shut from the other side and, with a heavy sigh, he wandered down the path back toward the town. The miller's daughter would help him pass the time.

Behind that heavy oaken door, the king of Powys was deep

in conference with his friend and most trusted advisor. At a great wooden table they sat, on which was set a spread of meats and other foods on great silver platters, though neither had eaten a bite.

"If this is true, Merlin, then we must move at once, for it may already be too late." King Constantine was an old man, his wrinkled and careworn face framed by thick lengths of steel-gray hair. Late in life did he marry, and fifty summers he had already seen when Uther was born. His own father, the emperor, he did not remember at all, for the great man been slain in Gaul when Constantine the Younger was but a year of age.

The other man in the room also was old too, though it seemed that all men saw Merlin differently. White as snow was his hair, said some, while others claimed it was iron gray mixed with black. Some saw a man stooped with age who walked with a stick; others a strong and active one who carried his staff like a weapon and who could ride or march all day. Perhaps those who knew him best saw him truest, for in Constantine's watery eyes, Merlin appeared ageless, somehow both old and young, and certainly neither weak nor infirm.

"It is true, Constantine, for with my own eyes I have seen it. When first this word came to me, I resolved to travel north and see the state of affairs for myself. Vortigern has indeed returned from exile, and he has not only forged an alliance with the Saxons; he is near to reaching agreement with the Picts. Indeed, as we sit here he may already have done so. The Picts are to have the north, the Saxons the east, and Vortigern the west and south."

Constantine thought silently, for Merlin had always been right, and his words were beyond doubt. Finally, he took a deep breaths and spoke clearly. "It is none too soon that we have called this council, and I pray we are able to reach agreement. For if we do not stand together, I fear we shall not stand at all. Indeed, even if all six kings here assembled join us, we may yet lack the strength to triumph. We must look for other allies."

As Constantine finished speaking, he was taken by a fit of deep, dry coughs. Merlin rose and filled the king's goblet from a golden flagon that had been set on the table. Constantine nodded his thanks and took a shallow drink, clearing his throat so he could again speak.

Before Constantine could continue, Merlin did, his voice brittle, as if he were speaking of something unpleasant. "There is but one potential ally with the strength to matter in this contest, and he is well known to both of us."

"Gorlois," Constantine responded, his face contorted as if he had tasted something bitter. "He is not my friend, Merlin, nor am I his. We have fought each other many times, as you well know."

"Needs may sometimes make friends from foes, for the lands of Gorlois also would fall under Vortigern also should he conquer all. He is no fool, Gorlois, nor will he relish the thought of bending his knee to Vortigern. He will listen to an entreaty, I believe. And though he is a vulgar man and I like him no more than you do, to my knowledge he keeps his oaths."

Constantine leaned back in his great oaken chair, eyes closed as he considered the situation. Ponder as he might, he could not think of an alternative. Finally, eyes still closed, he spoke softly. "I will dispatch ambassadors to his court at once." He paused for a moment. "I will send rich gifts also, for Gorlois is a vain fool, and such shall appease his pride."

Again, Constantine was taken by a fit of coughing, though it was worse this time, and he pulled a cloth from the table to catch the spittle. When finally he was done, he quickly balled up the small rag in his massive fist, but Merlin saw the spray of crimson splotches on the white linen.

Merlin's face softened, and he looked at his companion with warmth and concern. "Constantine, my old friend, you needn't hide the truth from me. For I know well your affliction. A potion of herbs I can make that will ease your pains. After the counsel I shall depart, for only in the deep woods grow the vines I need find. I fear it shall do nothing more than ease your discomfort and give you a bit more time, for I have no power to heal that which afflicts you."

"Is that your way of telling me I'm dying, Merlin?" He

laughed, which almost sent him into another spasm of coughing. Catching himself, he continued, "That my sickness is mortal is well known to me, good friend. I am old, and I have
traveled far and seen many things. I am content with my fate,
but I cannot die and leave my kingdom to fall to Vortigern. I
will not. I must conclude these alliances before I breath my last.
And your wisdom is, as always, sound. We must have Gorlois."

The treaty with Gorlois must be carefully drafted." Merlin's
expression was stern, thoughtful. "I will do it if you will permit
me. And it should be made as strong as possible, for though
Gorlois knows that Vortigern covets his lands, yet he still might
ally with him if he feels weak or threatened. We must bind Gorlois firmly to our alliance. Perhaps a marriage."

"You speak wisdom, Merlin, but I have no daughter, loath
as I would be to consign her to Gorlois' bedchamber. Nor does
Gorlois have a daughter to wed to Uther. Where shall I find a
bride to offer?"

Long they spoke, about many things - what barons of Constantine's had suitable daughters, the terms to offer Gorlois,
who should be sent to Cornwall to make the entreaty. When
they were finished, Constantine had one last matter he wished to
discuss. "I want to send an emissary to Rome, for I have not lost
hope that the empire may yet return to these shores."

Merlin looked at him doubtfully. "My friend, I fear that we
can expect neither imperial aid nor the return of the legions to
our shores. Many chances there were in the last century for a
strong and worthy man to invigorate the empire, yet all these
chances went to dust, destroyed by treachery and murder. Stili-
cho, Aetius, your father. I knew them all, Constantine, and all
were strong men and capable, yet each fell to an assassin's blade.
The small men, the deceivers, they have won, I fear."

"Alas, Merlin, you may be right, yet I feel compelled to try.
After Chalons, Aetius swore to me that he would march to Britannia and reclaim the land for the empire. We were to leave as
soon as he set things to rights in Italia. He rode south, but he
never returned. I beseeched him to take the purple, for I knew
Valentinian was unworthy and not to be trusted, and his mother,

that hellspawn Galla Placidia, even less. The army would have followed him, as would I. But Aetius, for all his petty scheming, was a loyal general of the empire, and he could not be persuaded. So it was that he was murdered by a jealous and unworthy master, and by the hands of Aetius' friends, Valentinian himself was slain in vengeance."

Constantine doubled over in another spasm of coughing, and Merlin leapt up to succor his friend. The coughing, which had seemed to be a severe attack, ceased when Merlin placed his hand on Constantine's back, as though the king were somehow soothed by his companion's touch.

Constantine grabbed his goblet and took a drink, clearing his throat forcefully. "Thank you, my friend. I am fine now. And, as I was saying, I cannot help but hope that another Aetius has risen in Rome and that the empire may yet be saved and restored to its glory. If this be just an old man's wistful musing, I know not, but we have had scant news from Rome since Aetius died, and none at all in nigh on ten years. It is long past time we know for certain - will the empire be restored, or are we truly alone?"

Merlin sighed softly. "I am not hopeful of success from such a quest, yet I can see no harm in trying. Whom do you propose to send?"

"I have considered it, and I have decided to send Uther. Alas, Merlin, I fear he and I have been as water and oil. I would that things between us had been different. I tell you truly, Merlin, that Uther is, in many ways, the most like me. All my sons are noble men and fill me with a father's pride, but my youngest was born with the lion's heart. Would that he were eldest, yet men cannot control such matters."

Merlin looked concerned. "Uther will not want to leave you when battle is in prospect."

Constantine's face betrayed a slight smile. "Indeed. But the boy must learn that duty and honor demand more than courage in battle. Uther is the youngest, so he is destined to serve his elder brother, and he must do so in many ways, not just with axe and sword. Perhaps such a journey will teach this to my son, for he will see many things and come to know a world larger than

Powys or Britannia."

"There is greatness in Uther." Merlin spoke abruptly, with considerable emotion. "I feel it strongly. Such travels, I believe, will give him much. I think your plan is a wise one."

They spoke a bit longer, but finally Merlin bade his friend to retire, for he was weak and fatigued, and the morrow would be a long and trying day. Taking leave of his companion, Constantine walked to his bedchamber, but he knew he would not sleep. My body is dying, he thought, but my mind is still good. I will see that my kingdom does not fall, by God, whatever I must do. Just give me the time, Lord, for there is much work ahead.

After his father had retired, Uther found Merlin sitting before the fire in the great hall. The advisor, some said wizard, sat quietly in a large oak chair. Next to him, on a small wooden table, sat a silver plate and a flagon of spiced wine. On the plate was a small honey cake, only half eaten. The room was quiet except for the crackling of the fire and the sound of the wolf-hounds gnawing on bones in front of the hearth.

Uther entered from behind, but as he walked through the doorway, without turning around Merlin laughed. "Ah, Uther, my boy. I thought you would find me. It has been too long. Much too long, my young friend. How have you fared since last I was here? When was that...midyear last? Yes, it has been far too long."

Uther stopped to play with the hounds, for they leapt up when he entered the room and ran over to greet him. "You have been missed, Merlin. Indeed, Caer Guricon is not the same when you are abroad."

Merlin smiled and motioned for Uther to sit. "Grave tasks I had to fulfill, and it is they that have kept me so long from the company and comforts of Caer Guricon. Indeed, it was a cold winter where I traveled long, and the warmth of this hearth and company would have been most welcome."

"War is coming, is it not, Merlin?" Uther walked past the dogs and took one of the other seats in the room. "For I have read many signs, not only that my father has called the council. He is deeply troubled, as I have never seen before." Uther paused uncomfortably before continuing. "And he is ill, gravely so, I fear, though he thinks he hides it."

Merlin tried to suppress a smile, for though he knew Uther well, the boy still surprised him. "He is ill, Uther, and it is indeed serious. I am going to make him a potion that will ease his sufferings, yet he is old and his time grows short."

"I feared it was so." Uther was somber, his voice gentle. "I have noted the difference in him for some time. Alas, I fear I have not been the son he wished me to be, and though I am who I am, I regret that I have been a disappointment to him."

"Nay, Uther," replied Merlin. "You are far wide of the truth, for your father is proud of you and loves you greatly. I have seen the two of you clash for years, to my great amusement, for he is more akin to you than to any of your brothers. Such it is that ofttimes like finds itself at odds with like, and more so when both are strong of will and spirit." Merlin saw the disbelief on Uther's face, but before the boy could respond, he spoke further. "Uther, as you trust in my word, believe me in this, for I speak the truth. Put your heart at rest, for we all have many trials ahead of us, and I would not have you troubled over grief that exists only in your mind."

Uther was silent, lost in his own thoughts about his father, himself, their many arguments. He got up from his chair and stood in front of the hearth, his eyes following the flickering fire. Above the hearth was hung a finely crafted sword, polished but well-worn, with a leather grip smooth from long use.

Uther's fingers traced the raised lettering on the hilt of his grandfather's sword. "Legio XX," he read softly to himself from the finely crafted etchings. The old man had died long before Uther was born, but he had achieved greatness. He had risen to become an emperor of Rome, only to be slain by his enemies through some unrecorded treachery. Uther never tired of listening to the stories of his famous grandsire, still remembered in these lands as Constantine II, King of the Britons.

Merlin let the boy think for a few moments before continuing. "Your grandsire was a great man, Uther, and though it was his fate never to see his newborn son, I think he would be proud of your father. Constantine has spent his life in the shadow of a sire who wore the purple, a man he never knew. Never has he held his achievements to be enough. But so it often goes with father and son. I would offer you some council if you will have it."

Uther had been running his fingers down the flat of the blade as he listened to Merlin, and now he turned to face his friend. "Of course, Merlin. Your counsel I always take to heart."

"Uther, ever have you and I been friends, for always I have seen in you much strength and virtue. You were born, I fear, with the heart of a king, more suited to an elder son than the younger. Yet, you are what you are, and 'tis likely that your eldest brother shall be king, and you shall be left to serve your family in whatever ways he deems best.

"Young though you are, I have never seen your equal in battle, yet to be a great warrior is not enough for a prince. For it is easy to fight any battle, even a hopeless one, and die with honor, yet far more difficult to forego conflict, or to treat with enemies and seek to make them allies. I would have you learn this and to understand more of such things, for though I know not where your future will lead, I feel that there will be greatness for you - and victory, and strife, and heartbreak. Be ready for all that comes, and know that not every foe will battle you openly on the field with armor and sword."

Uther was listening intently, for if there was anyone whose council the brash young prince valued, it was Merlin. Silently he returned to his chair and sat, the ancient oaken seat creaking as his great bulk settled into it.

Merlin leaned toward his young friend and spoke quietly but firmly. "I would pray thee to obey your father and do whatever he may bid you do, for now is not the time for a test of wills between you. Your road forward, I foresee, shall lead places you cannot now imagine and bring you great joys and sadness, glorious victory and terrible loss. But now, your father needs you, no less than any of your brothers, for his strength fails and he now faces a great struggle."

"So it is to be war then?" Uther spoke it as a question, but he did not wait for an answer. "And we shall be sorely pressed. Is this not truth?"

"It is." Merlin looked at Uther with admiration and approval. "More than you now know, for victory shall hinge as much on diplomacy and the search for allies than on courage in the field."

Uther frowned dismissively. "Bah! I am no diplomat to sit and bandy words with pompous lords when battle is in the offing."

"Indeed," interjected Merlin, "this is of what I speak. You are a prince of a great house, Uther, not a common soldier. Your honor and duty will demand much of you that you do not desire. If needs be you serve your father and people as diplomat, then so must you do."

Uther did not argue, yet Merlin saw the frown still upon his face. "Uther, think you the empire came into being long ages past simply by strength of arms? Indeed, have you learned nothing from your father's own recountings of his battles with Aetius against the Huns? Battles that would have been lost had Aetius not forged an alliance with his enemies to face the greater foe? Think you they wished to treat with old adversaries and seek their aid? Had Aetius and your father and their comrades thought as you do, Rome itself would be a generation in ashes now."

There was long silence as they sat together. Uther rose and threw a large log into the hearth, grabbing a poker and pushing it into place over the hottest embers. The wood hissed for a few seconds and quickly caught, and soon the fire was roaring, the rush of heat forcing back the chill of the damp spring evening.

Uther was the first to break the silence. "You speak wisely, Merlin, as always, yet I do not know if I can be what you seek. I have no tongue for such pursuits, nor the patience. But, I give you my oath that I shall try to complete whatever task is given me, for I am a loyal son of my house."

Merlin smiled. "Uther, my friend - for boy no longer seems a fit name for the man sitting here with me - I am proud of you, though not at all surprised. You surmise correctly that war and strife are coming, for the whole north is allied against us, and the barbarians from across the narrow sea too. We shall be sorely pressed to withstand their onslaught when it comes."

"We should strike first." Uther was almost shouting, his voice much louder then he'd intended. "For we shall take them unawares and seize the initiative." He softened his voice considerably.

"Indeed, my friend, your battle tactics are sound, and had we two legions of old assembled and ready to march I should agree with you. But think you, are we prepared for war? Last year's harvest was bad, ravaged by pestilence and early frost. Were the levy to be called now, and the spring planting abandoned, we would face famine by winter. Nay, we must have this year's harvest, as must our foes. After harvest, winter shall come soon, and the snows will make campaigning difficult. Thus, war shall not likely be upon us until next year, for beyond the harvest there is much else to prepare. This shall be no borderland dispute, but a battle for all of Britannia, and the smiths and armorers have immense toils ahead before a great army takes the field."

Merlin looked intently at Uther. "And allies we must still find, for we shall be overwhelmed without aid. This council shall end, as all such do, with half-promises and unfinished negotiations. Long after the kings have departed shall diplomacy continue, for though all will fall if they do not band together, still will they pick at old wounds and nurse ancient grievances. Great efforts and even more profound sacrifices we shall make if we are to withstand this test." Merlin stopped as if he was done, and Uther sat quietly, pondering the old man's words. Finally, Merlin spoke again. "I know not what part you are destined to play in all of this, my dear friend, but I feel that in some way it will be greater than you now imagine. Embrace your fate, Uther, and fear no challenge. You will find, I pray, that you are more than just a great warrior."

The two of them sat for a while longer, enjoying the fire, as the conversation turned to more pleasant and frivolous matters. As he usually did, Uther convinced Merlin to tell him a tale of times past. Though Merlin appeared to him much as he did to

Constantine, Uther knew that his mysterious friend was very old indeed, and he had known many of the great men of times past.

Finally, after talking long into the evening, Merlin rose slowly. "Well, my friend, I am not as youthful as you, and I have had a long and hard road of late. It is time for me to retire. I shall see thee again on the morrow."

With that, he glided quickly to the door and disappeared into the corridor beyond, leaving Uther to sit long into the night and ponder the words they had shared. The fire had burned down to ash before Uther finally rose and made his way through the near-darkness to his chamber, his mind still deep in thought.

Easter morning dawned clear and cool. The town church could not hold all those who had come for the council, so tents had been erected in a great field so mass could be held where all could attend. All except the nobles, for they celebrated Easter in the Pendragon chapel in the castle, where the kings received communion from Tremorinus, Archbishop of Londinium. Though aged and frail, the revered churchman had come at Constantine's bidding, and his presence added solemnity and weight to the council set to begin the next day.

Before him on their knees were seven kings, bareheaded and silent. Twice he passed before them, bringing them first bread, then wine, and when he was finished he bade them rise. When he had concluded the Easter mass, the archbishop led the assembled kings and barons in prayer for the success of the council. His voice was old and wavering, but there was strength still in it.

In conclusion he said, "And so, oh mighty God, we pray to thee to give this noble company here assembled the strength to save the land and people, for they fight in your name, and are humble and faithful servants to thee."

When the services were done the kings and lords retired to the courtyard, for everywhere there were tables laden with food and drink, and King Constantine feasted his noble guests. All around the courtyard of the castle were strewn garlands of early spring flowers, and the tables were set with plates of gold and services of silver.

In the town and the camps below, the retinues of the kings and the people of the town also celebrated, for Constantine had declared that all would be feasted from his stores. Over great pits in the green wild boar were roasted, and game birds were piled in great multitudes, for the hunters of Caer Guricon had ranged far and wide over the king's lands to prepare for the festivities.

Though it was Easter and declared a day of rejoicing, there was no break in the work for Constantine, for he was host to six other kings. On the morrow they would convene the council, and Constantine did not intend for any bad feelings to arise before it even began. He had seen more than one alliance shattered by an insult delivered at a feast or careless actions driven by too much wine.

Indeed, there was ill blood between some of those assembled, and Constantine and Merlin strove hard to keep the peace and good feeling. Disputes would be common enough when the council was in session, but today the king wanted his guests mirthful and relaxed.

Uther surprised his father, for he was among the kings all day, drawing from each stories of battles they had fought and even telling of his many escapes from the monastery, which brought King Pellinore and King Rience to great laughter when two had seemed about to argue.

Long was the day, and after the midday meal was finished there were minstrels and entertainments of every kind and a grand tournament, where Uther claimed the victory, besting Leodegrance in the final round.

At dusk the celebrations ended in the town and the camps, but in the castle there was a supper for the kings and their sons. All were in good spirits and the revels lasted well into the night. The last one to retire was Uther Pendragon, who had taken Merlin's counsel to heart and had impressed all present with not only his skill at arms, but also his honor and dignity.

The council was convened the next day after the kings broke

their fast together. The meal was simple after the feasting of the day prior, just bread and cheese and salt pork and fruits, and strong ale. When they were assembled, the arch-bishop led all in a prayer for their success and declared the council in session. Present in addition to Constantine and Merlin were the six other kings, all proud and lordly and each with his own concerns and goals.

Lot, king of Luthien far to the north, closest to the Pictish allies of Vortigern and most threatened by them. Lot was distrustful of the southern kings, and reluctant to commit any of his forces other than to his troubled border.

Urien, the youthful king of Rheged, no older than Uther himself and also a mighty warrior. Rheged was well north of Powys, straddling the great wall built by the Emperor Hadrian. Rheged and Luthien had been sometimes friends, sometimes enemies, though recent dangers had pushed them closer together. Urien had only recently succeeded his father and none knew his mind as yet.

Rience, king of Gwynned, just north and east of Powys, an arrogant and warlike monarch, not well-liked by his neighbors, most of whom he had fought at one time or another. A good warrior, but vain, he thought himself stronger than he was.

Vortiporius, even younger than Urien, who had just ascended the throne of Dyfed, along the coast west of Powys, after his father Aurelius was slain in battle in Ireland. He was aggressive and ill-tempered, and though just a boy he was clever and hard to read.

Ogyruan, father of Leodegrance and king of Cameliard in south, bordering Cornwall. Constantine and Ogyruan were close friends, and Powys and Cameliard had long been allies. He would almost certainly support Constantine, though the others knew this and would pay little heed to his entreaties, thinking he and Constantine to be of one voice.

Pellinore, king of the Isles, was also a warrior of great renown. He had allied with Aurelius, father of Vortiporius, for both claimed lands in Ireland and together they had sought to enforce their rule. Vortiporius blamed Pellinore for his father's

death for failing to aid him in battle. In truth, Pellinore was himself sorely pressed when Aurelius marched into an ambush, and
there was little he could have done, but the bad blood persisted.

Thus were these seven free kings of Britannia assembled,
for the others were pledged to the banner of Vortigern. To the
east the Saxon invaders held the coasts, and in the far north the
barbarous Picts hated all those of the south and would fight for
Vortigern so they might invade and pillage rich lands.

There was one other lord of import and power, and though
not sworn to Vortigern, he had refused to attend the council.
Gorlois of Cornwall ruled vast lands in southwestern Britannia
and commanded a veteran army, which he had used time and
again to bully his neighbors. A corrupt and devious lord, Gorlois was cruel, and he was liked by few. Most of those assembled
were relieved that he was not in attendance, but Constantine and
Merlin knew that Gorlois' army must be added to the alliance or
they would lack the strength to defeat Vortigern.

"Once again, welcome to each of you, great kings of Britannia." Constantine stood at the head of the table as he began to
address to the council. "My heartfelt gratitude to all of you for
accepting my invitation. It has been far too long since I have
seen some of you, my brothers.

"We are met here to discuss a matter of grave import to all
of us, for the usurper Vortigern is an enemy of each and every
lord here assembled. Indeed, many of you have fought battles
against each other, and some have met me on the field as well.
But though we have had disputes, we are all loyal Britons, and
I have asked you to come here because Britannia needs all of
its kings in this time of trouble. Vortigern invites the invader
to our shores as his allies and mercenaries. Already much of
the eastern coast has fallen. There were kings there, friends of
mine, and of some of you as well, who now lie unburied in the
smoking ruins of their castles.

"He rouses the barbarians of the far north to march south,
pillaging and burning as they go. Savage and godless, the Picts
are a deadly threat to all, and first to our northern brethren here
seated. Few of you are old enough to recall when I reclaimed

the throne of Powys from this usurper, after he slew King
Brochwel and dishonored and murdered that noble monarch's
daughter. Many of your fathers stood with me then and were
my allies, for they were outraged by Vortigern's fiendish deeds,
and their hearts cried out for justice.

"But now it is more than justice at stake, more than the
return of a single throne to one with rights to claim it. For this
time Vortigern has many times the strength he did when last I
fought him. Indeed, he has the power to crush every kingdom
and rule all of Britannia with an iron fist. Our disputes and
grudges are of little import, for if we do not stand together
then we shall fall, and those who survive defeat would live as
the usurper's slaves. I shall not live as such, and I will face the
enemy alone if needs be."

Constantine looked out over his guests as he spoke. "I am
known to all here assembled, and I have ruled longer than any
at this table. My father was not only imperial governor of Britannia, but also emperor of Rome, and I present this lineage to
support my claim to the high kingship. I ask all of you to join
our alliance and name me war leader so that I may again defeat
the usurper. I claim now no lands or spoil, no dominion over
you or the rule of your kingdoms, only your support in facing
this deadly foe."

Constantine paused, for he could feel his own weakness.
With every fiber of endurance left to him he struggled to stand
firm and speak in a clear and commanding voice. His body
ached, and his tired legs throbbed. But weakness was something
he dared not show here, for these kings would follow him only
if they thought he had the strength to lead.

"And you, brave kings of the north, Lot and Uriens, who
have fought the Picts many times. Think you that alone you can
defeat this dark coalition, for the savages from the north will be
streaming south ere long, and your villages and castles lie in their
path. And you, Rience, for your lands lie north and east of my
own, closer in both directions to our foes."

His gaze moved down the table. "You, lords of the south,
think you that if Lothian and Gwynned and Powys fall that

you shall be able to stand on your own? Nay, for if we stand not together our enemy will destroy us one at a time until none remain to challenge his rule."

Constantine paused again, resting for an instant while he allowed his guests to consider his words. "I propose, therefore, that we leave this council sworn and proclaimed to an alliance to meet the foe and drive him into the sea. Join me, my brother kings, and together we shall have the strength to gain our victory."

Finished with his opening speech, Constantine, his legs on fire with pain, slowly lowered himself into his seat. His voice had remained true. It had wavered perhaps once or twice, but nothing that would be unduly noted. He thought, how will I get through not only this council but the war that is coming as well? Blessed be Merlin's concoction, for it has kept my accursed cough at bay. And he promises me a stronger potion when he is able to find the plants he needs. Perhaps that will be enough, for Merlin is wise and resourceful. I pray it be so.

His thoughts were interrupted as King Rience rose to address the council. This is one you must watch, Constantine thought silently, for he may be trouble.

"I thank King Constantine for his hospitality." Rience spoke loudly, his voice firm, but more brittle and less commanding than Constantine's. "We all know his words are to be seriously considered, for he is a wise and noble man. Yet have we proof that this coalition is as dire as he tells? For many have tried to ally with the Picts, with naught to show for it other than bitter failure and murdered ambassadors."

Rience paused, his forehead furrowed as he looked over the table. "And if we send our armies to meet this enemy, how can we know that other foes, perhaps even some at this table, will not take advantage to settle accounts? Indeed, as our host declared, we have all had our battles among ourselves. If I commit all of my warriors, might another hold back seeking to gain advantage at home while we win the victory abroad?"

He moved his gaze down the table as he continued his speech. "Who shall lead the armies in the field? I declare before all that

I would follow Constantine, for he is a renowned warrior, and his lineage is great and noble. Yet we have heard stories that our host is ill. Pray tell, are we to follow one of Constantine's sons? Indeed, his sons are all noble and brave, yet have they the stature that six kings should serve under them?"

Constantine rose abruptly, though his body was wracked with pain, and he slammed his hand one the table. "Old I am, my friend Rience, with my greener days long past, yet strength I have remaining for one more war. Pledge your forces to this battle, and I shall lead them."

So went the council, for each king had his own fears and ambitions, and there would be much talking before any agreement could be reached. All through the day they bantered and into the night, when Constantine finally closed the deliberations for the day, bidding all to sup with him and return on the morrow.

Uther wandered through the camps, for the council was closed to all but the kings and their advisors, and he was bored. The dawn had been clear and cool, but by midday the sun had grown warm and Uther took off his cloak. The camps were busy with everyday tasks, cookfires burning and washerwomen kneeling along the river doing their daily work. In the distance he could hear a smith banging on his anvil, likely repairing some armor or weapon damaged in the tournament the day prior.

Uther was well known, for despite his young age he had already won great glory on the field of battle, and as he passed by commoners they jumped aside and bowed. He greeted them with a simple nod and continued on his way, walking slowly from the river to the edge of the forest. He was about to turn around and walk back to the castle when he heard his name being called.

"Lord Uther, greetings to you. Would you honor me by joining me for a flagon of ale?"

Uther turned and saw a familiar face. Lord Elisedd, one of his father's most important retainers, and a substantial baron in his own right.

"Lord Elisedd, it shall be my pleasure to join you. Indeed,

the day has warmed more than I expected, and some ale would be most welcome."

Uther walked over, and he and Elisedd locked hands on arms in a warm greeting. Elisedd called to his servants to bring ale and motioned for Uther to sit at a large table that was set before his blue and white tent.

A servant came rushing over, with a large flagon and two silver cups. Placing the cups on the table, he filled each and then bowed. Elisedd waved him off and, leaving the pitcher on the table, he hastily departed.

Uther and Elisedd talked cheerily, for though the baron was much older, they had met many times and were friends of a sort. They had taken the field together twice too, winning victories on both occasions. Elisedd was speaking of the council, for rumors were rife throughout the camps, but Uther's attention was suddenly lost to his companion, for he saw, partially covered by the flap of the great tent, the most beautiful girl he had ever laid eyes upon.

Elisedd soon noticed he had lost his young friend's attention, and then he realized why. He laughed gently at his youthful friend. "Ah, I see you have noticed my daughter. Indeed, you have seen her many times, yet perhaps not for several years." The baron, an amused grin on his face, called out. "Igraine, come here, for I would have you greet Lord Uther."

The girl Uther had been watching walked smoothly to her father's side. Indeed, this was no girl, but a woman of surpassing beauty and grace. A blue velvet gown she wore, with white lace along the collar and cuffs. Her coppery red hair glistened in the sunlight as it cascaded over her shoulders and down her back in tousled curls.

"Lord Uther Pendragon, my daughter Igraine."

Igraine bowed to Uther, and though she said nothing until bidden to do so, she smiled sweetly at the young prince.

Uther returned the smile but almost found himself tongue-tied. "Igraine, it is my great pleasure to see you. I trust your journey was a pleasant one." His speech was halting, nervous… very unlike Uther Pendragon.

She raised her head to look into his eyes. "Indeed, Lord Uther, I have enjoyed our travels and our stay here very much."

Her voice was soft and pleasant, and Uther spoke long with her, for he found he could listen to her voice forever. Finally, he took his leave of Elisedd and his magnificent daughter, for it was long past time he returned to the castle to see if his father had need of him.

He walked a bit and then looked back to get a last glance at her, and their eyes met, for she was doing the same. Uther Pendragon, who had coolly killed three men in battle at the age of thirteen found that his heart was beating wildly as he walked up through the town to the castle.

There he indeed found tasks that needed completing, and he set to work. There was a dispute between two lords that needed to be settled and, with his father in council and his brothers all busy, it fell to him. He listened to both, though the argument between them was tiresome and petty, and when they had finished, he made his judgment. The loser began to protest, but Uther silenced him with a cold stare, for despite his youth, all knew he was a great warrior and that his patience was short.

After he'd finished with the feuding lords, he had to deal with some merchants, for House Pendragon was preparing for war, and Constantine was buying every manner of provision and supply. The traders were as argumentative as the lords, and Uther had to carefully review the contracts with Carwin, his father's master of the treasury. It was many hours before all was resolved, and after he was done Uther sat on a bench in the courtyard and rubbed his aching forehead.

By God, he thought, rather would I face a dragon in single combat than these duties of kingship. Merlin was right - more there is to wise rule than prowess in battle, he thought to himself. Would I be able to master all of this? Perhaps it is best that I am youngest, for I shall be the sword of my house, and thus shall be my place. Let my brothers review accounts and settle petty feuds between vassals.

Still on his mind was Igraine, for he could not banish her visage from his thoughts. While listening to the lords or haggling with the merchants, never was she more than a moment from the forefront of his mind. Sitting on the bench he resolved to see her again, and after dark he slipped out of the castle and back down to the camps. He didn't want to cause any kind of commotion; he just wanted to see Igraine and have some time to talk to her. So instead of walking openly into the camp, he snuck around the rear of Igraine's tent and called to her.

"Igraine," he said several times in a hushed voice. "Do not be scared...it is Uther Pendragon."

His hand was pressed against the fabric of the tent, and finally he heard movement from the other side. He felt some-one pressing against his hand from the other side.

"Lord Uther." He recognized the voice at once as Igraine's. "It is late, my lord."

Uther pressed his lips against the tent. "Indeed it is. I would speak with you if you are willing. Can you leave the camp with-out anyone noticing?"

"Yes, I think so." She was whispering softly. "Stay where you are and I will come to you as quickly as I may."

Uther heard her move inside the tent for a time, and then there was silence. He stood there for perhaps fifteen minutes, listening to his heart thump as it had only ever done in battle. Finally, he heard soft footsteps approaching, and then Igraine stood before him. She was clad in a pale green dress woven from the finest material and decorated with delicate lace. Her hair was pulled tight, with an intricate braid running down her back. Ear-rings of gold and silver dangled from her lobes, and she wore a necklace of precious stones. Her fingers were adorned with rings, including one set with a magnificent blue sapphire. Uther took note and smiled, for surely she had not been resting in her tent so attired.

She bowed gracefully. "Good evening, my lord."

"I beg you, call me Uther, and I shall call you Igraine."

She flushed slightly, but answered quickly. "So I shall, Uther. Pray tell, what brings you out so late while all others sleep?"

She is bold, Uther thought with satisfaction. So different from the other women he knew, and so enthralling. What is it about her that so draws me in? "You do, my lady, for since we spoke earlier, you have been much on my mind, and I had to see you again." Too forward, he thought, you will scare her.

But she only smiled. "Indeed? I am most gratified that you feel so. Shall we walk? We could speak more at ease rather than whisper."

"I would be delighted," he replied. She began walking slowly, and he fell in beside her.

"I love the night." She looked up at the stars and the moon just rising, nearly full, above the silhouette of the castle. "It is so peaceful. Quiet, yet there is much to hear if you listen."

"Never have I thought about it before." Uther looked up at the sky as he spoke. "But it is indeed so."

She shivered slightly. "There is a chill in the air, for spring is still tentative, playing coyly with us."

Uther removed his cloak and placed it gently over her shoulders. "Until spring commits, we shall have to make our own way."

"Thank you my lor...I mean Uther. You are very kind. Though I venture that I see a side of you that not many have. I am grateful that you have shown it to me."

Uther stopped walking and looked at her. "And I have never met anyone like you, Igraine. You are different...special. Intelligent, indeed, and gracious and kind."

"You make me blush." She smiled, looking back at him. She started walking again, and Uther kept pace. "I have known of you as a hero for years now, but never did I imagine what you were actually like."

They walked long and spoke of many things. This is not proper, Uther thought more than once, for me to be alone with her at night. But he didn't care, for this was where he wished to be. Never one for doing a thing merely because he was told or expected to do so, he would not start now.

Finally, he realized with a start that the early dawn light was rising, chasing away the curtain of night. "Quickly...I must get you back to your tent before anyone awakes and finds you gone."

When they reached the edge of the camp, Uther peered carefully around, and seeing no one, he bade Igraine go back to her tent, lest she be caught.

"I shall return tomorrow night." He spoke softly to her, great kindness in his voice. "I promise. Forget me not before then." And with that he was gone, racing up the road to the castle as the morning sun cast its first tentative rays over the town.

Return he did, the next night and every other of the council, and each time, they walked and spoke until dawn, parting in the morning with greater longing and sadness. On the dawn of the day she was set to depart with her father and his entourage, she took Uther's hand and dropped something into it, closing his fist over the bauble. She stretched herself upon her toes, for he was much taller than she, and kissed him softly on the lips, before she giggled to herself and disappeared around the side of the tent.

Uther opened his hand and looked at his palm. In it was a beautiful silver ring with a perfect blue sapphire.

Just after dawn Uther awaited his father, for he was determined to speak with him about Igraine. He sat in one of the lesser halls where Constantine typically spent his days meeting with counselors and reviewing the business of the kingdom. Now, of course, he was also preparing for war, and his days had become longer, for there was not time enough to attend to all that needed to be done.

Indeed, the king's day was beginning early, for Uther had been sitting no more than ten minutes when he heard footsteps approaching. "Ah, Uther, my son." Constantine spoke as he walked through the door, his voice loud but hoarse from days of arguing at the council. "Glad I am you are here, for I would speak with you."

God, he has become old and frail, Uther thought, as he watched his father enter the room. The old man, once so strong and energetic now limped to his seat, as if each step were a misery. "I would speak with you as well, father."

"I have a task for you, my son, and I bid you do as I ask and not fight me. You and I have had many clashes, and though often I have wished for you to be more obedient, I have come to be proud that my son is a man of resolve. I would take back much of what has been said between us."

Uther opened his mouth to speak, but Constantine raised his hand. "Nay, my son, let me continue. For I would send you on a journey now, though I know you will not wish to go with war brewing. Yet I bid that you obey me in this, and that it not be a test of wills between us." He paused and looked into his son's steel-gray Pendragon eyes. "Uther, I ask you for your help on this. I need your help."

Uther was taken aback, for never had his father spoken thusly to him. It was strange, for he felt both strength and weakness in Constantine, as if great resolve was gathered to overcome crushing fatigue. Though he wanted to talk about Igraine, Uther could do naught at this moment but listen to his father's words. "What would you have me do, father?"

"The council has ended." Constantine's voice cracked as he spoke, and he paused to clear his throat. "Much have we achieved, though great efforts remain before us. Yet, the kings have made one demand...that I send an emissary to seek aid from the empire. I know not if this be a fool's errand or no, but I must honor their request, and in doing so I must send a delegation of high rank. Of all my sons, Uther, you have no wife to leave behind while you embark on such a long journey."

Uther winced at his father's mention of a wife, thinking again of Igraine, though Constantine did not notice, and he continued his entreaty. "Also, of all my sons, indeed of all my nobles, you are the greatest warrior, and I shall fear less for you on a long and dangerous journey. Go to Rome, Uther, and bring the emperor our entreaties that he aid us, as Flavius Aetius promised me so many years ago. Bring me back your report on the state of the empire, for we have had no word in many long years. I would that you do this just for me, for I would know myself if there is any hope of the legions returning. But I need you to do it for the council as well, for if we find there is no help from abroad, at least they will know for certain that we stand or fall on their actions."

Uther sat silently for a moment, surprised by what his father had asked of him. Were it not for the prospect of war and his feelings for Igraine, he would long for such a journey, for he sought adventure and never before had his father entrusted him with an important task such as this.

"Very well, father." Uther did not see how he could refuse. "I shall do as you ask of me. I shall go to Rome, and if there are allies there, I shall find them."

"Excellent." Constantine looked proudly upon his youngest son. "You have my full confidence, Uther. And you shall see many things, wonders that your brothers likely never shall. You will be forever changed by this journey, my son. I know, for I have been where you now go."

Constantine leaned over and put his hand on Uther's shoulder. "I have spoken with King Ogyruan, and Leodegrance will join you on your journey, for I wanted you to have a trusted friend at your back. Leodegrance will be a better king for what he experiences on these travels."

Constantine rose from his seat, though the effort was clearly painful. Uther got up also, and the two men embraced warmly. Uther had not mentioned Igraine to his father, for he thought to wait until he returned. He did not want her to mourn him if he was fated not to come back from his great journey, though little did he understand her feelings if he thought he could save her from grief if he fell. He resolved to ride to her father's stronghold and speak with her before he left, but he found himself compelled to depart almost at once and lost the chance. Less than a fortnight after his father bade him go, Uther was on the southern coast boarding ship for Gaul. Igraine would have to wait until he returned.

Merlin stood on a bluff and watched Uther's ship sail away. He spoke softly to himself. "There sails a servant of you, the new God, and he is faithful to thee. I feel that he shall be a mighty force in what is to happen, though I cannot divine what role he is to play. He will suffer terrible torment, I fear, and win great glory and power. I speak now to thee, oh God of the

Christians, I who am a relic of the old deities, whose power was in root and branch and raging rapid from the dawn of time. Into his hands, and those of his line, I shall place what remains of that power, that new and old may be as one to heal the wounds of this ravaged and bleeding land."

Chapter Two
The Great Journey

495 AD
The Narrow Sea

Uther Pendragon was strong and powerful, and despite his young age he'd slain many a foe in battle and never met an adversary he couldn't best. Until now. For the Narrow Sea was like no enemy Uther had ever encountered, and against its assault he lay prostrate, leaning over the wale of the ship in such distress as he had never known.

Leodegrance at first made playful fun of his friend, such a valiant hero reduced to infirmity. But so great was Uther's agony that his companion soon ceased his amusement and tried to sooth him any way he could. Leodegrance had spent many days on the fishing boats along Cameliard's coast, and he was not overly distressed by the sea's fury, rough though this crossing had been.

Uther's torment was prolonged by the need to sail south as well as east, for northern Gaul was said to be overrun by the Franks and, as such, too perilous a route for their small band. To the south the Visigothic king held large sections of Gaul and Hispania as Legatus of the emperor. Uther's father had fought the Huns alongside Theodoric the Visigoth, under Flavius Aetius. In the aftermath of battle, he had attended the great Gothic king as he lay mortally wounded on the field of Chalons. Likely they would receive welcome or at least succor in the court of the Visigoths, where Theodoric's son, Euric, ruled.

They would travel by sea to Aquitania, then across southern Gaul and through the mountain passes into Italia. Uther would have sooner fought through the guardians of Hell than stay onboard another moment, but he knew his duty, and he endured.

Through the intense discomfort he found himself thinking

time and again about Igraine. He could see her coppery red hair as it lay about her shoulders, beautiful in the sunlight. Her eyes, her lips, the sweet sound of her voice. He couldn't banish her from his thoughts for more than a few moments. Longtime companion that he was, Leodegrance could see his friend's distraction. Never had he seen Uther show any interest in a woman that outlasted a night's passion, yet this one clearly held him in her spell. Why not, he thought, for surely Uther would one day take a wife. Why not Igraine? She was of high birth and daughter one of his father's greatest barons.

"Ah, my afflicted friend, your body still fights the sea, but I fear your mind is not here. It is, I suspect, with a certain red-haired lady. Do I err?"

Uther's gaze shifted to his friend, his face ashen, looking as though even this bit of movement stirred his insides. "I cannot forget her, Leo." His voice was wavering, weak. "When we return, I shall make her mine."

"You are the son of a royal house, my friend, and you must marry. I have been betrothed since we played at battle with sticks, you and I. Igraine is the daughter of one of your father's greatest lords. It is a strong match."

"My father still hopes to see me in a priest's robes, my friend, and I fear he is as stubborn as I. But Igraine shall be mine, and if needs be I will disobey my father to make it so."

Leodegrance paused, considering the implications of such an act, but decided that counsels of patience and caution were best saved for another day. Hundreds of miles, and a long and dangerous journey lay between Uther and any fateful acts of rebellion. "Doubtless such will not be needed. I am sure your father will be pleased to see you married and settled."

"We shall see." Uther spoke then quickly thrust his head over the side and wretched, his whole body convulsing. "Gods," he rasped, "what could be left in me to come out?"

Thus went the journey across the Narrow Sea and down the Gallic coast, and it was days more before, at long last, Uther's eyes set upon the sandy shores of Aquitania. The ship made for a long stretch of open beach, and Uther was the first man ashore. Out of the surf he stumbled and onto the soft sand, where he collapsed and lay motionless in the sun.

Leodegrance laughed loudly. "Ah, my friend, I fear you have missed the solid ground under you."

"Leo, it has been days since I strode upon a surface that does not move. The sea, I fear is for others. My battles shall be on land, I trust, or I shall surely meet my doom."

They both laughed, and Leodegrance went to supervise the landing of their party, allowing Uther to rest. They had brought with them ten warriors as escort, along with a considerable supply train - food, tents, gold, gifts for the lords they would meet, plus horses and mules and servants to manage it all.

It took several hours to get everything unloaded, by which time Uther looked considerably less pale and sick. He even took one of the wineskins and drank deeply. On ship it had been a task to get him to take a few sips but now, suddenly aware of his thirst, he took it again and almost drained it.

"You look better, Uther, my friend." Leodegrance smiled broadly as he spoke. "And we have plenty of wine, so drink your fill."

Uther handed over the almost-empty skin. "I have done so already, for I didn't realize how thirsty I was until I started to drink."

Leodegrance looked up at the sun, hazy red and soon to set. "I know you are exhausted from the voyage, but I think we should march inland before making camp. We may attract pirates if we camp right along the coast, and while I run from no fight, our task is to reach the Emperor, not battle with barbarians and thieves."

Uther had a fragile smile on his face. "I am quite ready for anything." He paused, still looking a bit unsteady. "Or at least ready to ride my horse a few leagues."

They mounted, but rode slowly, for the servants leading the mules went on foot. They traveled from the beach and followed a sandy path winding slowly uphill. After an hour they found themselves along the top of a hillside and paused to look back over the sea. The sun was deep orange now, and low on the horizon, the reddish light rippling off the gentle waves. With a last lingering look, Uther turned and rode on over the crest of the hill, gratefully leaving the sea behind.

Another hour they rode, to the outskirts of a forest of tall, sparse pines. Near a small stream they ended their day's journey, and they set up the camp by torchlight. Soon they had a cluster of canvas tents pitched around a roaring fire, and the servants set to preparing the evening meal.

They supped on simple fare. Leodegrance ate a whole chicken, roasted in the fire, with loaves of bread with butter. Uther was more cautious, for though he felt better, he was still a bit uneasy where food was concerned. A loaf of bread he ate, and another wineskin he drained. They had brought apples from the autumn's first picking; they were small and hard, but good nonetheless. Uther was very fond of apples, and he finished with several, pronouncing them not quite ripe, but satisfying nonetheless.

With the meal over, Uther took his leave and retired to his tent, for his ordeal at sea had left him fatigued to the bone. He stripped off his belt and boots, and threw himself upon the pile of skins that would serve as his bed during the journey. He was soon in a deep sleep, disturbed only by a dream of Igraine. She was standing on a tower looking out at the countryside, tears in her eyes and her hair blowing in the wind. He awoke long after sunrise, and he found that a night on solid ground had done much to restore his constitution. He was troubled by his dream, but most of all he was hungry. Ravenous, as he could never remember being.

The smell of the cook fire drew him out of the tent, and he found the camp bustling with activity. Most of the tents were struck, and the cooking was well underway. Uther found a wineskin that had been hung outside his tent, and he drank deeply.

"At last." It was Leodegrance's voice, loud and cheerful. "I feared I'd have to leave you behind and go on myself."

Uther stretched slowly. "I had quite forgotten what it is like to sleep on solid ground. I shall, in future, remember to be thankful for that which I have always taken for granted."

"Indeed, my friend, you do seem to look quite like your old self. Come, let us break the fast together."

Leodegrance sat on the ground near the fire, taking two dark loaves from a small pile and handing one to Uther. He clapped his hands, and the servants began laying out a substantial breakfast.

"I did not see you eat but a morsel until last night from the day we set sail over a week ago. I guessed you would be hungry after a night's rest."

"Hah!" Uther bellowed loudly. "Hungry? Starved, rather. I wager I could eat a wild boar myself." He set to the food in front of him with commendable enthusiasm, beginning with the salted pork and cheese, then working through more bread, with mounds of butter, then apples and nuts, all washed down with flagons of excellent ale.

Finally, even his bottomless hunger was sated, and the servants quickly cleared the rest of the camp so the party could set out. Uther strapped on his sword and leather jerkin and, last of the expedition, he mounted his horse and declared himself ready to set out.

They agreed to make it a long day of travel, and to put some miles behind them before resting for the night. The path led first through the depths of the pine forest, though even if they hadn't the trail to follow they would have had scant trouble. The trees were tall and thin, with little or no underbrush, and the ground was flat. They kept on for some hours, skipping supper, and riding until the sun was well past its high point.

Eventually the forest became sparser, and they began to emerge into the country beyond. Over rolling hillsides they rode, and past houses, some great, others small, surrounded by vineyards and stands of olive trees. Some were occupied, but many seemed abandoned, and yet others were but burned shells. This was once a rich part of the empire, but it too had declined along with imperial power.

They had ridden for three days without encountering any but farmers and peasants, but on the fourth they were challenged. A group of riders, at least 50 strong, barred the road.

The leader rode out a few paces in front and called out for the Britons to halt.

Uther commanded the company to stop, and he rode forward. "Greetings, warriors. I am Uther, son of Constantine, of the house Pendragon. We are ambassadors from Britannia, come to seek an audience with King Euric of Toulouse."

The leader was richly arrayed and clad in mail. "I am Thudis, marshal of these lands that you cross, and though I offer you welcome, in times such as these I cannot allow your party to ride on unescorted. If you would continue on your journey I bid you to surrender your arms and accept our escort to Toulouse."

Uther answered Thudis' challenge, his voice loud and cheerful. "I greet thee, Lord Thudis, in the name of my father and king, Constantine II of Britannia." He held up a small metal disk. "Here is the seal of King Constantine. Gladly would we accept your escort, yet to surrender our weapons would be to yield our honor. We have come for counsel, not battle, and we are not arrayed for war."

Thudis sat upon his mount, studying the visitors. "Lord Uther, I mean no dishonor to you or your party, yet still am charged with defending these lands. You bear yourself with the honor of a princely house. I shall accept your oath on behalf of your party and allow you to retain your swords."

Uther put heels to his horse and rode forward toward the Visigoths. "My oath you have, Lord Thudis, sworn freely...and my thanks as well."

"Then let us ride together, and tonight you shall be my guests, for my villa is but a brief journey from here. If you are not averse to long marches, we can reach King Euric's court in three more days."

"Again, our thanks to you, Lord Thudis. We would be pleased and honored to accept your invitation. A night under roof would be most welcome." Indeed, Uther could think of few things more appealing than sleeping in a proper bed, at least for one night.

The two parties merged together, and continued down the road in a loose column, three abreast. Thudis rode alongside

Uther and Leodegrance, and they traded news and stories of their lands. From Thudis, they learned that the empire was in a far more parlous state than they had anticipated. The emperor they had expected to meet, Glycerius, had been deposed by the governor of Dalmatia, Julius Nepos, who had the support of the eastern empire. The Visigoths had warred on Glycerius, with great success in Gaul and less in Italia, though they had been at peace with Nepos in the year or more since he'd seized the purple. All the lands remaining to the western empire were in chaos, the legions of old but a fading memory.

Just before sunset they arrived at Thudis' house, a great old Roman villa perched on a hilltop. It was surrounded by grape-vines and olive trees, with outbuildings clustered along the base of the hill. Uther and Leodegrance marveled at the scale of the structure, all built of stone. Even at Caer Guricon, only the old keep was built even partially of stone; the rest of the castle and the town were of wood. The villa reminded them of the great houses in Londinium, though most of those were abandoned, and many had been scavenged for building materials. Thudis' villa, though, was occupied and maintained. It was old, and when closely inspected it was apparent that the newer repairs were of inferior workmanship to the old.

Thudis rode alongside Uther and Leodegrance as they travelled up the hill toward the main house. "I would be honored if you would sup with me, my lords, while I have rooms prepared for you in the villa. My servants shall see that your warriors and attendants are provisioned and given shelter."

Uther was momentarily uneasy. Separating the two of them from their escort would certainly make assassination easier. A glance over at Leodegrance confirmed to Uther that his friend had the same thought. They had known this Thudis only for the past few hours, and they were in a strange land far from home. Wisdom demanded caution.

But, Uther thought, Thudis had done nothing to arouse suspicion. His invitation was proper and courteous, and indeed, it was the least honor demanded when treating with noble guests. Thudis had been courteous and he bore himself with great dignity, as one born to rank and position. It was obvious that he was a Visigoth lord of considerable power and to refuse his invitation would be an insult. They did not come all this way, Uther decided, to offend the lords they met along their way, and he had never been one to allow caution or fear to influence his actions. He looked at Leodegrance, with whom long years of friendship had created an almost wordless communication, then turned to face their host. "Lord Thudis, we accept your invitation with great pleasure. Your hospitality is too kind, and we are most grateful to encounter a friend on our road, so far from home."

Their caution, in any event, proved baseless, and they shared a pleasant supper followed by an even more enjoyable night's rest in the accommodations provided by their host. The villa was very comfortable, even if it lacked the opulence it had clearly displayed in some past age. All around were signs of shoddy repairs over what had been once been flawless craftsmanship, but Uther and Leodegrance were awed nevertheless, for this Visigothic lord's residence, fading jewel that is was, outshone any in their native land. Darkness and the fall of empire had come late to these fertile lands in southern Gaul, but in Britannia night had fallen early, and the land was almost beyond living memory of richer times.

They departed early the next morning after a hurried but enjoyable breakfast. The trip to Toulouse was uneventful, and Thudis had arranged to stop for the night at the strongholds of other lords, so Uther and Leodegrance slept in beds each night. After the travails of the sea voyage, this journey was almost a rest for Uther, though they rode from dawn to dusk and covered near twelve leagues a day.

The terrain became rockier and hillier, and they passed within sight of several hilltop towns. Some of these seemed to be abandoned, or nearly so, while others were surrounded by hastily-built wooden stockades. The travellers came down through a section of rugged hills along a winding dirt trail that ultimately led to a paved road in the valley.

"This is the road to Toulouse." Thudis gestured to the stone path. "We shall spend the night at the villa of Lord Talric, a close friend of mine, and on the morrow we shall reach the city before the midday meal."

Uther was excited to be so close to the first major stop on his quest. This journey was the only thing of import his father had yet entrusted to him alone, and he enjoyed the feeling. Uther had also become friendly with Caradoc, Thudis' youngest son, who had accompanied them on the journey. Both were proud and brave, with ambitions more suited in that age to eldest rather than youngest sons, and they found much to discuss.

The night was passed merrily, for Talric was as gracious a host as they could have wished. After they feasted heartily and drained several casks of wine, they sat around the roaring fire and traded tales of battle until late into the evening.

Dawn came far too soon after a late night, and the band was ragged and tired as they set out from their host's pleasant villa. Before they left, Talric presented Lord Pendragon with a gift, for Uther had told the tales of his father's service with Aetius and Theodoric at Chalons. Talric, too, had fought in that epic battle, in Theodoric's guard, and he remembered the Briton, son of an emperor, who had succored his dying king. To Uther he handed a canvas wrapped bundle, which undone revealed an old helmet.

"From a Hunnic lord, my friend Uther, whom I slew on that very field not 20 paces from where your father fought alongside my king. I pulled it off of his head, which I had struck from the body."

Uther was moved by the gesture, but uncomfortable at the magnitude of the gift. "Lord Talric, your generosity to a guest is magnificent, but I cannot deprive you of such a trophy."

"Nay, Lord Uther, you must accept. For I am an old man, and my sons are all slain in battle. The Lord has seen fit to send me the son of another warrior who fought that great day, for many now forget what grave danger the anti-Christ Attila and his God-cursed horde posed to all civilization. Into your care I will now pass this keepsake, for perhaps you can sit with your father on your return and speak of the adventures of his youth."

Having taken warm leave of their host, the party rode quietly through the early morning light. The road wound between rocky hillsides and into lush valleys filled with farms and vineyards. This close to Toulouse there were few abandoned areas, and the homes and farms they passed were all bustling with activity, for it was well into harvest time. They made their way between a last pair of hills and rode down into a large valley. Before them lay the vastness of Toulouse, one of the great cities of the empire, and now the capital of Euric, King of the Visigoths.

Uther and Leodegrance stopped and stared in amazement, for city was like nothing they had ever seen, either in life or the shadowy world of dreams. Even Londinium, which they only knew as a nearly abandoned ruin, was at its peak but a small town compared to the vast city spread out before them. Toulouse was massive, surrounded by high stone walls and great bastions. From their vantage point they could see the maze of streets and endless blocks of buildings, the theaters, the fora bustling with cityfolk and, nearly in the center, the massive structure that could only have been Euric's palace.

The party rode swiftly down to the main gate. The guards were alarmed at first to see so large a group approaching, but Thudis and some of his men rode ahead, and spoke with them, after which they stood aside to let the band pass. Through the streets of the city they rode, and Uther, Leodegrance, and their companions looked all around them in wonderment at the structures and the crowds, so unlike anything they had before witnessed. Uther's father had tried to prepare him for what he would see in the heart of the empire, but still he found himself awestruck at what cities men could build.

Word of the visitors spread quickly throughout the city, and by the time they reached the palace there was a crowd gathered. Uther and Leodegrance followed Thudis into the palace, while the rest of the party waited. A rider had been sent ahead to advise the court of the approaching visitors, so they were not unexpected, and a richly-dressed chamberlain awaited them just inside the palace gate.

Uther held a small box, brought as a gift for the Visigothic king. It was the work of Powys' finest craftsmen, wrought of gold and silver and inlaid with amethysts brought back from the Pictish lands north of the great wall. Leodegrance carried an offering as well, a golden goblet, equally fine work by one of Cameliard's greatest metalsmiths.

They were led inside and down a long, columned gallery. The vaulted ceiling was at least thirty feet above their heads, and the walls and floor were of polished marble. Their steps echoed loudly on the glossy stone tile as they walked past large rooms on each side and stopped at a massive set of double doors. The chamberlain asked them to wait and bade Thudis to enter alone. Uther touched him on the shoulder as he turned to move toward the doors and handed him the amulet that Constantine had given him.

Thudis was gone for only a few moments before the double doors swung open to reveal a large room with a ceiling even higher than that in the gallery. On the walls hung tapestries depicting scenes of war and banners displaying colorful coats of arms. There was a central aisle, and on either side were small clusters of men, dressed finely in a variety of styles. At the far end of the room, seated on a large chair set upon a raised dais, was a tall man of perhaps 35 summers. His tunic was spun from golden fabric, and upon his head he wore a crown wrought from silver and gold. His brown hair was long, pulled to the side and fastened with a jeweled clasp.

They walked slowly down the aisle until bidden to stop by the chamberlain. They found Thudis kneeling before the king, but Uther and Leodegrance only bowed, for they too were of royal rank.

King Euric motioned for all to rise. "Uther Pendragon, greetings. You speak truth in what you have told Thudis, for this is indeed my father's talisman. Flavius Aetius was both enemy and ally to my house, but only to a friend would Theodoric have given this." He held up the golden amulet, examining it closely. "Thus I greet the son of my father's friend and ally. You are welcome here, Lord Pendragon, and I gladly offer you safe passage across my lands. Leodegrance, prince of Cameliard, greetings to you as well."

He paused as if considering his next words carefully. "But with welcome I shall also offer you tidings you may find ill, for things are not, I fear, as you hoped to find them." He paused again for a few seconds, seeking the words he wished to say. "You seek, I presume, to obtain assistance, or at least counsel, from the emperor to defeat your enemies and sooth the wounds of your troubled land. But all lands are now in turmoil, and the empire for which you search is all but lost. Indeed, where you now stand is no longer a part of it, for the emperor has recognized my independent kingship in return for the cession of Gallia Narbonensis to his direct suzerainty."

Uther was surprised by what Euric said, but he remained silent and listened as the king continued. "This emperor, Julius Nepos, is little better than a Dalmatian warlord, and the purple he owes to his wife and her uncle, Leo I of Constantinople, a year now in his grave. Aid he has naught to give, and to his counsel I would pay little heed. In Ravenna you will find him holding court, for Rome itself is long abandoned by the emperors. Twice sacked in living memory she is but a shadow of past glories."

Euric looked down at his guests, sympathy in his eyes. They had travelled far, in his estimation, for naught, and there was no joy in shattering their hopes. "You seek friends, and indeed you may find some in your journeys. I daresay you have found one in me, my lords. But allies with strength to aid you in your struggle, I think shall be elusive prey. In the wake of empire there is naught but strife and fear, and the lords who would assist you in greener times have their strength now tasked to preserving what they have, or seizing what they will from their neighbors."

He shifted in his chair, but his gazed remained fixed on his guests. "Thus is my counsel to you, and also this - that you stay with us for time in Toulouse as welcome guests. Our fathers were friends, and while yours yet lives, mine is long dead on a glorious field of battle. Allow me to honor him by feasting the son of his ally. Long has been your journey, and great pains and strife lie ahead, I fear. For now, I offer a brief respite. Let us eat, drink, and toast our ancestors."

Uther had remained silent, respectful of his host, for though he was also of royal blood, this was Euric's house and kingdom. The great Visigoth king spoke well and was obviously learned and wise. Here was a monarch of such majesty and power that the kings of Britannia seemed but petty lordlings in comparison.

"King Euric, for your kind words and warm welcome we thank you. We dared not hope for such hospitality on our long journey. For your wise counsel we are grateful. We shall consider it seriously, though still we are bound by our oaths to seek an audience with the emperor, whether our task be hopeless or no. You hospitality we shall gratefully accept, for our travels have been long, and are not yet ended. Your counsel on how best to reach Ravenna we would also request." He stepped forward and placed the small golden box on the edge of the dais in front of Euric. The warriors flanking the king tensed when Uther first moved, but held when they saw his purpose. Leodegrance followed Uther, and placed the gift from Cameliard next to that from Powys. "These small gifts we bring as tokens of our respect and gratitude."

Euric motioned to one of the warriors, who retrieved the gifts and handed them to the king. "Your gifts are indeed magnificent, and they are happily accepted. Henceforth they shall be treasures of my house. But now, I speak too long, for you are guests tired and worn from a long road. Rooms are prepared for you. Go. Rest and refresh yourselves for tonight we shall sup together and speak more of things."

Euric motioned to several men standing off to his side, and they stepped forward to guide Uther and his companions to their chambers. They were led deep into the great palace to large rooms, richly appointed. Hot baths had been drawn, and their own servants had been given admittance and awaited their commands.

When they had settled in and rested a bit, and washed away the dust from the road, Uther and Leodegrance spoke of what Euric had told them. If the empire were indeed on the verge of collapse, what purpose could be served by their continuing on? Should they trust Euric's word? Even if he were trustworthy, did he read the situation truly? Perhaps one great victory in the field would restore the empire's position, as it had a generation ago when Uther's and Euric's fathers had fought on the field of Chalons?

They were still speaking of such when they were called for supper, though such is a poor name for the feast that awaited them. At a great long table they were seated, with Euric at the head and Uther and Leodegrance on each side of the king. Thudis and the other lords sat next in line, in order of rank, Uther supposed. The tablecloth was woven of silken cloth, and the settings were of solid silver and gold. Many courses were served - soups, bread, venison from the king's own forests, game birds, wild boar roasted with onions. Long into the night they ate, and even longer they drank, draining cask after cask of the king's excellent wine.

They spoke of many things, for Euric's grandsire was the great Alaric, who had sacked Rome itself in vengeance after the emperor Honorius massacred the families of the Goths serving in the imperial army. This was the same emperor who had recognized Uther's grandfather's claim to share the purple, only to betray him to some unnamed murderer's blade.

They decided that Uther and Leodegrance would remain as Euric's guests for ten days, and then continue on to Italia, for they concluded that whether they had hope of success or not, they must follow their task through to completion. But, before they left, they would join a great hunt ordered by Euric in their honor.

For three days they rode far into the country, and slew many stags and two large boar, and Uther and Leodegrance became close friends with King Euric. Leodegrance asked many questions, for the kingship of Cameliard would be his one day, and he would learn what he could from such a mighty monarch. Uther, too, began to understand the difference between a powerful warrior and a great king. Though he did not expect to ever wear a crown, Uther swore to see Britannia united under the Pendragon. He would be more than a great fighter, he would study the arts of war and learn how to lead armies, for he could see now that there was more to achieving lasting victory than cleaving a few foes at close quarters.

At the close of the third day of the hunt, they rode back to the palace where tidings awaited them. Grim tidings indeed, for it was said that Orestes, the supreme commander of the army, had deposed Julius Nepos and driven him from Italia. The usurper proclaimed his son as emperor, and called him Romulus Augustus. All Italia was in disarray, and Vandal pirates swarmed the seas. The next day came more ill news. Snows had come early to the mountains, and the passes were closed. With their path closed by both sea and mountain, Uther and Leodegrance must perforce either turn back home or accept Euric's invitation to spend the winter as his guests.

Committed to completing their journey, the travelers accepted and spent the winter at Toulouse. It was a merry time for Leodegrance and the rest of their companions. There was revelry and also hunting and slave girls from exotic lands beyond imaginings. But Uther became pensive and partook little in the celebrations, for he wished to complete the quest and return to find Igraine and seek her hand.

To other pursuits his mind wandered too, for Euric was a learned and wise king and Uther, like most of the nobility of Britannia, was barely literate. Euric had shown them the great code he'd written, recording for all time his laws and commandments to the people. These were new thoughts for Uther, who had rarely pondered anything but battle and spoils.

Thus they passed the long winter, for spring came very late that year and it was nigh on mid-June before word came that the passes were open, and they could depart. At last, the travelers set forth to cross the rest of southern Gaul and then over the mountains and into Italia. An escort they had from Euric, which accompanied them to the border of his lands, and they were laden also with gifts from the king.

They crossed from Euric's kingdom into imperial lands, but they were not challenged, and they saw no legions or other soldiers. Thudis had bid them farewell also as they rode from Toulouse, for he had long now been away from his lands and was anxious to return. Caradoc, however, with his father's leave, joined their party. He had traveled these lands before with Thudis, and he guided them as they rode.

The trip across Gaul was pleasant and uneventful. The weather was splendid, and they rode long through the lengthening days. Two of the servants and one of their guards succumbed to the bloody flux, but otherwise they had little difficulty until they reached the mountains. Uther and Leodegrance had thought their homeland mountainous, but no great peaks such as these were there in Britannia. The range stretched on as far as they could see, and the paths that twisted their ways up and over the passes were narrow and treacherous.

The crossing of the pass was slow, and they lost two more of their number before they had finished. Summer was more than half over before they trod down into the fertile valleys of Italia. Euric had given them maps, for though they had a rough notion of how to reach Rome, they had no idea what course to follow to Ravenna. Following Euric's map, they set out for the city, which was indeed much closer than Rome itself.

They followed an old road that led over broad lowlands and through cultivated fields. Farmhouses were mingled with the occasional large villa, but many were in poor condition and yet others abandoned. They saw workers in the fields, but all fled at the sight of their party.

"Ere long we shall be met, I wager." It was Leodegrance who broke the silence and spoke what they all had been thinking. "For all who see us flee, and surely they have raised the alarm by now."

Leodegrance foretold truly, for before dusk that day they were challenged on the road by a large body of soldiers. The warriors were led by an officer wearing armor and fine livery, but the men were clearly barbarians, with tangled masses of long blond hair and naught for clothing but undyed canvas tunics and leather pants. Matching shields they carried, with alternating rings of red and white as their coat of arms. They carried a standard with a Roman eagle along with other symbols unknown to the Britons.

Uther rode forth alone and answered the challenge. "I am Uther, son of Constantine, of House Pendragon. We have come from Britannia to seek an audience with the emperor. We bear gifts and tidings of that land."

The officer looked upon Uther for a moment. "I am Antonius Arquellus, centenarius of the Numeri Heruli Comitatutus. I have been sent by Odoacer, commander of the imperial foederati, to whom reports have come of a band of armed men. It was feared that you were scouts for an invading army, for you have come from the direction of the Visigothic lands, and more than once have they attacked us."

"We are but ambassadors and seek naught but an audience with the emperor." Uther spoke loudly, but was cautious to keep his tone unthreatening.

The officer looked uncertain. Clearly, these were not the usual brigands and invaders to whom he was accustomed. "I cannot speak to such things. We shall escort you to Placentia, for the Magister Militum is there, camped with the army. It will be his decision if you are to be sent to the emperor."

The officer instructed them to turn about, for their destination lay in that direction. Antonius rode with Uther and Leodegrance, his men falling in all around the small band. Uther began to object about traveling in the direction from which they had just come, which he knew was away from Ravenna. Antonius, while flawlessly polite, was adamant - they must see the Magister Militum before they would be taken to Ravenna.

Uther looked at Leodegrance, and each knew the other's thoughts. They were outnumbered at least five to one and, apart from the odds, attacking the emperor's troops was hardly a promising way to win favor. Reluctantly, they resigned themselves to the inescapable.

They rode back only a short time, and soon they reached a crossroads and turned to the south. It was now nearly dark, but they only stopped for a brief meal, after which they remounted and rode by torchlight until the moon was high in the night sky.

"We shall reach Placentia within an hour," said Antonius. "A place shall be provided for you to make camp, and on the morrow you shall present your request to the Magister Militum."

"We thank you, Antonius Arquellus, for we are indeed fatigued." Uther's voice low and raspy, for he was exhausted from eighteen hours on horseback.

Before the hour had passed, they rode up to a large encampment, with many tents and long sections of wooden stockade. Uther could not begin to guess how many men were camped here, for he had never seen such numbers assembled. There were, in fact, over ten thousand soldiers in the tents and neat rows of rough wooden huts. The Britons were allowed to pitch their own tents on a flat area outside the main encampment and, while a detachment of soldiers patrolled the area, Uther and his companions slept uneasily, aware that they were being watched.

Sleep was welcome but all too brief, for just after dawn Uther and Leodegrance were summoned. Orestes, magister militum and patrician of the empire, supreme commander of the imperial army - and father of the emperor himself - would see them.

They were escorted to the center of the camp, where Orestes was seated outside of a large red tent. The imperial commander had a heavy build, and though he wore fine clothes, he was clearly of barbarian stock. Long tangles of dark brown hair hung down his back, and an ugly, crooked scar marred his cheek. Behind him hung great banners, and on either side stood two massive barbarian warriors, blond-haired and simply clad, like those who had escorted the Britons to the camp. Before him stood another man, broad-chested but short of stature, his long hair black as night and pulled back behind his head, held with a silver clasp. He was well-dressed in a red silken tunic belted at the waist with a golden rope and pants like those of the warriors, but finer and better made.

The shorter man spoke with Orestes, and though Uther was too far away to hear what was said, it was clear the discussion was heated. Finally, the standing man calmed somewhat, as if Orestes had said something to sooth his concerns. He pressed his arm across his chest and then extended it in a Roman salute before he strode away.

He walked right past Uther, and the two exchanged intense

stares. As he looked into the stranger's eyes, Uther could feel the man was trying to communicate something to him. There was more to the goings on in this camp than what was apparent at first glance. Uther's pondering was cut short, however, for they were bade to approach Orestes and state their business.

The great commander looked angry, though whether that was directed at them or a remnant of the just-concluded argument they knew not. They approached slowly and stood before Orestes.

"Greetings to you, Uther Pendragon." The Roman commander spoke in sharp, clipped tones. "And to you Leodegrance. Long have you journeyed, and therefore bitter shall be that which I must say to you, for you have come all this way for naught. Britannia, so many leagues distant, is of little concern to the empire. It has been a life of man since that land saw the imperial banners fly over its ancient strongholds and crumbing cities. I have given you an audience because you have come so far, but you shall not travel the road to Ravenna, for the emperor has scant interest as to the disposition of Britannia. Go then, and may God watch over you on your long journey home."

Uther was silent, for he had hoped, at least, that they would be given leave to present their case to the emperor. He looked briefly at Leodegrance and then back at their host. "Lord Orestes, I pray thee at least to hear our entreaties, for you may find that we offer strength as much as need. For Britannia, if united, could field a mighty force and return all of Gaul to the imperial fold. My house has served the empire in past generations, and may do so..."

Orestes interrupted Uther. "Ah yes, Uther Pendragon. Speak you of your grandsire, weakling who lost the throne, or your father, who fought so bravely in the imperial ranks at Chalons? Yes, Arquellus has told me all. I know of your lineage. Know you that I too fought at Chalons? Indeed, at the side of the great king of kings I battled all that long and bloody day. And what deed was truly done that day? For Valentinian was a weak and feckless emperor, while Attila was strong like the iron of the Earth. Had not your confederation of enemies joined together for one day, Attila would have marched to Italia and wed the princess Honoria, for she had consented to the marriage, and indeed she besought Attila's succor that he march to Ravenna and rescue her. See you not the strength such an emperor would have brought, instead of the weak parade of fools that followed? For Aetius was the only man of strength left to Rome, and his sovereign rewarded victory with treachery and murder. So seek not to impress me, Lord Pendragon, with the exploits of your father, for it shall avail you but little."

Uther and Leodegrance were silent, for it was clear they had no friend in Orestes and could expect no help. These were bitter words after so many arduous travels, and they were greatly grieved. Uther felt his anger rising at the insults, but this was neither the time nor place for that.

Orestes looked upon them silently for a moment. "Though we are not allies, I am not so uncouth as to refuse hospitality to tired travelers. Go back to your camp, for you shall be fed and re-provisioned for your trip home. On the morrow, my men shall give you escort back north so that you might make the passes while the weather is fair. Good bye to you, Uther Pendragon, and to you Leodegrance. Fair thee well."

With that Orestes turned and began to speak to one of the men to his side. Uther and Leodegrance knew they had been dismissed, and they turned to follow the guards back to their camp. Orestes was good to his word at least, for they were brought a midday meal and mules laden with provisions for the trail.

They ate sparingly and in silence, dispirited as they were by the reception they had received. The afternoon they spent readying themselves to depart the next day, and in the evening more food was brought, and they supped together before retiring early. Uther was roused from dark dreams by a hand on his shoulder, and he leapt off the bed and reached for his sword. In the flickering torchlight he saw Antonius Arquellus and the man he'd seen arguing with Orestes.

"Fear not, Uther." Arquellus spoke softly. "We are not assassins come in the dark, though indeed such men were sent to your camp this very night by Orestes. My men have slain your intended murderers and are now guarding your tents. Lord Odoacer has come and would speak with you."

The smaller man moved forward and nodded to Uther. "Lord Pendragon, it is my honor to bid you welcome. As Arquellus has said, my name is Odoacer. I am gratified that my men were able to put an end to the insidious plot against you and your party. Orestes is a usurper who deposed the emperor to instill his own son on the throne. He has brought the army to the edge of rebellion, and that cannot be allowed. This unhappy empire stands now on the precipice of cataclysm, for another decade of civil war and man shall lose the light of civilization, as your own wounded land has already in great part. For tell me true, that the great Roman cities of Britannia stand as abandoned ruins and the all the lands are ruled by warlords and petty kings who war with each other while pestilence ravages all."

Odoacer looked up briefly as Leodegrance entered the tent. "Welcome Leodegrance, prince of Cameliard. Greetings and good health to you." He paused, moving his eyes between Leodegrance and Uther. "My lords, Orestes shall not live to the morrow, and I shall assume command of the army. I pray thee forget Orestes and his anger, for though a Roman citizen, he joined the Hunnish king of kings many years ago and sought power at the side of an invader. He is bitter and without wisdom."

As he spoke, Odoacer glanced back and forth between Uther and Leodegrance, not wanting to show disrespect to either. "I will treat with you after the deed is done, for though we have no strength to offer Britannia, I would share words with you before you depart, and if you will indulge me, perhaps ask your help."

With that, Odoacer took his leave with Arquellus following, for it was to be a busy night for them. Arquellus was true to his word, and fifty of his warriors guarded the camp of the Britons. Uther and Leodegrance sat up, speaking softly in Uther's tent, for it was in neither of their natures to rest while great matters were decided. But this was not their land, and they did as they were bidden. They guessed it was just after midnight when they heard the sounds of fighting within the main camp, which lasted but a few moments and was done.

At dawn they were called to come to the main camp, and they broke their fast with Odoacer and Arquellus at a long table erected in front of Orestes tent. As he bade them take their seats, Odoacer spoke. "The usurper, Orestes, is dead, slain as he attempted to flee. I command the army now."

They spoke as they ate. "Please accept our regards, Lord Odoacer, and our wishes that your future be filled with glorious victories." Uther's voice was genuine, for Orestes had proven himself a deceiver and assassin, and Odoacer had treated openly and honestly with them.

Odoacer looked up at Uther. "Thank you, Lord Pendragon. I would speak with you, for though I have no strength to spare I would offer you counsel if you will accept it." Uther nodded silently.

Odoacer looked at Leodegrance, then at Uther. "I have seen the empire in the west descend to the brink of savagery. Many years has it been since any but usurpers and thieves donned the purple. On the morrow I march on Ravenna. The emperor Romulus Augustus, Augsutulus we call him in mockery, shall be compelled to yield the diadem. I shall not wear it myself, but I shall send it to Constantinople, to the eastern emperor, and I shall rule Italia in his name. No more shall petty lords seeking the purple plunge the wasting land deeper into darkness."

Odoacer paused for a moment as if he were trying to divine the thoughts of Uther and Leodegrance. "I would bid thee to return to Britannia devoted to this task - to unite your land by whatever means you must, for if petty kings wage eternal war the whole will sink into darkness and despair. It is you, the great lords of Britannia, who will answer to God if your homeland falls to savagery, just as my soul will be called to account if I seize the diadem and Italia slides into darkness."

Uther and Leodegrance were silent, considering Odoacer's words. He only spoke what they already knew in their hearts. Britannia was dying as its lords squabbled among themselves, and the people suffered. The land was beset by invaders who could be defeated only by a united people. If the Britons would not be slaves they must be masters. Finally Uther spoke. "Lord Odoacer, your words are truth, and we shall return and purpose ourselves to uniting the land, whatever sacrifices that quest may require. If we must slay every errant lord and king we shall do so."

"Good, good," said Odoacer. "And now, if I may, I would ask that you do a service for me, for I would be merciful, but I fear I need your help to do so. Augustulus is but a boy, forced into the purple by his father, who wished to rule through his son. I would spare his life, but such a course is fraught with risk, for alive he may inspire resistance and rebellion by his father's allies. I would have you take him to Britannia, and swear your oaths that he shall never leave your island. Do this, and I will grant him mercy and give him to your care."

Uther and Leodegrance shared a quick look, each nodding assent to the other. "We shall grant your request, Lord Odoacer, for I see the wisdom and mercy in it. This child emperor shall travel with us to Britannia, and I shall pledge that he will remain and never again set foot in Italia."

Thus agreed they finished their meal, discussing less weighty matters as they did. When they were done, Uther and Leodegrance returned to their camp to prepare, for on the morrow they would depart with the army and march to Ravenna.

The march to Ravenna was uneventful, and there was no opposition to Odoacer. For seven days they journeyed, and as they neared the capital the fertile farmlands and vineyards gave way to marshes and bogs. The army was greatly slowed by the terrain, and Odoacer decided to ride ahead with a small force. He invited Uther and Leodegrance to join him, and so with a group of 200 horsemen, Uther Pendragon rode to witness the deposition of the last Roman emperor in the west.

Ravenna was another marvel to Uther, like Toulouse, a vast city unlike anything else he had ever seen. The emperors had lived mostly in Ravenna for nigh on seventy years, and the city displayed the opulence of its imperial station. Ravenna opened its gates at Odoacer's command, for as swiftly as he had journeyed here, news of what had transpired traveled faster.

Through the broad main streets they rode, all the way to the imperial palace. Odoacer's men burst through the massive gilded doors, but they met no resistance, for all the guards had fled. They led the emperor out into the square before the palace in front of Odoacer who, mounted upon his horse, stared down intently at his imperial captive.

The emperor was but a boy who had seen no more than twelve summers, and though he expected nothing but certain death, he stood proudly before Odoacer. The warriors who had dragged him out waited, for they too expected the command to slay the boy.

But Odoacer did not give that command. Instead, he looked upon the emperor silently for a moment and then spoke, his voice imperial. "Your father, Orestes, is dead. Romulus Augustus, as you call yourself, hear my words. You have usurped the throne, and you have no right by succession or victory in battle or ordination by God to rightfully claim the purple."

Romulus did not answer, but stood straight and did not back away. His legs, perhaps, wobbled somewhat, for he was terrified. But he drew the strength from within himself to stand fast and face his death with pride and dignity.

Odoacer continued, "Yet, I perceive more the fault of the father in this than the son, for I do not hold you to account for the deeds of Orestes, the traitor. A son's obedience to his father I will not punish if I need not. I do not seek your life, boy, and if you accept my terms willingly I shall grant it back to you." Romulus looked up with surprise on his face, for the first time betraying emotion, though still he said nothing.

"First," said Odoacer, "you shall renounce the imperial throne and all claim to it, now and forever. You shall surrender the diadem and all tokens of the office. Second, you shall depart Italia, never to return."

Odoacer motioned toward Uther. "This is Lord Uther Pendragon of Britannia. Soon he shall return to his homeland, and you will go with him as his ward, for he has agreed to accept this charge. The rest of your life you shall live in Britannia, and you shall make your oath here and now never to return and always to obey Lord Pendragon. If you agree to these terms I will spare your life; if you refuse, it is forfeit." Odoacer paused for a moment, allowing the boy to consider his words. "Decide now."

The boy-emperor stood for a moment, still silent. He had steeled himself to face death, and now he was offered life, though he must give up all he knew and travel to a faraway land. His legs almost gave way under him, but he found the strength to stand firm. He looked up at Odoacer and spoke with as much dignity as he could muster. "I accept your terms."

The emperor was escorted to his rooms, for Odoacer ordered that he not be dislocated until it was time to depart. He was kept under guard but made comfortable, and no harm was done to him. The imperial diadem and the other emblems of empire were carefully packed into a great chest. True to his word, Odoacer sent these on a ship, with many guards, to Constantinople. Henceforth there would be a single emperor, and Odoacer would rule Italia as legatus and king.

In the weeks after the deposition, Uther and Leodegrance spent much time speaking with Odoacer, for though he was by birth a barbarian, they found him to be lordly and wise, and a friendship of sorts grew between them. Alas, there would be little time for this brotherhood, for one morning Odoacer called his guests to break the fast with him and to speak of things. Odoacer was leaving for Rome on the morrow to receive the acclamation of the senate and their recognition of his kingship.

"I would have you join me, my friends, but alas I fear you will find yourselves compelled to decline. For even this morning when I awoke shortly before dawn, I felt the chill of autumn in the still morning air. If you ride with me to Rome, you will find yourselves unable to begin your return journey until spring. For I fear you would already find the mountain passes closed by the time you could reach them. Thus, if you would depart this year I will make ships available to you at Vada Sabatia to sail you to Euric's lands. From there you can make your way back to Britannia. But you must depart soon, or you will find the sea closed to you as well. The Vandal pirates are like to take advantage of the disruptions in Italia ere long."

Uther was silent, for he longed greatly to see the legendary city of Rome. But already when they had departed Caer Guricon the clouds of war were gathering, and he thought of Odoacer's earlier words. Britannia must be united, lest a dark age befall the people. Though his heart longed to ride to Rome with Odoacer, he knew he must return home. He had been gone too long already. He looked over at Leodegrance, and he could tell his friend thought as he did. For their personal longings were of little import; only their duty mattered.

"King Odoacer, though I long to see Rome, your counsel is again wise. Duty and honor call us home, I am afraid. War I am sure has come, and we should have returned long ago. With your leave, we too will depart on the morrow and gratefully accept your offer of a ship to take us to Gaul, for anything that speeds our way is welcome."

So it was that Uther Pendragon and Leodegrance said their farewells to Odoacer, now king of Italia, and rode west to the far coast, and there took ship for Gaul. With them they took many gifts, for Odoacer had been generous and had laden them with many treasures.

West of Toulouse their ship took them, for they wished to reach the coast and set sail for Britannia before the full fury of winter was upon them. They were grieved, though, that they would not see Euric again, for the king had been kind to them. The sea would never be friend to Uther, but his distress was greatly lessened from the first voyage, and he was in good spirits. Returning home for him was also returning to Igraine.

The deposed emperor, Augustus, was quiet during the voyage. In truth, he missed the diadem little, for he never truly ruled and was only his father's figurehead. Yet he was but a boy, torn from family and country, and on his way to an unknown land.

One day just before the ship reached shore, Uther took the boy aside and spoke with him. "King Odoacer bade me to take you as my ward and see to your needs, and I shall abide by this oath. I see in your eyes great sadness, and from this I shall give you a new name, for you can no longer be Augustus. Henceforth you shall be known as Tristan, which in the native tongue of my land means sadness. This, so that you will never forget what you have lost, for it will always be inside you. Yet I pray that you find a place with us, and discover your way to joy and contentment."

But even as he said it, Uther did not believe that such would be Tristan's fate. There was a sad destiny to this boy, and Uther could feel it, that his life would be hard and his end tragic. After they spoke Uther sat alone and pondered his feeling. Finally, he whispered softly to himself. "Uther, you sound like Merlin with all this talk of destiny. The boy will write his own fate." But he did not believe it, for the feeling was still there.

When they reached the shore, Caradoc led them to Thudis' villa, for they had landed not more than two day's journey from there, and they wished to bid farewell to the Visigoth noble who had been a good friend to them.

"We shall deliver you to your father's door, Caradoc." Uther's voice was sad, wistful. They had come to think of Caradoc as one of their own, and the parting would be bitter. "I shall indeed miss you, my friend."

"Nay, Lord Uther, I wish not to remain here. Rather, I bid you allow me to accompany you to Britannia, for there is naught for me in Gaul but for my father to find some position of little import. My elder brothers shall manage our family's holdings, and I would not be an appendage, for my heart craves more. My blade shall find use in your service, I believe, for you have many battles to fight."

Surprised, Uther thought for a moment before speaking. "My friend, you are surely welcome in Britannia, and I should be honored to have your sword in my service. Yet, I could not accept such without your father's blessing, for he has been a friend to us, and good and true."

Caradoc smiled and laughed softly. "Lord Uther, my father will be only too relieved to find a place for his youngest son, for he shall have trouble enough doing so for the elder ones. He has six of us."

And so it was, for though Thudis would sorely miss Caradoc, he knew his son's heart and mind were too great for whatever trivial post he could hope for in the Kingdom of Toulouse. He thanked Uther and said his farewells to his son, with whom he dispatched ten warriors to serve as guard. Leaving the villa they rode west, to a coastal town where Thudis had told them they would be able to hire a ship, and from there they set sail to Britannia. Anxious they were, for they had been gone more than a year, and they longed to return home and see what that time had wrought. Uther ached to join the battle he knew must have begun. And there was Igraine as well, who had never been far from his thoughts.

Chapter Three
The Great Storm

475 AD
Caer Guricon, Capital of the Kingdom of Powys

King Constantine sat at a rough wooden table as his counselors argued boisterously with each other. He was silent, listening to all, but his mind was on other matters. Allies he needed, and more than he now had. For his spies had confirmed Merlin's greatest fears. The Saxon invaders and the northern Picts had both allied with Vortigern, and they would take the field in the spring. Against this rising force there was no hope, not unless added strength be found.

The council had ended just as Constantine had expected, with half-hearted commitments and grudging cooperation. More diplomacy would be needed before the alliance was a reality, but he was confident that all six would join him in the end. Indeed, they had few options, for all he had said about them being crushed one by one was true.

At the far end of the table sat Merlin, impassive and unreadable, as silent as Constantine himself. The counselor, wizard some said, had returned just after dawn. Two weeks he had been gone, for he had departed Caer Guricon the evening the great council ended and had not been seen until that morning.

The rancorous debate between his advisors became too much for Constantine, for his patience was strained and the pain in his body was torturous. Finally he could take no more. "Out! All of you begone, for you wail like women!" They looked at him, suddenly silent, most of them frozen with stunned expressions on their faces. Constantine leapt painfully to his feet and howled again, even louder. "Out, I said. Now! Leave me, or by God I shall send all of you to hell!"

The shocked counselors hurriedly rose and scrambled for the door, knocking over chairs and dropping sheaves of parchment in their haste. Merlin merely sat quietly, though he couldn't suppress a slight grin. "You may be ill, my old friend, but you still rage as well as ever. I fear that you have aged them all a decade this morning."

Constantine's rage abruptly gave way to amusement, for he could not stifle a small laugh at Merlin's remarks. "Indeed, and I fear I shall regret it, for they were bumbling old fools already. Were they ten years older, gone entirely would be their minds." The king fell back hard into his chair. "Lighter is my heart that you have returned, my trusted friend, for I fear I shall have great need of your help."

Merlin rose and walked across the room, stopping before Constantine. From his robe he pulled a large vial filled with a sickly green liquid. "Let my help begin then, with this." He gently placed the glass vessel on the table. "I have journeyed deep into the ancient forests to find the plants I sought."

Constantine took the vial in his hand and looked at it for a few seconds. "What a revolting potion. Does it taste as bad as it looks?" He pulled the cork and took a sniff. "Or as bad as it smells?"

Merlin placed his hand softly on the king's shoulder. "'Twas not your palate I sought to appease, good friend. Take you this potion when you rise and before you retire each day, for it will ease your pains."

"My thanks to you, Merlin, for I shall have such need of what strength I can muster."

Merlin smiled warmly at his old friend. "I promise that you shall once again mount your horse and lead your warriors into battle. Though I fear that you will indeed curse my name when you taste it."

Constantine laughed at Merlin's jest, and a coughing spasm overtook him, though just for a moment. When he recovered he spoke, his voice strained but clear. "You know me well, do you not? Again, my thanks to you. If it banish my weakness I shall relish anything, even your foul-tasting elixir."

"Constantine, know you that this is the limit of my abilities, and though it is enough to give you relief for a time, I have not the power to heal what afflicts you. The time you gain is but borrowed, I am afraid. Indeed, when this potion has exhausted its strength you shall find yourself weaker than before."

The king looked at Merlin with a grim smile. "Worry not, my friend. Well-resolved am I that this will be my last adventure. My time grows short, for unlike you, I have aged with the passing years."

Merlin's eyes seemed for a moment to be gazing dreamily into some unseen visage, though where his mind drifted, Constantine knew not. "I have aged too, my dear friend, for once even Merlin was young and the world seemed a great mystery to unravel. Many trials have I weathered since those days, and bitter struggles have I endured. My time nears its end too. Indeed, I can feel the changes in the world, and I know not what lies ahead. I too awaken each day to weariness where once it was excitement. But this struggle we shall share, good King Constantine, and together we will do what we must to save this troubled land."

Constantine smiled, but it quickly gave way to a frown. "And what we must do now, is to draw Gorlois into our alliance. Without his strength added to ours, I fear we have no chance. Unless Uther brings back aid from the empire there is no other ally to be had. And we both know that Uther's quest is hopeless. We had to try, but I think there is little chance for success."

"I think you are correct, and I too believe we must have Gorlois fighting with us. Indeed, all the more so for he is the one lord to whom I can imagine Vortigern extending an offer. His lands are far south, and Vortigern could offer him handsome conquests and yet still rule most of Britannia. Alliance with Vortigern offers more to Gorlois than we can match, yet it compels him to trust in his new ally after the rest have fallen. And after we are no more, there would be little to stop Vortigern from overrunning the south as well."

Constantine had a sour look on his face. "Gorlois is an untrustworthy, foul-tempered, and course man, but he is no fool. He will not ally with Vortigern, for he knows he shall retain what he is given only so long as his new friend needs him. My fear is he will wait too long pressing us for the best terms, for his greed is great, and indeed exceeds his wisdom. We must forge a true alliance with him rather than a hasty arrangement. Long has he sought recognition as king of Cornwall, and that we shall offer him on behalf of all of the monarchs of the alliance."

Merlin nodded. "Indeed, you would use his vanity to ensnare him. For such an offer gives him naught that he does not already possess in every practical manner. He rules Cornwall as a king, he calls himself such, yet he craves that you and the other kings do so as well. Of course, a title will not be enough. He will want lands, gold, some type of reward."

Constantine frowned again. "No doubt he will have further demands, but he has long wanted the recognition. Once it is offered, he will be easier to treat with. And I shall try to bind him to my kingdom beyond a simple treaty."

"A marriage? Indeed, we have spoken of this before." Merlin paused to see if Constantine was going to propose a candidate. When the king remained silent, Merlin took a breath and continued. "I was thinking of Lord Elisedd's daughter, Igraine. For he is one of your highest and most loyal vassals, and his daughter is a suitable choice. An ideal one, in fact, for she is quite beautiful."

Constantine looked up and slapped his hand on the table. "Ah, Igraine. She is beautiful indeed. You think Gorlois will desire her when he sees her, and be thus more pliable. Indeed, perhaps we can add lust to vanity on our list of diplomatic tools."

Merlin looked down sadly. "It will be a bitter fate for the girl, for Gorlois is foul and callous. I fear her married life would not be a happy one."

"She will do her father's bidding." Constantine's tone was suddenly imperious. "Just as Elisedd, her father, shall do mine. If this is the price she must pay that we may save Britannia, then so be it, for is it a greater sacrifice than that of the warrior who dies on the field? She is a lord's daughter, and if she marries Gorlois her son will be a king. It is a good marriage for her, loftier than she might have wished for."

Merlin was still hesitant. "Still, though you are right, I still cannot help but grieve for a young girl so consigned. What must be, must be, but I am saddened by the choice. And what of Uther?"

Constantine looked up, surprised. "What of Uther? What has my son to do with these matters?" Merlin looked down and was silent for a moment, as if he was considering what next to say. "Merlin?" Constantine repeated himself impatiently. "What of Uther? Of what do you speak?"

Finally, Merlin let out a deep breath. "Constantine, I believe that Uther is quite fond of the girl. Of Igraine. He snuck down to her father's camp to see her several times during the council, though he thought he did so unnoticed. He went on the voyage at your bidding, but I feel he has intentions toward her when he returns."

"That boy has never shown interest in any woman beyond bending a serving wench over a table. Now he thinks he will just pick a wife from among my lord's daughters?" Constantine was annoyed, and the topic brought to his mind recollections of past arguments with his youngest son. "No. I shall not see my alliance falter over some infatuation of Uther's. No doubt he will happily drown his sorrow with the smith's wife or the cooper's daughter, and that will be the end of it."

Merlin fidgeted uncomfortably. "My friend, Uther and you have ever been at odds, but there is more to the boy than you now see. There is great strength in him, of character as well as body. He shall play a greater role in what is to come than you believe."

"He is my son, Merlin, and he has the strength of the Pendragon. Think you I would have sent him to the empire had I doubted that? If Uther wants a wife I shall find him a suitable one, but it shall not be Igraine. For you would not have suggested her were there other options. For Gorlois we need a bride of great beauty who is closely tied to my house, yet of noble enough birth to appeal to the man's vanity. There is no one else."

"It is true." Merlin spoke sadly. "No other option could I see, for I would not have suggested Igraine were there. But I fear that Uther will be more deeply troubled than you believe. Indeed, I feel as though I betray my friend, and yet this we must do, lest all fall to the usurper."

"I shall send for Elisedd and Igraine at once. Ambassadors I will dispatch to Cornwall on the morrow. If all goes well, we shall travel to Tintagel Castle as soon as can be arranged. Thus I, who have claim to the high kingship, shall journey to Gorlois, still but a duke, for I shall put aside my pride and rights of precedence. It shall be more than just Uther's lusts that are sacrificed for this alliance. I pray we can bear the hardship that is coming, for it will weigh heavily on all of us before morning comes again."

Merlin nodded, and the two sat silently, for each was lost in thought. Finally, Uther called to his chamberlain, bidding him send word to Elisedd that the king wished to see him and his daughter. And he called for messengers to deliver his letters to Tintagel Castle.

"Father, I beg of thee, no! I pray thee, do not consign me to such a fate." Igraine's voice was piteous as she beseeched her father. Her face, normally beautiful, was red and raw from her tears, and her magnificent hair was a hopeless, knotted tangle.

"Daughter, stop this foolishness at once. We are bound to do the king's bidding; you know this. He has commanded the betrothal, that if Duke Gorlois accept his alliance, the marriage shall bind the houses in treaty and friendship. Gorlois is to be recognized king. Indeed, my daughter, you shall be a queen, and your son shall rule all of Cornwall. 'Tis a wonderful match, above that which I could have arranged for you."

Igraine whimpered miserably. "But father, there is another who has my heart."

Elisedd turned abruptly and started at his daughter. "What do you mean, daughter? For I have given my blessing to no suitors. Of whom do you speak?"

Igraine was silent, head turned to the window, her watery eyes staring listlessly at the landscape. It was a fine early summer day, and the sun was glistening off of the golden fields. Yet

Igraine saw only darkness. They were guests in the castle tower at Caer Guricon, and she looked down by the river, where her family's camp sat just a month before.

"Daughter, you will answer me." Elisedd's tone was more forceful this time.

Without turning to face her father, Igraine spoke softly, barely above a whisper. "Lord Uther, father. It is Lord Uther that I love."

"What has happened? Are not the serving wenches and village girls enough for the young lord's fancies that he must play with the heart of my daughter?"

Igraine turned and looked at her father. "Nothing has happened, father." She tried vainly to hold back more tears. "After Lord Uther visited us in our camp he returned and spoke with me. Three more times he came to see me, and long we spoke. I have his heart as well, father, I know I do."

Elisedd's anger had flash hot, but now it waned, and he walked over to Igraine and put his hands gently on her shoulders. "Igraine, you are my only child. In your eyes I see your mother looking back, bidding me to watch over you. Since she was taken from us, you are all that is left to me, and I have indulged you. Anything would I do for you, yet this is the duty of your station. There is naught either of us can do to change this destiny."

Igraine was silent, though she looked up at him, and in her eyes he saw terrible, aching sadness. He opened his mouth to continue, yet no words would come. Finally, he continued, his voice broken and halting. "My sweet daughter, Lord Uther may not even return, for he is on a perilous journey."

He saw the tears welling up in her eyes again, streaking down her pale cheeks. "I say this not to hurt you, but yet it is truth. Even if Lord Uther should return, naught is the chance that you could be together. For if this alliance is not made it is likely that all of Powys, indeed, all of Britannia, shall be plunged into darkness. Know you Lord Uther well enough that you cannot imagine his father's kingdom falling while he yet lives. No, Uther Pendragon will not outlive defeat. Many would he slay in a hopeless struggle, and yet be overthrown in the end by the multitudes and himself finally slain.

"And even should this not come to pass, no way is there that you could be betrothed to him after we had refused his father's command. Think you King Constantine would consent to the marriage of his son to the daughter of a disobedient and treacherous vassal?"

Finally Igraine spoke, her voice faint but clear. "I beg thee, father, to give me some time alone, for I must make peace with this cruel fate." Her voice was sadness itself.

Elisedd's mouth opened as if he were about to speak, but again, he could not easily find the words. Igraine put her fingers to his lips. "Please, father. I blame you not, nor doubt your love. Please leave me. Just for a short while."

Elisedd paused briefly and then turned to walk away, his face a mask of pain nearly as acute as that his daughter wore. He stepped to the door and stopped momentarily, turning as if to say something else. But he was silent, and after a brief glance back at Igraine, he opened the heavy oak door and walked out into the hallway.

Igraine sat on the edge of the bed, her hand absentmindedly rubbing the soft fur bedcover as she thought. Sure she was that Uther felt the same as she, yet did that matter? For all her father said was true, and indeed, if she refused to marry Gorlois and the alliance faltered, would she be responsible for sending her love to his death in a hopeless war? Uther Pendragon would never yield to an enemy, she was certain of that...not even if she begged him to do so.

Igraine was intelligent, and as a result of her father's indulgence, she was educated as well. Her thoughts and desires screamed for release, trapped though they were, for she was also the dutiful daughter of a noble lord. Could she refuse and bring dishonor on her family, and perhaps even punishment and retribution onto her father? Certain she was that no joy or happiness lay in the future King Constantine had decreed for her, only pain and longing for lost love. Yet, she cared more for other things than her own happiness - for her father and family, for the land, which would surely suffer if Cornwall did not join the alliance. And mostly for Uther, her love, who she knew would fight to the death no matter what the odds, for to yield was not in him.

What will happen to father, she thought, for if I obey I will be far away in Cornwall, and he will be alone. Elisedd had never truly recovered from the loss of Igraine's mother, dead these last ten years from a fever which nearly took the daughter as well. He too will go to war, she thought, but if he returns, what joy will be left to him?

She thought of Uther, far away on whatever trail she knew not, and she prayed that he be safe and return unharmed. "Forget me, my love," she said softly to herself, "for fate has played us as fools. Forever shall I love thee, yet together we can never be together, and I would not have you suffer as I do. I pray you find happiness and some woman to love who can give you the sons I now cannot."

She closed her eyes and lay on the bed, for even the will to sit upright drained away from her. On her side she lay, sobbing softly to herself, resigned to her fate yet lost in despair.

Tintagel Castle stood stark and imposing, silhouetted against the red light of the setting sun. A great stone keep, built on the foundations of a ruined Roman coastal fort, Tintagel was the home of Gorlois, Duke of Cornwall. Tintagel was a marvel to behold, a vast fortress rising darkly above the crashing sea. Built upon the cliffs, with water on three sides, Tintagel seemed to mock any who would seek to assail it. Gorlois was known throughout the land, for though not yet regarded a king, he ruled nearly all of Cornwall and had more subjects and commanded more warriors than any monarch of Britannia, save Constantine.

A great procession now approached the castle, moving slowly along the winding road in the fading light of dusk. At the front rode the heralds, carrying the blue and silver banners of House Pendragon, for King Constantine himself was come to visit Gorlois. With him rode Lord Elisedd and his daughter, for Igraine was to be presented to Gorlois as his prospective bride. Also in the party were the counselors of King Constantine and the other monarchs, for the final terms of alliance were to be concluded during this visit. If Gorlois accepted Igraine and the terms of the treaty were agreed upon, the wedding would occur in the spring at Caer Guricon, at which time the grand alliance would come into being.

For half a mile the party stretched, with wagons, servants, and 100 men-at-arms riding two-abreast on the twisting, narrow road. Seventy leagues they had ridden, and they had left Caer Guricon a fortnight before. Their stay would be brief, for though the weather had been fair, fall would soon give way to winter, and Constantine wished to return before the snows came.

The summer had been lost to endless negotiations, with emissaries journeying furiously between Caer Guricon and Tintagel. Gorlois had been difficult, as Constantine and Merlin had foreseen, and the scribes were kept busy recording and revising the many terms of the treaty. Through tireless effort, they had finally drafted a document that all parties seemed like to accept, for Merlin had ceaselessly visited the kings, seeking their agreement. Many respected Merlin greatly for his wisdom and were wont to heed his words. Others feared him as a wizard quick to anger, and this too he used to his advantage. Even Constantine he manipulated somewhat, for though they both sought the same result, Merlin was the more able to ignore grudges and past grievances. Never would he betray Constantine, but his guidance he provided both openly and through subtler means.

When they arrived at Tintagel, the great gates were thrown open, and Gareth, Gorlois' marshal greeted the party, bowing before Constantine and welcoming them with great ceremony. "Greetings to thee, King Constantine, most noble and welcome visitor. And to thy entire party, lords, counselors, retainers... welcome to all."

Constantine flushed with rage, for it was an insult, and a calculated one, for Gorlois not to meet him personally. Merlin foresaw this, and he was next to Constantine when the king was about to speak. "We thank you, Lord Gareth," declared Merlin, cutting off Constantine's pending response. "King Constantine is most anxious to see the duke, for long it has been since they have broken bread together, and he has much to speak of with his new ally."

None but Merlin would have dared interrupt Constantine, and indeed, the king felt a brief rush of anger toward his advisor and friend. But Constantine felt Merlin's gentle touch on his shoulder, and his rage subsided, for he realized what his wise old friend had done. By speaking to Gareth he had preserved Constantine's honor, for Merlin had acted as an intermediary just as Gareth had done for Gorlois, turning back the duke's attempt to place himself above the king. "And now we pray you present us to the duke," Merlin continued, "for far have we traveled to seek his counsel and company."

The royal party was escorted into the keep, where rooms had been prepared for them. They wished to refresh themselves and shed their stained travel clothes, for Gorlois had bid them join him for supper in the great hall. The men-at-arms and servants were billeted with Gorlois' own guards, as there was no room in the main tower for such a multitude.

When they had prepared themselves, they were escorted to the hall. Constantine was clad in a rich blue tunic embroidered with the silver dragon of his house, and on his head we wore the golden crown of Powys. Beside him stood Merlin, wearing a simple gray robe and carrying his staff.

Elisedd walked behind them, attired similarly to Constantine, and at his side was Igraine, wearing a green silk gown that shimmered in the flickering candlelight. Her hair was intertwined with strands of small gemstones, and her beauty was surpassing. This was all the more amazing, for little time had her ladies to prepare her. That beauty was cold, though, lacking its former warmth, and her green eyes had lost their luster. Of old they had sparkled like emeralds, but now they were dead, beautiful still, but more like jade, solid and without depth.

The great hall of Tintagel Castle was a massive room, the timbered ceiling rising 30 feet above the stone floor. A long table had been set up, and standing before it was Gorlois, master of Tintagel and Duke of Cornwall. He was clad in a yellow and green tunic, for these were his colors, and around his neck he wore a great medallion wrought of fine gold. Modest of height was Gorlois, but broad in the shoulders and heavy of build. His face was dominated by a huge and misshapen nose, and a jagged scar ran down the right side from his forehead to his jaw. Long thin strands of oily hair hung irregularly from his large head.

"Constantine, my old friend, it has been far too long since we have broken bread together."

"Indeed, Gorlois, much too long." Constantine ignored the impropriety of the overly familiar greeting.

Gorlois looked approvingly at Elisedd and the striking young woman standing at his side. "And this must be Igraine. She is indeed beautiful, as your counselors have said so earnestly insisted. Perhaps they even understated her loveliness. Lord Elisedd, with your permission, I would have your daughter seated next to me that we may begin to acquaint ourselves. Of course, you will sit with us."

Elisedd nodded his assent. "Of course, Lord Gorlois. Igraine would be most pleased to sit beside you at supper."

Gorlois smiled. "Then let us be seated, for I would be a poor host indeed if I withheld supper from my guests who have traveled so far to see me." He looked to his chamberlain. "Supper is to be served immediately."

Gorlois sat at the head of the table, with Igraine and Elisedd flanking him. Constantine was seated at the far end, with Merlin on his right. To his left sat Gorlois' top counselor, Hugh the White. Constantine was more or less silent during supper, listening as Merlin and Hugh sparred over the final treaty provisions. He smiled to himself, for though Hugh was a wily and capable advisor, no man got the better of Merlin.

Constantine looked across the table and saw that Gorlois was quite taken with Igraine. He had known the girl since she'd been born, and he knew her to be intelligent and capable. Sadly, he thought, Gorlois would only appreciate her great beauty and ability to give him sons. He found himself wishing that he could have arranged a better marriage for her, for he knew she would have little happiness with Gorlois. Indeed, if Merlin was right and Uther was taken with the girl, she would have made a fine daughter-in-law, and such a wife would have done his son much good. Alas, it could not be so, for fate had intervened and set the girl's destiny. Igraine would seal the alliance in her marriage bed, and nothing could be allowed to prevent that.

Igraine sat next to Gorlois and tried to maintain the smile it was her duty to wear. She had no appetite, and she pushed her food around, eating just enough so no one would notice. Gorlois asked her questions, and she gave him the short and simple answers she knew he expected, for it was clear he was not a man to appreciate a woman's intelligence. Little would he want from her, save her body and his heirs. Such a life would be enough for some, she supposed, for this was a good match, and her son would rule vast lands one day. She thought sadly, should that be enough for me? Am I but a foolish girl to imagine more? She tried to resign herself to her fate, but her heart ached at the emptiness of it all. And try as she might, she could not banish Uther Pendragon from her thoughts.

There have been women, she thought to herself, who have commanded their own fates, and set their own destinies. How many times had she heard the king speak of Galla Placidia? Though Constantine hated the woman and cursed her to hell, it was clear that she'd led her own life, made her own choices. How does one do that, she wondered. For I must betray father and king and country to escape this bitter fate, and indeed, my love Uther would need do the same. Nay, she thought to herself, I cannot betray my family and lord, neither can I allow Uther to do so for me. I shall marry this crude and foul lord and give up hope of happiness in this life.

Thus resolved, Igraine tried her best to feign interest in Gorlois' stories, for in his own conceited way he was trying to win her affections. At last, though it had seemed to her the night would never end, Constantine bade his host to excuse his party, for they had journeyed far and were greatly fatigued.

Her father escorted her to her chamber, where her ladies prepared her for bed. Long after the supper had ended, she lay awake, staring at the crescent moon through the window, for sleep eluded her. She was resolved to do her duty, yet in her heart was naught but the cold ache of utter hopelessness.

"Go you now! For you must reach King Urien and tell him of this." Lord Arailt spoke with great effort, for he was hurt to the death. He lay in the new fallen snow, under a massive oak where his retainers had carried him, mortally wounded, from the field. His face was crusted with blood and his chest rent open by the blow that had struck him down. His ripped chainmail shirt dangled loosely from his mangled body. His blood-soaked cloak lay over him, for it was fearsomely cold, and his distraught warriors sought to comfort him any way they could.

Around him they stood, but five of the five hundred he had led there, and the only ones who still stood with their lord. Despite his command, none moved, for they could not bring themselves to leave their master to die alone in the bitter cold. Behind them lay the battlefield, now a hillside covered with broken swords, tattered flags, and the shattered bodies of the fallen, silent but for the moans of the dying and the screeching of the carrion birds.

Arailt spoke again, blood welling from his mouth as he struggled to form the words. "Do you hear me not? Begone! All of you! To the king, for you must tell him the Picts are all united, and they move south in great force. Go now, before you are trapped. I need no man's help to die."

The warriors finally heeded their lord's commands, and they ran south through the deep forests, leaving Arailt, a lord of the Kingdom of Rheged, Marshal of the North, as he bid them do. Yet too late they were already, for the woods were full of Pictish warriors hunting for survivors from the battle. Together they encountered a group of three, tall warriors clad in filthy plaid tunics, now stained with blood, their painted faces framed by rough hanks of greasy brown hair. Wounded already were the five soldiers of Rheged, and ill-fit to battle new foes. They fought with courage and desperation and prevailed, though four of them fell slaying their enemies.

The last of the warriors, Caelin, was but a youth, and this

had been his first battle. Now he was all that remained, and leaving his slain and dying comrades, he made his way south through the woods. His only hope was in stealth, for he had twice been pierced by Pictish spears, and he had not the strength remaining to face even a single enemy. Through the bristly snow-covered brush he made his way, listening carefully to avoid the roving bands of his foes.

For five days he staggered onward, first through the forests and then the hilly country to the south. Finally, he emerged into the open plains of Llwyfenydd then, half-blind, delirious with exhaustion, and frozen to the bone he reached the fields on the outskirts of King Urien's capital at Carlisle. Across the frozen River Eden and to the gates of the town he stumbled, and falling to his knees he gasped his message. "I must see King Urien, for I have been sent from the field of battle by Lord Arailt, Marshal of the North, who has been slain by the Picts."

The gate guard ran out with a skin of water, putting it to Caelin's mouth and urging him to drink. Calling madly to the townsfolk who had begun to gather at news of the new arrival, he enlisted two of the largest men, and bade them help him carry the youth to the king's stronghold.

Inside the city, many of the buildings near the old Roman walls had been taken down and replaced by small cultivated fields. Others stood empty, partially dismantled for their stone and building materials. It was clear that many more people had lived here during imperial times, and though the old walls were still maintained and guarded, the inhabited sections could have fit in half the space within.

Over the frozen mud of the rutted main street they bore Caelin, for Urien's keep lay at the far end of the town, adjacent to the southern wall. Nervous townsfolk gathered along their route, for Caelin's words that the Picts had attacked and the Marshal of the North was dead were spreading rapidly. The guards at the keep took Caelin from the townsfolk and carried him inside. Into the king's throne room they bore him, and they put him into a chair and wrapped a fur covering around his shivering body.

A moment later a door in the back of the room opened and King Urien entered. Tall was Urien, with long red hair and pale skin. Clad in a crimson tunic, leather pants, and boots, and covered with a fur-trimmed cloak and gloves, the king trod silently toward his throne. Young was Urien, of fewer years even than Caelin, though his bearing was noble, and deftly did he carry the weight of kingship.

Caelin, seeing the king enter, recovered somewhat from his delirium and attempted to rise, his face contorted in pain as he tried, without success, to stand. Urien, seeing the wounded man stir, raised his hand. "Nay, honorable warrior. Do not rise, for it is clear that thou has done thy duty and rendered service to make any king proud. I pray thee, sit and tell me what message you bear from Lord Arailt."

Caelin took a breath and then spoke, struggling to keep his voice even and strong. "My king, I stand before thee and offer my fealty, now and always. Come I from the northern borders, for there has been a terrible battle. Word had come to Lord Arailt that the Picts had been burning villages and carrying off slaves. Thinking this to be a raid, Lord Arailt called out the northern levy and marched against the foe."

Caelin's voice began to falter, his throat still parched. Urien motioned, and a servant brought a cup to Caelin. "Drink," said Urien, "and gather yourself. For a terrible ordeal have you had."

Caelin drank, a sip at first, and then deeply. When he had finished, he cleared his throat and continued. "I thank your majesty. To Carlisle, Lord Arailt sent a messenger, but likely he was slain, for we did not know at the time that the whole of the forest was full of Pictish warriors.

"North we marched, five hundred strong, and when our scouts found their host we formed for battle and charged. Our attack pushed them back, and we burned their camp and claimed the hillside. Yet this was naught but a trap, for the force we fought was only a tithe of their true strength, and next they assailed us from all sides. Banners from all Pictish nations we saw, for they have banded together it would seem. Though always there have been raids, never has this happened before that they fielded such a force. There were twenty of them to each of us, and we were surrounded. In a circle we fought, and many we slew, though our battle was a hopeless one. Finally, our circle was broken, and in small groups we fought on. In the end, Lord Arailt fell, surrounded by the bodies of foes he had slain."

Caelin paused for a moment and took another drink from the cup. "His guards had all fallen, and alone he was fighting when he was pierced by a Pictish spear and staggered back from the force of the blow. I saw, and I was running to him when a giant Pict swung his greatsword. Lord Arailt had dropped his guard as he fell back, and I saw a great spray of blood as the enemy's blade tore through my lord's armor and rent open his chest. In horror I watched, and then I screamed and ran forth to avenge my master. Three of us were upon the great Pict warrior, and together we overthrew him, for his strength was such that no one of us could have bested him.

"Into the woods we bore Lord Arailt, though it was clear his wounds were mortal. Resolved we were to stay with him while yet he lived and defend his body against defilement if needs be, but he ordered us to come to you and speak of what had happened. Five of us set out south together, and four were slain on the journey. Providence and God's good grace saw me to your majesty that I might fulfill my lord's last command."

Urien sat silently for a moment considering what Caelin had told him. Indeed, this was grave news, for if the Picts, who had always warred against each other more than they did against his realm, were united under a single banner, he would be hard-pressed to stop them. "Caelin, we thank you for your devotion in delivering these dark tidings. Wounded we can see you are, and we would have your hurts tended now. Your lord died a hero, and we shall honor his memory. You we would have join our own guard, for such valor and loyalty is to be recognized and rewarded."

Caelin again tried to struggle to his feet, for the king's kindness overcame him, and he was shamed to be sitting in his sovereign's presence. His strength, alas, was not equal to the task, and again the king waved for him to rest and remain in his chair.

"What of the northern levy what losses were suffered?" There was great worry written on Urien's face as he spoke.

Caelin replied slowly, painfully. "I know of nary a man save me who escaped the field, though some may have done so that I did not see. Our losses were grievous, and it must be that at least nine of ten who fought on that hillside still there remain."

Urien maintained his strong countenance, for he was king, and fear he could not now show. Yet shocked he was at the terrible losses, and unnerved at the size and ferocity of the enemy host. When he spoke he said naught but this: "Caelin, it is past time I saw that your wounds were mended and you were fed and rested. Again, my gratitude for your devotion. We shall speak again when you have slept." He turned to one of the guards. "Prepare a room and bear him hence. His wounds are to be tended, and he is to be fed. Then he is to rest. Let none disturb him."

The guard called into the hall, and a moment later several servants came in bearing a litter on which they placed Caelin and bore him out of the throne room. Behind them the great doors closed, and King Urien was left alone with his counselors.

"Call up the levy at once. All warriors of Rheged are to assemble at Carlisle, for we shall need every sword. Send out the runners to each county, and tell my lords that they are commanded to be here with all their warriors in three days, for we may have no longer than that before we are besieged. They are to march day and night if needs be." He turned to his chamberlain. "Prepare two riders, for one I shall send to King Lot and the other to King Constantine. If we are assailed by the Picts, so must Lot be, or else in grave danger of attack. No friend was he to my father, yet the northern barbarians are a foe to both of us. Indeed, at the council at Caer Guricon, he and I clasped hands and vowed to aid each other against the Pictish enemy. We shall hold him to his oaths."

Urien dismissed the counselors to complete the tasks he had given them, but long he remained, considering stratagems he might employ, for he had no thought about how to fight so mighty a foe. Finally, he retired to his chamber and took out parchment to draft letters to Lot and Constantine, for help he would surely need if he was to prevail.

In the days that followed Caelin's arrival, there was much activity in the court of Urien. South to Caer Guricon he dispatched his best rider, and indeed, to the other capitals he sent messengers as well, beseeching his prospective alliance partners to march north to his aid. Northeast to Luthien he send his missive as well, though he knew well that if he was sorely pressed, King Lot must needs be under even more dire threat.

Much was done to prepare the city for a siege, and in this the king had an advantage, for he had already been preparing for war, and the storehouses were bursting with grain. Weapons and armor were stockpiled, and the walls had been made ready for defense. Warriors began arriving from Arailt's doomed force, and it became apparent that, while the battle had indeed been disastrous, far more soldiers had escaped than Caelin had guessed. Fully a third of those who'd marched with Arailt yet lived, and these were now rallying at Carlisle.

Across the river, north of the city, was the old Roman fort at Uxelodunum, built centuries before along the great wall. Urien ordered that it be readied and garrisoned, and he rode north to view the progress himself. Along the wall built by the emperor Hadrian he planned to delay the enemy. Though his forces were far too small to man the massive fortification, he would compel the enemy to besiege both Uxelodunum and Carlisle, lest they leave hostile forces intact in their rear. The Picts would be strongest in battle in the open field and weakest when attacking fortified places. He would give them two sieges to undertake.

Behind the warriors trickling in from the north came the refugees, townsfolk and farmers fleeing the invaders, miserable and hungry and destitute. Urien grieved for his people, but he ordered that none be allowed to enter Carlisle, sending them instead further south to survive as they could. His capital would likely endure a siege, and he could feed no more mouths, lest all should fall.

By the end of the third day after Caelin's arrival, over 1,800 warriors of the levy had reached Carlisle, adding to Urien's

guard of 300. Five hundred men the king placed in Uxelodunum, along with enough store to last a year. The fortress
would lay in the rear of any army besieging Carlisle, and the king
commanded it be held at all costs. There he placed Owain, his
father's brother and a warrior of great renown, and bade him
defend the place to the last.

At dawn on the fourth day his scouts returned, bringing the
news that the Picts had indeed come in great numbers. Over the
wall they poured, and toward Carlisle they streamed, ten thousand strong. At first they ignored the fort, but Owain attacked
them from behind with 200 mounted warriors, inflicting great
slaughter before he withdrew, his own losses slight.

The foe then divided into two groups, the smaller assaulting
Uxelodunum and the larger hurling itself against Carlisle. For
two days, ill-equipped for attacking fortified places, they threw
themselves at the walls, with crude ladders hastily built from
felled trees. In a battle frenzy they charged and charged again,
heedless of losses until finally they pulled back, leaving 1,500 of
their number dead or dying beneath the walls. For two days and
two nights the king was on the fortifications, fighting with his
men, and many foes did he slay. On the last day, Caelin found
the king on the wall and bade his permission to join the fight,
though his hurts were still unhealed. A Pictish chieftan he slew
before his wounds opened again and he was borne back to the
keep.

Of old the Picts would have retired after such losses, but
now they built armed camps around the city and the fort, and
settled in to enlist hunger as an ally. Urien was dismayed, though
he had expected nothing else. Whatever force had forged this
alliance among the Picts also directed their strategy. The king
knew he could hold for a time, yet he also knew that starvation
and disease would sooner or later give the enemy the victory
they sought, unless relief came to break the siege.

At dusk on the third day King Urien stood atop the tower
of his keep and looked out over the fields of the south. Camps
he saw, as the invaders surrounded the city, and when the fading
light finally failed he watched their fires twinkling in the gather-

ing darkness.

He spoke softly to himself. "Constantine, our fate is in thy hands. It was you who proposed alliance. Ride now to my aid, and save my people and I, for one, shall acclaim thee high king. Thus I swear before God."

Constantine awoke to someone banging on the door of his chambers. He looked through the window and saw that the sky was still dark, lit only by the stars themselves. "Enter."

The heavy oaken door creaked open and Arwel, his chamberlain, entered cautiously. The counselor was a tall, slender man, not much younger than Constantine himself. He bowed to the king. "I beg your pardon for awakening you, sire, but news we have had that I thought you should hear at once."

The king sat up uncomfortably, for his body was wracked with pain in the mornings before he drank Merlin's elixir. The room was lit only by the candle Arwel was holding, and Uther felt around the night table for the small vial. Finding it, he put it to his lips and took a sip of the vial concoction, feeling the pain driven away almost at once.

"What news? Don't just stand there. What has happened?"

"A rider has arrived from King Urien. A parchment for your majesty he bore." Arwel set the candle on the small table next to Constantine's bed.

Constantine rose and held out his hand. "Give me the message." The chamberlain hesitated for an instant, and the king demanded it again. "Now, for we have no time for delay." He took the folded parchment that Arwel held out to him and looked down at the unbroken wax seal. It was the mark of Urien; he recognized it well. Reaching for a dagger from his nightstand he broke the wax and read the note. Constantine's eyes widened, and the dagger he still held slipped from his grasp and dropped to the floor. "Assemble my counselors immediately. And is Merlin at Caer Guricon still, or has he departed? If he not be here, send riders seeking him. Tell him I bid him return at once, for I would speak with him if I may."

The counselor bowed again and hurried through the door

to carry out the king's orders. After him Constantine bellowed. "And send my valet at once!" Arwel had already sent for the Huarwar, the king's valet, and ordered food to be brought to his chamber, just as he'd already sent messengers to awaken the counselors. He resolved, nonetheless, to check on things himself and make sure all was underway.

A quarter hour later, Constantine was dressed, and he walked out of his chamber, leaving behind the breakfast Arwel had sent, untouched save for a few bites of bread and a cup of spiced wine. The king strode purposefully and quickly, for Merlin's potion had worked its magic yet again, and he felt strength in his legs as he had not for many a year.

When he reached the great hall he found his counselors already gathered, awaiting his arrival. He nodded abruptly as they greeted him. "All of you are aware of what has happened, I trust? I need not point out how serious this is, I am certain, for you all know we did not imagine that Vortigern could be ready to attack until early summer at the soonest. We have much work to do."

Constantine and Merlin sat alone, speaking of what had happened. "I underestimated Vortigern, Merlin, and he has defied winter and stolen a march on me. Caught unready we are, for our forces are ill-prepared to take the field as yet." He unrolled a large map depicting all of Britannia, showing each kingdom, and all the rivers, roads, and old forts. "This map is a great treasure, Merlin, for there is none like it possessed by any other lord. It was left by my father, and it depicts all terrain and fortifications in the land. I have made great efforts to see it kept current."

Merlin looked at the map with a grin. "I have seen this map before, though never have you shown it to me. I remember when your father commissioned it, though he did not live to see it finished. Some of the borders have changed since the initial drafting." Merlin was staring at the map but not seeing it, for his mind was in another place, another time. "I remember the day your father set sail, Constantine. It was dawn, and the sky was gray. In the cold drizzle I saw him for the last time, and we bade each other farewell. He was in good spirits, for he left to seize an empire, but my mood was leaden, for the portents were evil. I tried to convince him to stay, but though he trusted my wisdom, he was blind where ambition was concerned. As if it were yesterday I can see his ship vanishing into the dreary gray horizon."

"Are you worried I too will ignore your counsel, Merlin?" Constantine managed a slight grin.

Merlin glanced up at his friend. "Nay, Constantine, for no counsel do I have for you now. I know not what to tell you to do, nor how to react. I fear that if we respond immediately, unprepared as we are, we will be defeated. Yet if we wait until we are ready, we may see our allies destroyed one by one, leaving us too weak to prevail."

"Have you read the portents ill, my friend?" Constantine wasn't sure he believed in all of Merlin's mysticism, but he knew better than to ignore anything the old man said.

Merlin sat silently for a moment, thinking. "I cannot see whether victory or defeat awaits us, yet I divine that great loss and sacrifice lay ahead. And certain I am that Uther will play a vital role."

"My son is indeed a great warrior." Constantine allowed himself a brief prideful smile. "But can one fighter, however skilled, make such a difference? Perhaps I should not have sent him away."

"Nay." Merlin put his hand on Constantine's arm. "I feel that he was meant to go. It may be that some wisdom he gains on this trip will affect him in some way. Or perhaps he will return at the right time to play his part. I know not what will happen, but I feel Uther's quest was necessary, and it will serve us in some way."

"Which does not change the fact that we must now decide what to do now." He sat silently for a few moments, thinking. Slowly his expression changed, and Merlin could see his friend had made a decision. "With no clear route, I must choose to support my friends. Urien will fall without aid; that much is certain. And of Lot we have heard naught. I must send forces north without delay."

Constantine looked down at the table, studying the well-crafted map carefully. He could make out the differences between the original markings and the various updates made over the years. The newer writing was brighter and easier to read, the old faded and harder for his aged eyes to see.

"I cannot commit fully to the north, though, for the Picts are far from the only force at Vortigern's command. Still he has his Saxon allies, and there are many Britannic lords who have sworn to him." Constantine's faced contorted in disgust. "Treacherous dogs." He pointed on the map to an area well east of Powys. "Here shall I send a contingent, for I hope to deceive Vortigern into thinking we invade in great force. Perhaps by this stratagem, he will be unnerved, and consequently he may pause and give us the time we need."

Merlin, who had been silently listening, finally spoke. "Do you not take a great risk in so dividing your forces? Caer Guricon you could hold for some time with a small force, allowing you to send a large army north to break the siege of Carlisle. Then, you could concentrate your forces and attack to the east."

Constantine considered Merlin's words. "Indeed, my friend, we take terrible risks no matter what course we choose. For if was stand on the defensive in Caer Guricon, with only a small force held back, what is to stop Vortigern from striking King Rience…or Cameliard to the south? Such a strategy would yield all initiative to the usurper, and indeed, he has already seized the advantage. Also, if we hide behind our walls, what of the people? Shall we leave the towns and villages to Vortigern's mercy? Do we stand atop our battlements while our nations burn?"

"They will burn in any event, my friend, if your armies are defeated in the field." Merlin's voice was grim.

"There is no good choice for us, Merlin, for we are in grave danger. Yet if it must be a choice of evils, then the choice is mine. I would stake all on aggressive action rather than cowering behind my walls."

"Constans will go north with half of our levy, and I shall send word to King Rience to dispatch a contingent of his forces to join them on the march. I shall them to move with haste, for surprise is essential to offset the enemy's numbers."

"They will indeed be heavily outnumbered." Merlin's tone remained dark, somber. "If they do not achieve the surprise you seek they will be at great risk, far from home and ill-supplied. You take a great risk."

"I would send a larger force if I dared, but I must defend Powys and also dispatch men to the east as a ruse. I shall send 300 spears under Antonius, with orders to move rapidly and create the appearance of a much greater army. If we are fortunate, Vortigern will hesitate, and we shall gain the time we need."

Constantine glanced up from the map where he had been focusing, and looked Merlin in the eye. "I would send you to Tintagel if you will go, for we must convince Gorlois to support us now. The wedding, I fear, will needs be postponed, but his armies in the field we must have without delay. He will be difficult and hesitant to help until the kings have gathered and acclaimed him. There is no one with a better chance to convince him. If he consents to send a force north, I myself shall lead them to augment Constan's army."

Merlin sighed. "Of course, Constantine, I shall try. But Gorlois is ofttimes unreasonable. I am uncertain of my chances for success."

"We have no other choice, my friend, for there is no prospect of convincing all the kings to abandon their strongholds now to attend Gorlois' wedding and coronation. Indeed Urien is besieged and Lot likely cut off entirely. Gorlois has demanded that all be present at the wedding to acclaim him king before he releases his forces. He must relent on this demand."

Merlin nodded. "I shall go and prepare, for I leave on the morrow."

"Fare thee well, my friend. I fear that no road is safe now, so I will send fifty men at arms with you as escort."

Merlin nodded his thanks and took his leave of the king. Walking down the corridor he thought grimly to himself, for he had grave concerns about Constantine's strategies and feared that the coming months would bring great hardship and challenges. His vision of events to come was cloudy, and he was uneasy. Through it all, Uther kept coming to his mind. What great part, he thought to himself, are you destined to play in this saga, Uther Pendragon?

Chapter Four
Two Kings

496 AD
Southern Coast of Britannia
Near the Ruins of Noviomagnus

Uther was the first to leap over the wale of the ship, landing chest deep in the icy cold surf. The voyage home had been a bit easier on him than the outbound journey, but he was still glad to have his feet touch solid ground. They'd had to pay extra to hire a ship, for winter had almost begun, and the risk of the voyage was greater. The crew still had to sail back to Gaul, so they insisted on landing here on the southern coast rather than spend further days at sea. It took little effort to convince Uther to ride more and sail less.

Beyond the narrow sandy beach there was a wall of rock rising irregularly above the sea. While the ship was unloaded, Uther climbed along a rugged path to the top of one of the outcroppings and peered inland. He looked out over a small plateau with rough grassy patches, mixed with smaller rock formations, and beyond this there were rolling hillsides as far as the eye could see.

Leodegrance walked partway up the path. "What see you, old friend, save a way to avoid the unloading."

Uther laughed and turned to look at his companion, but as his eyes moved across the panorama they caught something hazy in the distance. His head froze, for he recognized the shadowy image as a column of smoke, and behind it he saw another. And another.

Leodegrance saw Uther's reaction and hurried his way to the top of the cliff. "What is it? Riders?"

"No. Columns of smoke. Villages burning, I would guess. It would seem war has come already, at least to the south."

Leodegrance scaled the last section of path and stood next

to Uther, gazing out over the hillsides at the dark, shadowy pillars rising into the sky. They were becoming denser and easier to see. "By my reckoning, we are not far from Cameliard. If there be open war here, my father will know. We must ride to Caerleon without delay."

Uther looked up and down the coast, finally pointing east. "There the cliff is much lower. Likely we can find a path the horses can climb."

Down on the beach Caradoc was supervising the unloading of the horses and mules and the organization of provisions. With Caradoc's guards added to the surviving warriors and servants of Uther and Leodegrance there were nearly thirty in the band, and it took half the day to unload them and prepare to ride. They ate a quick and cold midday meal, for Uther and Leodegrance were insistent that they travel as far as possible by nightfall.

About a league east they found a break in the cliffside, and there a twisty, but manageable pathway leading off the beach. Shortly they were up on the plateau and making much better time than they had on the soft sand. Long they rode, and on their way they found three villages, all of them burned to the ground. In each they found the villagers slain, and it appeared that many had died in great torment. There were charred bodies lying next to burned stakes and disfigured corpses strewn about.

At the last village they found a battlefield, for there were ten Britannic warriors lying slain along with eight of the Saxon invaders. They dismounted and looked closely. One of the warriors carried a standard they didn't know, a red hawk on a black field. Six of the bodies had been hideously disfigured after they had been slain. These bore the coat of arms of Cameliard.

Uther leaned over and picked up one of their shields, staring at it somberly. "Indeed, these are your father's warriors, and if I read their arms correctly, they are from his personal retinue."

Leodegrance's voice was cold as ice. "You read correctly, my friend. The fiends have dishonored the dead. We must find whomever did this." There was death in his tone.

"Then we should ride now, for I swear these tracks lead-

ing off are not two hours cold. Perhaps we can catch them in
their camp if we follow without rest." It was Caradoc, who was
kneeling on the ground along the path leading from the village.

"Can you track them?" asked Uther.

"Indeed, for little have I had to do most of my life save hone
my skills at the hunt. It will be harder in the darkness, but they
have left a sloppy trail, easy to read. This way they rode." He
pointed northeast.

They mounted and set out, following Caradoc's instructions.
Many times he dismounted to read the ground more closely by
torchlight, and twice he had them turn back and change their
course, but he never lost the trail.

At two hours past midnight he called quietly for them to
stop. He turned to Uther and Leodegrance. "They are very
close, perhaps just over this next rise. We should go forward on
foot to scout."

The three of them dismounted and drew their swords.
Silently, they crept forward, crouching low as they reached the
top of the gentle hillside in front of them. In the small valley
below was a camp. There was no moon, and all they could see
was illuminated by the dying campfires. It was a large camp; that
much they could tell.

"At least three score warriors I would say, perhaps more."
Uther whispered softly to his companions. "We are outmanned,
yet surprise would be our ally."

There was blood in Leodegrance's eyes, and Uther needed
no words to know his friend's heart. "Caradoc, half our swords
are your men and not ours. It is not for us to command them.
What say you?"

The Visigoth looked at his two companions, and in his
expression was steely resolve. "You are now my brothers, and
your battle is mine as well. Let us send forth the word to your
enemies that you have returned."

The three of them silently clapped hands together and crept
back down the hillside. Uther ordered the servants to remain
until he came back to retrieve them and commanded the warriors to follow. They would attack at the gallop and slay as many

as they could before the foe was roused and able to resist. Those with torches were to set the tents aflame. Uther forbade battle cries until they were in the camp and fully engaged. Tristan he ordered to remain, for the boy was still too young, and he had no time to watch over him in this fight.

Uther and Leodegrance were in the fore, with Caradoc at their side. Behind came their men, also three abreast. Over the hillside they rode, torches held high and swords drawn, and then they were in the camp. Uther rode past a large red tent and let his torch fly through the open flap, and he plunged into a group of the enemy who were sitting around the embers of a fading camp fire.

They rose with shock, just as Uther's blade struck. The first fell, his chest cleaved open and his collarbone shattered by the mighty blow. Again and again the massive sword struck, and Uther's enemies died amid great sprays of blood, their screams of alarm quickly silenced. Five he had slain before any even fought back, and still did he ride forward, killing all those he could find.

Leodegrance rode to the right of Uther and cried, "Cameliard!" His first blow struck at a warrior just bringing his spear to bear, and it took the man's head clean off. Next he rode at a group of three Saxons who were running toward Uther. His sword clanged on his target's shield, yet so strong was his blow that he broke the Saxon's arm, sending him to his knees.

All through the camp the fighting raged, and sounds of sword striking sword reverberated through the still night air. The enemy tents were ablaze, and half-naked warriors stumbled out into the paths of the attackers. The surprise was total and the battle a massacre. Ten minutes after it had begun there were two score of the enemy dead or dying, and the rest had yielded and dropped their weapons.

Among the captured were ten Britons, all wearing the black and red insignia they had seen in the sacked village. Caradoc's men guarded the captives, and the Visigoth prince, who had been dismounted in the fight, stood before Uther.

"Know you what men have we lost, Caradoc?" Uther was

covered in his enemies' blood, and he wiped his face with a rag as he spoke.

"Yes. One of your men was slain, and another wounded seriously, though I think he will live. One also of my men was slain, and two injured, though neither of those grievously."

Uther let out a deep breath, "God has been merciful to us this night, for we have prevailed more decisively than we dared hope. And we have avenged the destroyed villages."

The camp was searched, and they found a bag of copper coins, and a box full of trinkets of little value, likely all the treasures that had been possessed by the villages. Near the center of the camp they found a pole sunk into the ground, and chained to it were half a dozen women. They were of various ages, and all were naked and shivering in the frigid night. One, a girl of no more than twelve summers, lie dead, burns on her body and her thighs covered with blood. Uther called for his warriors to unchain the women and give them their cloaks. Other women did they find in the tents, similarly assaulted. He sent a messenger to bring up the servants and the mules, and ordered that the women be given water and food.

The prisoners, huddled together miserably, called for mercy, falling to their knees before their captors. Leodegrance looked over them with contempt in his eyes. "And what of them?"

Uther stared at the distraught captives, his gaze like the face of death. "Behead the Saxons." His voice was ice.

"And the Britons?" asked Caradoc.

Uther called to a pair of his warriors who stood at his side. "Gather brush," he told the two men. "Burn them alive."

His arms burned with exhaustion, and his legs were numb from the cold, but King Urien swung his blood-soaked sword yet again, and another Pictish warrior fell from the wall onto the frozen ground twenty feet below. All day the enemy had been testing the walls of Carlisle and the resolve of the men of Rheged, but the defenders held firm and repulsed every attack with a river of Pictish blood.

For ten months, Carlisle had withstood the siege, and Urien, the young king, was the heart of the defense. Everywhere he was, wherever the threat was greatest. Anywhere his men lost heart, at whatever point the enemy was pouring over the walls, there was the king, his great sword singing the song of death to the invader.

Caelin also had won great honor, for he had slain a score of foes, and twice he had made his way through the night to carry the king's messages to Uxelodunum, half a league away across the river. The great fort still held out as well, and Owain, the king's uncle who commanded there, had three times sallied out to burn the enemy's camps and steal their supplies.

Yet a pall of gloom lay over the town and sapped the strength of the defenders. More than half their number had been lost, and even arming every old man and boy, they would soon be unable to hold the walls. They were down to a quarter loaf of bread and a small piece of salt pork daily, and that was for the fighting men. The townsfolk got even less. The horses had long ago been eaten, and now even a rat was such a prized meal that a man might be murdered for it.

The enemy had suffered greater losses, that is true, and for a brief time Urien thought his men might break the siege. His hopes were dashed the month before when the enemy's ranks were swelled with new arrivals. Another band of Picts, perhaps two thousand strong had joined, and from the south, bearing strange black and red banners, came an army of Britons, at least three thousand strong, which joined the besieging forces. It was thus that all of the foe's losses were made good, while Urien still gazed south each day in vain, looking for the help that had been promised him. Naught had he heard either from Constantine and his alliance or from King Lot of Luthien, whose domains lay north and east of Rheged.

Pestilence raged in the city, and nightly the dead were buried in great pits, hastily covered with a few shovels of dirt. Stories had come to the king of corpses devoured by starving towns-folk and of human bones found sucked dry of marrow. Twice Urien himself had been down with the fever, and the last time it had come close to taking him. But his resolve remained strong.

Three times he had refused offers of terms if he would open his gates, and he swore that only marching over his body would the enemy have his capital.

Next to the king, one of his men strained to push over a scaling ladder, and Urien joined him and helped topple the thing, dumping three Picts onto the rock-hard frozen ground below. All along the walls the enemy were breaking and falling back to their camps. A ragged cheer went up among Urien's men. They had held once again.

The king walked slowly down the narrow stone stairs from the battlement, his guards falling in behind him. Well have we done, he thought, yet still I will soon have to abandon the walls and pull the defense back to the keep itself. He knew that when he gave that order he would be consigning the townsfolk to a hellish fate, for he could not take them all into the keep. The Picts were savages in the best situations. What horrors would they inflict on the peasants after almost a year of siege and five thousand of their number slain?

His thoughts were grim as he walked back to the keep, and he ordered the guard on the battlements reduced to the minimum number, for he could not bear the thought of his men freezing all night on the windswept walls. They had torn down almost all of the timber buildings, yet the supply of firewood was not going to last the winter. For almost a fortnight, the men on the walls had gone without fires, and Urien had commanded that none serve more than two hours a night in the bitter cold before being relieved.

Back at the keep Urien walked to his bedchamber, for he had ordered the hearth in the massive throne room left unlit. The wood consumed there in a day could keep a hundred of his soldiers warm, and thus was his priority. His chamber was warm, the fire in the small hearth crackling noisily. On the table was set the king's dinner, a roast fowl, with bread and butter, and a flagon of hot spiced wine. Urien poured himself a cup of the wine and tore a leg off the fowl. He sat in the chair by the fire and sighed deeply, feeling the warmth bring feeling back to his legs. He took a drink of the wine and savored the hot liquid

sliding down his throat, driving the chill from his bones. Urien
called to his chamberlain and ordered that Caelin be brought to
him, then he ate sparingly of the leg of fowl while he waited. A
few moments later there was a knock on the door.

"Enter."

The heavy oaken door swung open and Caelin walked
in. The young warrior was clad in a simple tunic and a heavy
woolen cloak. Around his head was tied a coarse bandage, partially soaked through with blood. He stood rigidly before Urien.
"You called for me, sire?"

Urien looked up and stared at Caelin intently. The two had
become close, perhaps because they were nearly the same age
and, though both young, each had proven his worth in battle.
Indeed, Caelin had shown himself to be a warrior with few
equals, and Urien had lost count of the foes he had slain.

"Yes, Caelin. I wanted to speak with you. But first, have
you eaten?"

"Yes, sire, I have finished my evening meal."

"And what was that, pray tell, a crust of bread? I am fatigued,
my friend, but not blind. To my eye you weigh two stone less
than when you staggered into this keep ten months ago. I would
not have you lose the last of your strength, for you have become
one of my greatest warriors."

"Still have I the strength to serve my king and realm." The
young warrior stood proudly. "The day that not be so, let God
take me."

"Nonetheless, eat." Urien motioned toward the platter of
roast fowl.

Caelin did not move. "That is your majesty's supper, and you
should finish it, for you need strength even more than I."

"I am quite finished with it, Caelin. Sit. Eat."

Caelin wavered, and did not sit until Urien motioned a third
time. Finally he lowered himself into one of the chairs and
took a small portion of fowl onto a plate, though with Urien's
encouragement, he soon set to the entire bird and devoured it,
leaving naught on the platter but bones sucked clean.

Urien rose and walked to the table. Taking the flagon, he

poured more wine into his cup, filling another as well and handing it to Caelin. "Drink, for this will warm you and take away
the chill."

Caelin drank deeply of the hot, flavorful wine, and he savored
the feeling of warmth as he swallowed. He had indeed been
famished, and the meal and the wine brought strength back to
his aching limbs. He hadn't realized how weak he had become
until the meal restored part of his constitution. "My thanks to
your majesty. You are too kind."

"Caelin, you have merited my kindness on more occasions
than I can easily recount, yet there is one other task I would have
you undertake, if you will accept it."

"Sire, I shall gladly accept any task you give me, and I shall
succeed or die in the attempt."

Urien smiled. "Such I knew would be your response, yet I
would have you know what I intend before you agree. Into this
keep you came, wounded and frozen and half-dead, true to your
oath to bring me Lord Arailt's final words. I would now have
you undertake such a quest again, for I must know why we have
heard naught from King Constantine and the other monarchs.
I tell thee truly, Caelin, I believed that Constantine would long
ago have ridden to our aid, yet we have received not so much as
a message from the south. The King of Powys is an honorable
man, and in his word I trust. I must know what has happened."

Urien took a drink of wine and walked over to the hearth,
warming his hands at the fire as he continued. "I would send
you south, to make your way through the enemy's forces and
journey to Caer Guricon. Deliver my message to King Constantine and beseech his assistance, for we cannot hold much longer
on our own."

Caelin rose from his seat and stood rigidly before the king.
"I am at your command, sire. I know not how to slip past so
numerous a foe, but if my body and soul may achieve it, then
it shall be done. I shall reach Caer Guricon, and then I shall
return...with or without the army of King Constantine."

"Nay, Caelin. If you find no help then do not return, for if
we have no relief we shall fall, and I would not have you return

from so perilous a journey only to perish in a lost cause."

Caelin opened his mouth to protest, but Urien raised his hand imperiously. "We shall not argue, for would you obey your king or question his commands?" Urien could see that Caelin was troubled by his final order, yet the young warrior said nothing and just stood silently before the king. "Go now, and rest, for tomorrow you shall leave as soon as it is dark."

Caelin bowed and left the king's chambers as ordered, walking slowly to the common room where he was billeted. He lay on the pile of straw he had called a bed these past ten months, but sleep wouldn't come despite his exhaustion. I will be forever shamed, he thought to himself, to live in the free south if my king be fated to die in the ruins of his capital. For several hours he rolled about fitfully, until at last fatigue won out, and he fell into a restless sleep.

The next night, with a pack full of provisions, a heavy fur cloak, and a small bag of gold, he crawled silently through a secret door in the south wall. The moon was but a tiny white sliver, and the night was nearly black as pitch. Slowly, carefully he made his way past the camps of the enemy and then, climbing over a steep hillside, he found the old Roman road and headed south.

For five days they rode north and west, and finally, as they cleared a steep hillside, they saw Caerleon in the distance. The stronghold of Leodegrance's family for four generations, Caerleon was a massive fortress, which of old had housed an entire Roman legion for three centuries. Now it was the seat of Cameliard, and one of the greatest strongholds in Britannia.

No more Saxons had they encountered, but they surprised a small group of Britons bearing the black and red banner, and they put them all to the sword. All save one, the leader, whom Uther questioned, learning much of who they were and from where they came. The prisoner did not survive the questioning.

Warriors of Vortigern's army they were, and allied with the Saxons. Their lords had charged them with laying waste the country and instilling fear in the villagers to break their will.

Five kings had sworn to Vortigern, and to their levies he had added every turncoat and sword for sale he could find. From the furthermost north to the southern coasts his forces were in the field, and all of the free kings were hard pressed.

As they reached to the gates of Caerleon they were challenged, and Leodegrance rode forward, calling to the captain of the guard by name. "Folant, have I been gone so long that your forget me, whom you trained to fight?"

The captain was a fearsome giant clad in black mail, his wiry hair and beard half black and half gray. At the sound of Leodegrance's voice he ran forward from the portcullis and fell to his knees. "Sire, you have returned." He turned his head and shouted back to the gate-guards, his voice choked with emotion. "The king has returned. All hail King Leodegrance."

Leodegrance was taken aback, and he quickly dismounted, walking over to Folant and bidding him rise. "Of what do you speak, Folant, for my father is king in Cameliard."

The captain rose and stood before Leodegrance, and tears streamed from his eyes. "Alas, my king, for your father is dead. Slain in battle on the eastern marches two moons past. You are now king of Cameliard."

Leodegrance stood silently, for he was overcome with emotion. Grief for the loss of his father, shock at the realization that he was now king, uncertainty as to what next to do. It was Uther who spoke next, for he had dismounted and run to his friend's side. "Make way, men of Cameliard, for long has your king journeyed, and he is fatigued. You have awaited him, and he has returned, and he shall lead you, yet first the son must mourn the father." He walked with his silent friend through the gates, waving aside the guards who barred the way.

The captain accompanied them into the fortress, ordering the gate guards to return to their posts. Word spread quickly, for the warriors of Cameliard had been leaderless and despairing, and the return of their young prince, now king, rallied their spirits. Along their path the soldiers and craftsmen and servants of Caerleon gathered and, bowing low, they paid homage to their new king.

Finally the party entered the great hall, and the thick wood double doors were shut, leaving Leodegrance, Uther, Caradoc, and Folant alone. Leodegrance sat in one of the heavy oak chairs, not the king's seat, and looked up at his guard captain. "Tell me now, Folant, all that has happened." He motioned for the giant to sit.

The great warrior stood nervously, but sat when Leodegrance motioned to him once again. "Well, sire," - Leodegrance cringed when Folant called him "sire" again - "there were raids along the eastern marches. Saxons, and other warriors too, attacking villages, killing, burning, carrying off women. It started just before the harvest. Your father, God rest his soul, would have none of it, and he took half the guard from Caerleon and rode east. He was a wise man and a good king, your father, and he knew there would be more trouble, so he called up the levy before he left, ordering them to assemble at Caerleon.

"Behind he left me, to hold Caerleon and organize the levy, so what I know of the fighting in the east is from the men who returned. He ranged all along the eastern frontier and drove off the raiders, slaying many. Then he learned from a captured Saxon, that the women who had been taken were being held in a camp just east of the border. You know what sort of man was your father, sire. If there were subjects of his in danger he would be there in an instant. So off they rode to free the prisoners.

"But it was a trap, for when they reached the camp they found the women, but all had been slain after much torment. Doubtless, your father realized it was a trap, but it was too late, for they were beset by enemies from all sides. Long did they fight, and finally they cut through the enemy, yet in this last fighting the king was surrounded by enemies and overwhelmed. The last of the guard turned and fought, reclaiming his body before they left the field. One man in ten returned, but they brought the body of the king, and now he rests in the tomb of his fathers."

The room was silent for a moment. Leodegrance was briefly lost in memories, but he forced himself back to the present. "No Saxon chieftan lured my father to his death. The hand of

Vortigern is clear in this matter. Our business now is vengeance. You said my father called the levy - where are they? I saw none but the normal guards when we arrived."

Folant looked nervously at Leodegrance. "Sire, with your father slain and you gone for so long, no one knowing where, the lords were confused and without a leader. Finally, they dispersed and returned home to protect their lands the best they could. I took to myself the power of regency and commanded that each leave a tithe of their men here to replace those lost with your father. I sent a messenger to Caer Guricon, for King Constantine had been at war in the north, and had bidden your father to guard the south. I begged instruction from him, but as yet we have heard naught. I pray that you approve of my actions, sire, for I meant not to overstep my place but only to preserve Caerleon for you until your return."

"Approve?" Leodegrance placed his hand on the captain's broad shoulder. "Folant, you have acted wisely and loyally. Indeed, you have held Caerleon, for if you had allowed its defenses to weaken we may have arrived to find the fortress taken and its gates barred to us. For surely, Vortigern has spies, even in Caerleon."

Leodegrance thought for a moment about his next actions, for he was new to kingship and, truth be told, he did not know what to do. His heart cried out for vengeance, yet marching foolishly east only invited disaster. No doubt Vortigern expected such an action from the young king and had already prepared another trap. Yet he must display boldness, for he could not appear weak and indecisive before his lords, lest they lose confidence in him. Indeed, their morale was already shattered by the defeat and death of the old king.

Uther sat silently as well, for this was Leodegrance's kingdom, and it was for him to decide on his next course. Uther would help his friend any way he could, but also now his thoughts drifted to Caer Guricon. Folant had said that Constantine had been in the field, yet there had been no word for some weeks. Though he had only obeyed his father's wishes, Uther was now regretful that he had been gone, for it seemed that events had progressed faster than had been expected. He wanted to stay at Caerleon to aid his friend, but he knew now that he had to return to Caer Guricon as quickly as his horse could carry him. He would leave on the morrow.

Finally, Leodegrance broke the silence. "Folant, call the levy again, for though we shall not march off recklessly, it is clear that war is upon us. Each lord is to leave one man in five to guard his stronghold, and march with the rest at once. I would have the army assembled in a week."

Leodegrance turned to face Uther. "My friend, sure I am now that you will return to Caer Guricon as soon as you may. My father always regarded Constantine as high king and supported him in all things. Bring to your father my regards, and tell him that I also look upon him as the rightful ruler of all Britannia. I shall look to the defense of Cameliard, but also I await council on our joint course of action."

Uther nodded. "With your leave, I shall depart in the early morning, and take none with me that I may ride swiftly and arrive as soon as I may."

Caradoc, who had been standing silently, finally spoke. "Lord Uther, I shall ride with you if you permit it, for I will not slow you, and you shall have at least another sword should we encounter trouble on the road."

"I am honored by your offer, my friend. I intend to ride day and night with no rest."

Caradoc smiled. "Indeed, I thought nothing else. I shall keep up with you, and you shall have one friend, at least, protecting your back."

"Then it is resolved." Leodegrance spoke forcefully, but Uther knew his friend was troubled and uncertain. "The rest of the party may stay at Caerleon as long as they wish. Indeed, I am grateful for the skilled swords. For you, my friends, since I have but one fleeting night to be your host, let us at least share a decent meal, and then I bid you both retire, for you have a long and hard road ahead of you."

They supped together, and then Uther and Caradoc retired. Long was the night, though, and filled with troublesome dreams.

Burning towns and ruined fortresses did Uther see, and battle-
fields of horrendous carnage. Many times he awoke, soaked in
sweat despite the cold night air.

Leodegrance had risen early to bid them farewell, and he
didn't appear to have gotten any more sleep than Uther during
the night. Well-packed provisions he had ready for them, and
gold too, for he and Uther had used that which they'd brought
on their trip. The fastest horses in Caerleon he put at their dis-
posal, and when they were ready to depart he said an emotional
farewell to his traveling companion of more than a year.

He stood alone in the dim pre-dawn light and watched
them ride away. Long after they'd ridden up and over the hillside and disappeared from view he stood and looked out where
they had gone, for he was deep in thought about war and kingship and friends. When, he wondered, would he next see Uther
Pendragon?

Through the muddy main street of Caer Guricon he rode,
for Uther had returned home after many months abroad. All
around the town were pitched the tents of the levy, for the
warriors of Powys were called to the king's banner. Yet no
fresh levy was this, for he saw the debris and tattered flags and
wounded men of an army that had seen battle. And fewer tents
there were than he remembered from the last time the army was
assembled.

He rode up the path to the great dark bulk of the castle and
as he reached the top he found the gates closed tight. Dark
figures stood guard on the battlement above the entry and on
the walls.

"Open the gates."

"Who goes there?" The reply was harsh and impatient. Half
a dozen guards looked down threateningly from the crenellated
wall above the gate.

"It is Uther Pendragon, knaves, and if you do not open the
gate at once I shall climb up there myself and teach all of you to
respect my commands!"

He could hear the excited banter among the guards, and a

familiar voice crying out. "It is Lord Uther. He has returned."

Uther recognized the speaker - Caer Guricon's captain of the guard. "Indeed, Kelven, and I have come too far to be patient of delay now, so open the gate. I would see my father at once."

There was a clang as the bolt was removed and a great creak as the massive oaken doors slid open. Uther and Caradoc rode through and up to the castle courtyard. Jumping off his horse, Uther turned to Caradoc. "Wait for me here, my friend, for I would speak alone with my father."

Caradoc nodded then dismounted and took the reins of his and Uther's horses. "I shall attend to our mounts and await your return."

Into the keep Uther strode, and halfway to the great hall he came upon Merlin. Though troubled over all he had seen since his return, Uther could not help but smile when he saw his old friend, clad as always in a counselor's simple robes. Merlin returned the smile, but it did not last on his lips, for he seemed consumed with worry.

Uther embraced the older man warmly. "Merlin, it is good to see you, old friend. It has been far too long."

"And pleased I am to see you." Merlin warmly returned Uther's embrace. "Long have you traveled, and much no doubt have you seen. There are many tidings to tell, and mostly ill, though your father should speak of these to you."

"And while I long to sit by the fire and tell you of my travels, no further should I delay seeing my father, or I shall once again be scolded for frivolity. News from here in Britannia I bear as well from across the sea. Know you that King Ogyruan is dead and that Leodegrance now rules in Cameliard?"

"Aye, for the news of the king's death had reached us, yet it is good tidings at least that Leodegrance has returned, and Cameliard again has a king."

"So where is my father, Merlin, for I shall present myself at once."

"He is in his bedchamber, Uther." Merlin looked down sadly. "For his health fails him quickly now, and I fear his time is short indeed."

Uther's smile faded, for he had been worried about his father's health even when he left the year prior. He took leave of Merlin and hurried to the king's chamber. Knocking softly on the door he said, "Father? It is Uther. May I enter?"

"Uther? Come in, come in." His father's voice was frail and thin, barely audible through the door.

Uther swung open the heavy wooden door and walked slowly inside. King Constantine lay in his bed, his body covered with furs. Slowly and painfully he turned his head toward the door. Uther was shocked, for the king was gaunt and pale, a few sparse wisps of white hair all that was left of the thick mane he'd had but a year before.

"Uther, my boy. I knew you would return in time." He spasmed and began coughing, red mist spraying from his mouth.

Uther ran over and knelt at his bedside. He grabbed a rag from the small night table and wiped the blood from his father's lips. The old man reached out with a skeletal arm and put his withered hand on Uther's. "Be still, father." Uther spoke softly, soothingly. "I am here."

"Nay, Uther." Constantine's voice was hoarse and rattling. "There is much to speak of and little time. Listen now, for a great deal has happened while you were gone, and many burdens have fallen on your shoulders. War has been kindled in all of the land, and greatly have we suffered in the field. All of your brothers are slain, Uther. Before yearend, you shall be king of Powys."

Uther stood there, stunned, staring into his father's rheumy eyes. "All? How?"

"Constans slain, leading a force north to relieve Carlisle, for Urien has been under siege these ten months. In the forest they were attacked and turned back, and though they fought their way out, your brother was mortally wounded by a spear thrust and died a fortnight later here in Caer Guricon."

The old king's voice was brittle, burdened by weakness and by the grief of a mourning father. "Constantine was murdered in his camp by one of his men, for alas there are traitors even in our ranks who have taken Vortigern's accursed silver to betray their rightful lords."

Constantine coughed again, struggling to clear his throat and continue. "And Antonius fell with all his men, defending the eastern approaches when they were assailed by the enemy. None survived to return, so little do we know of what there occurred."

Uther looked down at his feet, his expression one of pain and regret. "I should not have departed, for in the end, little did we achieve. The empire is lost, and indeed there is no longer an emperor in the west but only a barbarian king of Italia. Here was my place, in the field with my brothers, and Leodegrance's with his father."

"Nay, Uther," replied Constantine, "for you did as I commanded. And now we know that never shall the legions return to our shores. Britannia must thus have a high king, lest through division and warfare we descend into darkness. This is your birthright, Uther, for you will soon be the last of the Pendragon. I charge you with this task, my son, for you are already the greatest warrior in Britannia. I beg your forgiveness, for I fear I have left you little power to enforce this claim. Our arms are defeated and demoralized, and I die knowing I have failed. My last hope is that my son may take up our banner and prevail where I have not."

Uther's mind was reeling, for so much had happened in these last few days. He put his hand gently on his father's head. "There is naught to forgive, father, for I will do as you bid. Yet, you will recover from your ills and live many more summers."

Constantine's lips formed a fragile smile. "Nay, my son. God calls me. Indeed, without Merlin's potion already would I be in His kingdom. But alas, even Merlin's wisdom has its limits, and the elixir no longer has power to hold off mortality. More swiftly comes the end now, for so Merlin warned me it would be when first he brewed the potion. Worry not for me, Uther, my son, for I fear not death. Tired I am, and ready to leave this life. I regret only that I leave you naught but strife and war against bitter odds."

"We shall prevail, father, and I swear to thee that the Pendragon shall defeat Vortigern and claim the high kingship of Britannia. Whatever may be required of me, I shall prevail."

The old king smiled at his son, but only for a second, for he had one more burden to lay upon Uther, and now he wished he had chosen another course. "Uther, there is one other thing we need speak of. For it involves Elisedd's daughter Igraine." Constantine was half-blind, but he could see his son well enough with his clouded eyes to tell he had judged wrongly, for in that moment he knew that Uther loved the girl, and his heart ached for what he must now say.

While Constantine paused, Uther could not hold his tongue. "Please father, do not tell me she is somehow stricken. God, please let it not be so!"

"She is well, Uther." Constantine's voice was thick with despair. "Yet for you, I fear, these will be bitter tidings, for betrothed to Gorlois of Cornwall she is. Indeed, had war not come upon us so early, she would be already married."

Uther gasped in his shock, his mind racing to grasp with this news. "Then she has not yet been married? For you are king, father. I beg you, give not your consent to the match Elisedd has arranged. As king, thus is your right."

Constantine paused, then struggled to make himself say what he had to. "It is not Elisedd's doing that has made this match; it is mine, and undertaken not by choice. For Igraine is the cost of alliance with Gorlois and with Cornwall. Her wedding shall seal the treaty between Cornwall and Powys, and Gorlois shall recognize the Pendragon as high kings, aiding us with all his forces."

"No!" Uther's cry was a mix of anger and despair. "It shall not be so. I would sooner slay Gorlois than lose Igraine to such as him!"

Constantine gripped his son's arm with all the scant strength that remained in his withered hands. His body wracked with pain, he spoke through another fit of coughing. "Be silent, Uther! For a king you must be and not a lovesick boy. A full third of our warriors have been lost, and the enemy overwhelms us on all frontiers. Without the forces of Cornwall to aid us there is no hope. None. Kingship is a heavy burden, my son, heavy indeed. Yet it is your sacred duty, for the people will need you. You will be high king of Britannia and unite this ravaged land. Unless you allow Vortigern to have the victory."

"I cannot. I will not lose her."

"Then you would allow your kingdom to fall, and when you are dead with your warriors on the field, what shall become of Igraine? Shall she die too, or be spoil for the conquerors? For you will be her high king as well. Will you protect her or, by having her yourself, will you fail her and all your subjects? All of Britannia?"

Uther buried his head in the fur covering on his father's bed and sat silently, the only sound in the room, Constantine's struggled breathing. Finally Uther spoke, his tone dark with despair. "When are they to be wed?"

"Within the fortnight, for even now Gorlois journeys to Caer Guricon to claim his bride. Uther, you must pledge to me now on your honor that you will not attempt to stop this union. Were there any other way I would embrace it, but there is not. Indeed, now Gorlois would take insult were we to renege and likely there would be war with Cornwall as well as Vortigern. Cameliard would be the first to fall. Would you betray Leodegrance and allow him to bear the brunt of Gorlois' vengeance for your love of a woman? Would you see your friend dead in the ruins of Caerleon?" Uther knelt before the bed and was silent. Constantine continued, rasping through the rattling congestion in he chest. "Uther, swear to me, for this is my last command to you."

Uther rose, slowly, stiffly, as if all strength had drained from him. He stood over his father and looked at the frail and dying man and realized that the burden had already passed to him. If Powys should survive and prosper or if its people should be conquered and reduced to slavery, all this was now on his shoulders. He had never thought deeply about the responsibilities of being king, for never had he expected the crown to fall to him. But now he thought to himself, I am already king, in all but formality. All is on a knife's edge, for if I do not take command then no one shall.

In that instant was born Uther Pendragon, high king of Britannia, for within him grew a terrible, steely resolve. Though still but eighteen years of age, the boy was gone, in its place naught but the dread warrior king. In that moment he recalled Odoacer's words, and he knew that he would unite Britannia under his rule, whatever the cost. He would water the field with his enemies' blood.

"I swear to you, father." Uther's voice was like ice. "Igraine shall marry Gorlois." Thus were the last words Uther Pendragon ever spoke to his father. He turned his back on the wretched old man and walked out into the corridor.

Uther sat at the oak table in the great hall poring over a large map. On it were small flags representing the best guesses at the location of enemy forces. His gaze was focused on the cluster of markers around Carlisle.

"We must relieve Urien, for if Carlisle falls we lose our bulwark in the north. Thus, there we will strike in force and break this siege. Yet we must also deceive the enemy, lest he discover how weakly held Caer Guricon will be once the army has departed."

The advisors around the table were silent and gloomy, for they saw no way to engage the might of the enemy. On all fronts they were outnumbered, and his victories of the past year had emboldened their foe and swelled his numbers. Terrified lords, who might have sided with Powys and its allies, submitted to Vortigern's rule out of fear.

"Gorlois shall arrive tomorrow." Uther spat the words with disgust. "I shall insist that his forces be at Caer Guricon and ready to march north by the new moon. This alliance is dearly bought, and I shall demand the full support for which we pay so heavily."

Kelven, the captain of the guard of Caer Guricon finally spoke. "Lord Uther, what of our lands and those to the south. We are no less sorely beset here than in the north. How can we hope to hold back the foe if the army marches to relieve Carlisle, and Gorlois' forces too?"

"Perhaps we can conceive of a strategem that will serve our need." The voice came from the great entryway, where stood Merlin, just arrived to sit in the war council.

Uther looked up at the new arrival. "Your wisdom would be most welcome, Merlin. What thoughts have you on this?"

Merlin paused. "I would speak with you alone, my friend, for I have words just for thee."

Uther stood abruptly and walked toward the entry where Merlin stood. He turned briefly, addressing the assembled advisors. "Continue preparing the plans for the march north." He clasped his hand on Merlin's shoulder and bade his friend follow. Out of the main doors they walked and through the courtyard to one of the bastions that overlooked the town below.

"Alone we are now, Merlin. So what plans have you that cannot be shared with the council?"

"A plan I do have, and while I trust the council to a point, also I doubt not that Vortigern has spies, even in Caer Guricon. That all of your brothers were taken at disadvantage and slain seems to me too much to grant to fate alone. I would bid you to be cautious in whom you place your confidence."

"And can I trust you, Merlin?" asked Uther plainly.

"Thus do you speak like a true king, my friend." There was weariness in Merlin's voice. "Yet do you truly doubt my friendship and loyalty?"

Uther looked down at his feet. "Nay, Merlin. All my life have you been there for me. Yet so much has happened, and I know not whom I can trust. For fear as well as disloyalty can sap the strength of my army." Both were silent for a moment, then Uther glanced at his companion. "So what is your strategy, Merlin?"

"There are opportunities for deception as well as battle. For you have just returned, and though no allies were you able to find, your foes do not know this. From the coast you rode to Cameliard, and on your way you assailed and destroyed several of the enemy's raiding parties."

"This is true, Merlin, but no more than six or seven score did we slay. And, indeed, we were outnumbered in the largest fight."

Merlin placed a hand on Uther's arm. "Ah, but put yourself in the enemy's place. The only remaining heir with a claim to the high kingship has returned, for surely by now Vortigern is aware you are back. He lands, with what allies or forces you know not, yet along his march, all of your forces have been wiped out where before they ranged without hindrance. What might you think? What fears would grow on your mind?"

Uther listened attentively, for he began to divin Merlin's plan. "Deception…that must be our weapon here and in the south. Yet can we truly convince the foe that we leave strength enough here to meet him and still march with enough power to relieve Carlisle?"

"It will place a heavy burden on Leodegrance," said Merlin, "for he is one of those you can trust with the truth, and I fear great risk will fall upon him as he plays his part. For you, yourself, will certainly need to go north. The army is demoralized, and only you can restore its spirit. Leodegrance you must leave behind to hold Cameliard and Powys."

Uther stood silently, thinking, grasping at the threads of a plan. "Caradoc." he finally said, more loudly than he had intended. "A Visigothic nobleman I have with me, and his guard. Though the warriors we have left behind in Caerleon. A friend he is, and sworn to my service. They be but ten in number, but might we not create an army of Gothic shadows, come to our aid under Caradoc, the great Visigothic prince?"

"Indeed, such was my thinking. This is the tool we shall use if this Caradoc be willing. We must begin immediately, for your friend must be heralded as a great visiting prince. Vortigern's spies we shall enlist to our aid, for no doubt they will quickly report of this foreign lord welcomed into Caer Guricon. He must be included in councils, and there must be much talk of his army. We will present his few men as a personal guard and but a fraction of his total strength."

Uther smiled grimly. "This plan could work, I daresay. For Caradoc is of noble bearing, and he will be easily accepted as a great prince. We shall use this deception to forestall the enemy in the east and south while I march to Carlisle with the levies of Powys and Cornwall." Uther's smile left him as he spoke of Cornwall, and Merlin understood, for he knew the great price of this aid. Silently they stood together, and Merlin knew what dashed hopes Uther now pondered.

"Uther, I would ask something of you…that you will do as I bid you and not ask of me any questions."

Uther looked confused, but he nodded at once. "Merlin, with my life I trust you. What is it you would have me do?"

There is a small house in the town, just off of the main road past the orchard. It is recently whitewashed, while all the others around it are dark-stained wood. Know you of what I speak?"

"Yes, I think so. I believe I have walked past the house before."

"Then I bid you meet me there, just after dusk when darkness comes. Do not delay or knock on the door. Just enter. And let no one know where you go."

Uther did not understand why Merlin would make such an odd request, but he knew the old man did nothing without reason, and he had promised not to question. "Very well, Merlin. I shall do as you request."

Merlin just smiled briefly and nodded.

Uther returned the nod. "But now, I shall go and speak with Caradoc, and enlist his aid in our plan."

Uther slipped out of the castle just after dusk, taking a secret passage known only to a very few. Although Merlin had not asked him to disguise himself, he decided that discretion was probably wise. He wore a simple gray hooded tunic, with only a small dagger for a weapon. With the hood drawn over his head he made his way through the town, finding the house of which Merlin spoke. Looking around him and seeing no one, he pushed open the door and walked inside.

Standing in the room was Merlin, and next to him a slim figure clad much as Uther himself was, also with a hood drawn. Uther gasped when two small, pale hands reached up and pulled back the cloak to reveal Igraine's face.

Merlin spoke, his voice gentle and sad. "Uther, Igraine, I deeply regret that your destinies have demanded such painful sacrifices from each of you. I would, if it were in my power, release you from your fates, and pray you might find happiness together. Alas, there is naught that I can do, save perhaps grant you a brief time together, that you shall not be totally denied each other. This night only shall you have, and I promise that none shall disturb you nor discover your secret. You are safe tonight, but come the morn, your time together must be ended. Just before dawn shall I knock three times on the door. Uther, you must then leave and return to the castle. I will bring Igraine back to her chamber, and none shall know she was ever gone."

He slipped quickly through the door and was gone, leaving Uther and Igraine alone, with only the flickering light from the hearth illuminating the room. Igraine stood nervously, looking at Uther, but saying nothing. Uther knew he should leave, but no force of will could he muster that was strong enough to move him. Merlin, he thought, I know not if this be an act of mercy or a dagger in the heart, yet I am grateful.

Finally, he could restrain himself no longer and, walking hurriedly across the room, he embraced Igraine, her lips urgently meeting his as she fell into his arms. Afterward, Uther could not remember how long they just stood in each other's arms, though he never forgot the feeling of her lips or the scent of her hair.

Slowly, he unbuttoned her tunic, letting the loose garment drop to the floor, and he took her into his arms, carrying her to the bed. For that night they belonged to each other, and the dismal fate that awaited them did not exist. They did not sleep, for fear they would lose a moment together, and as the night grew old they lay quietly together, savoring the warmth of each other's bodies. They spoke little, for what could they speak of but that which the morrow would bring?

When the three knocks on the door came, Uther had been waiting, and yet he felt as though his blood had frozen. Their last moment together was heart-rending, and Uther held her tightly, as if he could push away fate as long as his grip remained strong. Finally, with a last gentle, lingering kiss, he left her wordlessly.

After Uther had slipped out, Merlin waited for a moment to give Igraine time to dress, and then he entered the room and led her back to the castle. By whatever wizardry Merlin possessed, they walked back into the castle unseen, slipping through the secret entry and up to Igraine's chamber. Her ladies still slept, and whether it was providence or Merlin's machinations that made them slumber so soundly she never knew.

"Thank you, Merlin," said Igraine softly. He voice was sweet, yet in it was great sadness. "For though my fate is a bitter one, now Uther and I shall always share a part of one another. You have given me a memory to sustain myself, whatever this cruel life brings."

"Sustain you both it shall, for whatever befalls you, know that Uther Pendragon loves you as strongly as you love him." Before he left, Merlin reached into a pouch in his robes and handed Igraine a small vial, glass worked with delicate gold. "Drink this in a goblet of wine at your wedding, and do not forget. It will not harm you, but it will make you bleed, and by this Gorlois shall believe that you were still a maid in your marriage bed. For never can he know of this night, or that you love Uther Pendragon."

Igraine took the vial and bade Merlin farewell. As he closed the door behind him she lay on the bed, clutching the small bottle, and began to cry.

Gorlois, duke of Cornwall, and his entourage rode through the main gate of the castle at Caer Guricon to horns blowing celebratory fanfare. He was in good spirits and spoke cheerfully with his advisors, for on the morrow he would be wed to the beautiful Igraine, and then he would be acclaimed king of Cornwall, and be so recognized by the seven kingdoms of the alliance.

The ceremonies were originally to have taken place the past spring but were delayed when war erupted in the north and east. Initially, Gorlois had demanded that all seven kings be present to accept him as one of them. He had long been resentful of their unwillingness to recognize him as king despite the fact that he wielded greater power than all save Constantine. After months of diplomacy, he had relented, for the kings were in the field with their armies and unable to attend. Parchments he had from all, attesting their assent to the agreement. All save Urien, who was besieged in his capital, and Lot, far to the north and cut off from Powys by the enemy armies.

In the one of the minor halls sat Uther Pendragon, totally silent, his face like carved stone. In a chamber in the tower lay his father, King Constantine, the architect of the alliance. But Constantine now faced his final struggle and, too weak to stand or even speak more than a few words, he had ceded control of all affairs to his only remaining son. Now Uther was charged with welcoming Gorlois and presiding over the wedding and other festivities...and sending the woman he loved away to Cornwall as another man's wife.

He was alone, for he had chased the terrified servants away and ordered his counselors to leave him. But now it was time to greet his guest in the great hall. Uther rose slowly from the heavy oak chair, his legs leaden. His face showed no emotion, just deadly resolve in those steely gray eyes as he walked silently out into the corridor and made his way to the great hall.

Chapter Five
Dragon of Winter

497 AD
Winter
Caer Guricon, Capital of the Kingdom of Powys

Uther stood in the courtyard of the castle at Caer Guricon, his vassal lords and allies standing in a rough circle around him. The day was gray and overcast, with a brisk wind that made the bitter cold all but unbearable. The lords were clad in heavy fur cloaks and thick winter boots, yet all shivered in the deep winter chill. All save Uther Pendragon.

Uther stood like a statue, impervious, it seemed, to cold or discomfort, clad all in black save for the blue and silver Pendragon arms emblazoned on his tunic. Under his mail shirt, hidden from view, was a silver ring with a blue sapphire, hung from a chain about his neck. His gray eyes were cold and emotionless, and the features of his face were as chiseled marble.

"We march tomorrow. Have your contingents ready, for we set out at dawn." His tone was cold, imperious. A low mumbling sound arose from the assembled lords, not so much a reply as a ripple of discontent. Uther paid it no heed and turned to leave when one of the lords mustered the courage to speak.

"Lord Uther," - for though he commanded as regent, his father still lived and he was not yet king - "always shall House Pendragon command our loyalty, yet I must ask you to reconsider this command. You allow us to leave only one man in ten to defend our estates, and when we return it may be to wasted lands and burned castles. And you insist that we march out in mid-winter on short notice and ill-supplied. How many will perish from the cold?"

The voice was that of Lord Arven, a troublesome sort, wont to seek advantage whenever he could. Uther turned his head, and his ice cold gaze fell on the complaining vassal. Arven stood fast, but cringed under that deadly stare, for whatever they thought of their young heir, all here gathered had seen him in battle.

"It is decided, Arven." Uther spoke with grim finality. "The time for debate is passed."

Uther started to turn his head to leave when the stubborn lord protested yet again. Those around him who had seen Uther's stare leaned away nervously and prayed for him to be silent, yet Arven would not be stayed.

"Lord Uther, I cannot consent to leave my estates unprotected and allow my men to die by the roadside in the winter snows. Allow us to leave one man in three, and delay this march until spring, and we shall follow you anywhere. But I shall not blindly march to my ruin." Arven stood defiantly, having worked up his courage to take this stand.

The lords near Arven cringed, for they expected an outburst of rage and invective in response to the rebelliousness of the vassal. Yet Uther was silent; not a word passed his lips. He merely stood, still as death for a long moment, and then, in a motion so quick no eyes could follow it, he pulled his sword from the scabbard and swung the blade with deadly effect. So swift was the blow that Arven had not the time to gasp before his head was struck from his body and fell into the new fallen snow in a shower of blood.

There was a collective gasp of horror from the assembly, yet no one else dared speak or even look directly at Uther, who stood there calmly, still holding his bloody sword. After a moment, Uther turned and started back toward the castle.

"Dawn," he said as he walked away. "We leave at dawn."

In an instant, he was gone, leaving naught behind save the stunned assembly and his deep footsteps in the bloodstained snow.

Merlin stood in the great hall, alone in the quiet predawn hours, thinking about recent events. He was troubled by the change in Uther since Igraine was wed to the newly crowned king of Cornwall. The boy had always been a great fighter, yet also he had been joyful and caring. Now he was cold and as hard and unyielding as granite, totally without mirth, without mercy, without pity. He saw naught but his charge - to unify Britannia - and he was determined to do so at any cost. Merlin feared for his humanity.

"What have we done, Constantine?" he said to himself, his voice barely audible. "What have we created? I fear through heartbreak and love denied we have unleashed something terrible."

Merlin had thought to accompany Uther and the army as it marched north to Rheged, but Uther had other thoughts, and bade his counselor to remain behind. "Leodegrance and Caradoc are charged with deceiving the enemy," Uther had said. "Your wisdom and cunning would greatly aid in that endeavor. You would do me tremendous service if you remained and committed yourself to that effort."

Of course he was right, thought Merlin, for little could you offer to the army in battle. Better you remain and help mislead the enemy. "Old fool," he said, talking to himself again, "you just wanted to keep an eye on Uther. But he needs not your oversight, for he is wise and strong, and though heartsick and hurt he will be fine." Thus he said, but what he truly believed he was not sure.

The sound of heavy footsteps from the hallway distracted Merlin from his thoughts, and he looked behind him just in time to see Uther trod quickly into the hall from the main corridor. "Greetings, Uther."

"And mine to you, my friend." Uther's voice was clear and strong, but without emotion. "We are agreed, are we not, that you will remain and help Caradoc and Leodegrance hold Powys and Cameliard?"

"I shall," said Merlin.

"My thanks to you then, for I shall feel less concern if you are here to advise. Indeed, Merlin, I would have you accept the regency in my absence if you will."

Thus occurred a truly rare event, for Merlin was surprised and caught off guard. He who had advised many kings and spoken in a hundred great councils was momentarily without words. "I shall accept your charge, my friend." Never before had Merlin agreed to take direct control over the affairs of those he advised. I owe you this, my friend, he thought.

"My thanks to you. There is no one in whom I have greater confidence." Uther then took his scabbard off his belt and laid his sheathed sword on the council table. He walked over to the fireplace, feeling a slight warmth from the prior evening's fading embers, and grabbed his grandfather's sword from the mantle. He pulled the blade partially from the sheath and looked at the polished steel briefly, then slammed it back in place and hooked the ornate scabbard to his belt in place of the one he had removed.

"This was the blade of a king of Britannia, of an emperor. He spoke partly to Merlin, partly to himself. "It shall see battle once again as this nation is united. The land may have but one high king, and all must swear fealty to him. To me. They will yield or I shall leave them as a feast for the carrion birds. My father used diplomacy; Vortigern used fear. I shall use both. Those who do not recognize me as high king shall lie buried under the ruins of their shattered strongholds. Those who oppose me shall answer to God for the sufferings of their subjects, for the bloody scourge of war that is visited upon their farmers and townsfolk. For villages burned, for children slain, for the women taken by the bloody hand of the soldier. The sin be upon any who fail in their allegiance to their high king."

The deadly resolve in Uther's voice surprised even Merlin, who stood in silence listening. What Uther was becoming he could not know, for never in all his many years had he heard a man speak with such terrible resolution. He feared for the Uther Pendragon he knew so well, yet he found himself believing his friend would prevail in his coming wars and gain a kingdom. Whether it would cost him his soul, Merlin knew not.

"Your father awaits you, to bid you farewell and give you council. Long has he been awake, for he knew you would be departing with the sunrise."

"I have naught to say to my father." Uther's tone was icy. "I have paid my price for this alliance, he shall pay his."

"Uther, Constantine has not many days left. He will likely die while you are on campaign. Would you depart without having words with him?"

"My father and I have had our last words." Uther walked to the door, then paused and glanced back. "Fare thee well, Merlin." With that, he walked into the corridor and out into the courtyard, leaving his troubled friend and advisor standing silently in the great hall.

Leodegrance sat his horse atop a hill and looked down over the forces deployed in the valley. For weeks he and his allies had played their game, convincing the forces of Vortigern that Caradoc was a great Visigothic prince, come to Britannia with his army to support the alliance. Confusion they had spread through the enemy's ranks, and now Leodegrance had decided the time had come to strike. Before him, arrayed for battle, was the levy of Cameliard, and alongside his men were drawn up the forces sent from Cornwall. Half of Gorlois' troops marched north with Uther, while the balance remained to defend the south.

The young king of Cameliard had positioned half his horsemen on the right of the army, retaining a force of picked men with him on the hill as a reserve. In the center he had placed the main body of Cameliard's warriors, armed mostly with axes and swords, and alongside them, the spearmen of Cornwall. On the left, under Gareth, the Lord Marshal of Cornwall, stood Gorlois' heavy horse. In all, more than four thousands of warriors awaited the command for battle, and yet this was not all their enemies saw. For marching along the hill behind Leodegrance, as though moving to outflank them, the enemy saw a large force of Visigothic warriors, their round shields emblazoned with brightly colored coats of arms.

At the head of this force rode Caradoc, wearing armor and a tunic of incredible richness, and surrounded by nine bodyguards. With him, in the foe's estimation, was his marshal, though had the enemy been able to see through the hooded cloak he wore they would have recognized the old man beneath. For Merlin rode with Caradoc, playing the role of his general, and the army they led consisted of every kitchen servant and farmhand they'd been able to assemble.

For weeks, every craftsman in Powys and Cameliard worked at Merlin's behest, fashioning large round shields in the Visigothic style. Now this phantom army took the field, and marched from the hill, in full view of the enemy, into the forest, as if moving to cut off the foe's retreat.

Catigern, commander of the force that faced them, stared nervously at the army arrayed before his. Younger son of Vortigern, he had been appointed Marshal of the South and charged with bringing the southern kingdoms to heel. He had unleashed his forces on the countryside and spread terror among the peasantry and townsfolk, undermining their morale and their resolve to resist. Finally, when he gave battle he ambushed and destroyed the force sent to meet him, slaying hundreds, including the King of Cameliard. Victory was within his grasp before the young heir returned to rally his forces and avenge his father. Worse, he brought with him allies, a Visigothic warlord and his army, and with their aid he destroyed the raiding parties. Now emboldened, the new king had taken to the field in force and marched east to confront Catigern's army.

Catigern was worried, for though he still had the advantage in numbers, the margin was far less than he had thought it would be. Why, he wondered, would Leodegrance come out of his fortresses and meet a superior army in the open? Even with the forces of the Visigothic prince standing against him, Catigern had half again the numbers of his enemies. Unless there was another surprise that Leodegrance kept hidden, waiting for the right moment. Another ally? A traitor in Catigern's army?

What he did not consider was that Leodegrance was a different sort of man than he. Catigern was a bully, and his courage was fed by having the upper hand. A fair fight he would try to avoid, and one where he was outmanned would completely drain his resolve.

Leodegrance was a hero - aggressive, determined, and indefatigable. He chafed at inaction and would jump at any chance to fight his enemy. He knew not how long the ruse with Caradoc would fool his foe, nor did he trust in the alliance with Gorlois lasting indefinitely. Now he had the enemy confused and two thousand troops of Cornwall at his back. He would strike.

He would have attacked already, but he wanted to give the foe the chance to see his false Visigoths. Now the decoy troops were almost out of view in the forests on the right. He gave a command and one of his standard bearers dipped the flag of Cameliard - the signal for the cavalry on the wings to charge.

The horsemen of Cameliard, the barons and landowners, spurred their horses forward, screaming cries of bloody vengeance for their slain king. They faced a company of mounted Britons wearing the red livery of Vortigern, and behind them a large force of Saxon foot. Leodegrance's nobles thundered across the valley with such ferocity the enemy horsemen were momentarily shaken, and they hesitated before they countercharged. The men of Cameliard thus had the impetus and they crashed into their foes, throwing javelins then savagely slashing with their swords. The enemy horsemen fought back for a moment, then wavered and broke, fleeing in disorder with Leodegrance's men in pursuit.

On the other flank, the nobles of Cornwall faced the larger contingent of Catigern's cavalry and the two forces locked in a bitter and confused melee. Leodegrance watched the fighting on both flanks and, as the infantry lines in the center crashed into each other, he led the hundred mounted men he'd kept back on the hill around the left. With the king in the forefront, they charged into the flank of Catigern's cavalry. Engaged to the front and flank, and overwhelmed by the ferocity of Leodegrance's charge, they broke and fled.

Catigern was unnerved by the fighting on the flanks, though he had Saxon noble infantry positioned as a reserve behind both, and those troops had formed shieldwalls and prepared to face the victorious enemy cavalry. The battle in the center was much more in his favor, as his numbers were greater, and his position was uphill from the attacking forces. Now was the time...

he would commit his infantry reserves and break then enemy center before Leodegrance's horsemen could fight through his shieldwalls.

"Lord Catigern!" The cry came from a young warrior riding hurriedly to his position. "The camp is under attack from the woods. They are behind us, my lord!"

The Visigoths, he thought bitterly, just as I feared. If Caradoc's army attacked them from behind while they were still fighting to their front, not one man in ten would escape. "Sound the withdrawal." His voice was cracking and high-pitched from fear. "Retreat. The army will retire."

The horns blew and all across Catigern's host the confused and startled warriors paused and gave ground. Fully engaged, they found it difficult to retreat, and they fell back slowly, still fighting. But confusion and fear sapped their morale and within a few moments panic began to spread. First in small groups, and then all across the line they dropped their weapons and fled.

Most of the infantry in the center escaped, but the Saxons posted on each wing were almost wiped out by the pursuing cavalry. Only a few survivors reached the woods and relative safety. Catigern himself was overcome with fear and fled the field ahead of his army, whose retreat became a confused rout of abysmal disarray. In their desperation to escape, his forces left their camp and all their baggage and fled for their lives.

In the woods near the abandoned camp stood Owin, master hunter and gameskeeper to King Leodegrance. He and fifty of his fellows emerged from the dense woods from which they had been throwing javelins and pretending to be several thousand Visigoth warriors preparing to attack the camp. Owin was tall, more than six feet, and gray of hair, for he had seen five and fifty summers. He had served three generations of Leodegrance's house, but never had he rendered greater service than that which he and his hand-picked fellows had done this day. The plan was Merlin's, but it was Owin and his men who had seen it done.

Into the empty camp they swarmed, and if they took the chance to pick out the best of the spoils, such were the fortunes of war. Owin was sitting on a felled log and enjoying some of Catigern's finest ale when King Leodegrance rode up to the camp. With the king was Caradoc, who had convincingly played his part in the ruse, and Gareth of Cornwall. Owin leapt to his feet and bowed to his king. Leodegrance's arm was bandaged, and his tunic was torn in several places.

"Greetings, Owin. Good service have you given this day my noble woodsman. Indeed, this day you are a hero of Cameliard."

Owin bowed deeply. "You are too kind, sire. My life has been service to your noble house. I am yours to command, now and always."

Leodegrance smiled. "Today my command is simple, for if you and your band of freebooters have not yet had your pick of loot from the camp, then I bid you take what you will, for well have you earned it this day." A cheer went up from the hunters and woodsmen who were close enough to hear the king's words. Owin bowed again and walked back to his men, for while they had indeed already plundered the camp, he thought there would be no harm in appropriating bit more with the king's blessing.

Leodegrance, meanwhile was receiving riders sent from across the field. The foot in the center had lost heavily against the more numerous foe, and while the mounted companies had fared better, still he had over 400 slain in total, and many more wounded. It took many hours to count the enemy dead, and while Leodegrance never knew how many wounded had fled, on the field lay over 1,200 of the foe, most of them killed as they tried to flee. The army of Catigern was defeated and dispersed, and it would be many months before the south was again under serious threat of invasion.

"We must pursue." Gareth's tone was arrogant and prideful. "The enemy flees in disarray."

Leodegrance sat atop his horse in silence for a moment, as if considering his options. "Nay, Gareth, for though I also long to follow and destroy the foe, we know not what other forces await to the east. Indeed, the army we have just faced was beaten largely by deception and not force of arms, and despite their losses here today, they still outnumber us greatly. Our appointed task is to hold the south and to protect our lands and people, not to invade far to the east, away from our support and supplies. I ache to give the order, but as king I must consider more than my heart's longings. We shall return to Caerleon and regroup. At least until we can send scouts east to truly determine what we would face.

Gareth wore a sour expression, for he clearly did not agree with the king, though for once, the troublesome lord kept his tongue and obeyed without question. He took his leave of Leodegrance and rode off to organize the Cornwall forces for the march back to Cameliard.

Leodegrance dismounted and sat on the log that Owin had left, and he sighed heavily. His page handed him a wineskin, and he drank deeply from it, wiping his lips with his tattered sleeve. Well, Uther, he thought, we have held the south for you, at least for now. Fare thee well, my friend, in your battles in the north.

Uther's men had marched three days, and great was their misery, for the weather had turned colder still, and a foot of snow fell. Men struggled to move forward, and each step was bought with pain and perseverance. But Uther would not relent, for since Caelin had arrived at Caer Guricon, he was resolved to save King Urien no matter what the cost. Everywhere in the host Uther seemed to be, rallying the men and driving them forward, and little did it appear he slept. Nothing he asked of his soldiers that he himself did not endure, and by this example - and by ruthless discipline - he kept his ragged army together and moving. Over a mile they stretched, two abreast on the narrow old road.

Each day men died, and any who fell from fatigue were soon frozen where they lay. Faster even than the men perished the horses, and while Uther left his castle with 400 mounted men at arms, over 100 of the great warhorses had already succumbed. The smaller pack mules fared better, but they too were dying, and men had to carry what load a fallen animal had before.

Uther rode with Caelin, and all day he questioned the young warrior regarding the siege. Again and again he asked about the enemy's numbers, their dispositions, the state of King Urien and the defenders within the beleaguered city. Slowly they continued north, fighting the weather every step. Their exertions were past the endurance of normal men, and only Uther Pendragon's iron will held the army together until a fortnight and a day since they'd left Caer Guricon, when even his mighty resolve seemed no longer force enough to press the men onward.

"The ruined inn!" It was Caelin who shouted excitedly. He pointed toward the fire-ravaged wreck of an old building. "I passed this hulk no more than four hours after I left Carlisle. We are but a half day's march from the city."

Uther halted the column and ordered that the camp be made at that spot, though several hours of daylight remained. He intended to surprise the Picts, and he would not chance moving closer until the morrow, when they would attack. Word spread rapidly through the army that they were near to their destination, and the news of the early stop to the march was greeted with great joy, tempered almost immediately by Uther's order that no fires be set. He would not allow smoke to warn the enemy of their presence, so he and his soldiers would endure without.

The troops ate their cold supper and covered themselves the best they could to pass the frozen night. For Uther, there was no sleep, and he wandered the camp, watching the men trying to stay warm under whatever piles of coverings they could find. He spoke to any he found still awake, giving words of encouragement before sending them off with orders to rest.

Uther pulled his fur cloak tighter about him and looked up at the starry sky and the moon's tiny sliver. Tomorrow it will be new and the night black, he thought. Perhaps darkness is the ally I seek. We must have surprise, for we will be outnumbered, and we cannot long stay in the north. We have other enemies to face ere long. He fell to his knees and softly prayed. "God, grant us victory tomorrow, and give me the strength to unite this bleeding land. All that is important to me I have sacrificed to this fight, and my blood also I shall give if that be thy will. I beseech thee to instill strength into my soldiers hearts, lest their courage fail them on the field. Help us smite the heathen enemy whose banners are stained with the blood of thy children."

All through the night Uther walked about the camp, thinking, planning, strategizing. By the first flickering rays of dawn's light, he had resolved on a course of action, and as his lords rose he collected them, and together they broke their fast as he laid out his plans.

It was long past midday when the army broke camp, for Uther wanted to reach the enemy after darkness had fallen. Before beginning the march, they did much preparation, for each man was given a torch, and all were fully arrayed for battle as they left camp. There would be no stop, no time to prepare later - they would attack immediately upon reaching the enemy.

Caelin rode in front with Uther, and he directed the army stealthily to the reverse slope of the ridgeline south of Carlisle. Orders were passed throughout the host, and in each company men kindled fire pots and the torches were lit. Weapons at the ready and blazing torches held aloft, Uther's army awaited the order to charge. They were arrayed with mounted troops in the first line and infantry behind, and in the forefront, ready to lead the attack, was Uther Pendragon himself.

He turned upon his horse and looked upon the rows of flickering torches…his army ready to attack. "Now is the time, my brave warriors. For this we have marched through snow and ice and over the bodies of our fallen brothers. For you who fought last year, your vengeance is at hand, for to this enemy we shall be death incarnate. Nowhere would I rather be than here, at the head of this fearsome host. Curse those who sit before their fires this night drinking spiced wine, for it is we who wield God's bloody sword. Bring me no prisoners; let not one of them live. Follow me, and charge home crying Britannia!"

With that Uther spurred his mount and galloped over the crest of the ridge. Throughout the host a great war cry came up, and as one the mass surged forward. Many cried "Britannia," as Uther bade them, yet still more screamed, "Uther" or "Pendragon," as they surged up and over the crest and down the hillside.

The lookouts in the Pictish camp stared in stunned silence

as a storm of fire swept over the hillside toward them. They screamed and sounded the alarm, but then the flaming death was upon them. First came the horse, over 200, carrying javelins and torches. Into the camp they thundered, hurling their spears and torches with deadly effect, then drawing swords and slaying any they could reach. Uther's sword, the blade of an emperor, struck again and again, and all around him were heaped the bodies of those he'd faced.

More and more Picts emerged from burning tents and ran from the other camps, but hundreds were cut down, and the rest broke and fled, running back toward the city and away from this new doom that had fallen upon them. From the battlements atop the wounded city came a cheer, soft and ragged at first, but growing. Soon there were hundreds of warriors on the wall screaming wildly as Uther's men sliced through the foe, pursuing the routing survivors as they broke right and left around the walls of Carlisle.

Just as the fleeing Picts neared the walls, the south gate opened, and King Urien charged out at the head of 150 men at arms, riding the last mounts in Carlisle. Trapped between the two converging forces the enemy threw themselves to the ground begging for quarter. Uther looked upon the miserable Picts huddling together groveling for mercy, but his heart was ice. "To the sword," he screamed again and again. "Put them all to the sword. Every one." It was but a few minutes before the bloody work was done, and nary an enemy warrior remained alive outside the south wall, but only the wretched camp followers - women and children who cowered and awaited their fate at the hands of the victors.

But the battle was far from done, and Uther rode to King Urien and hailed his royal cousin. "Well met, Urien, my brother. Will you ride with us around your fair city? For to the northern end we now go to finish what here we have started. Then behind him, to the host he issued his cry. "Around the city! To the north! For our work is not yet done this night."

Uther did not await Urien's stunned response, for the King of Rheged was shocked to see him at the head of the relieving army, and no words came quickly. In an instant, Uther was gone, riding around the walls to engage the foe on the other side. "To the northern wall," Urien called to his own men. "Follow Uther Pendragon!" And with that Urien rode off after Uther, drawing his sword and shouting again, "Follow Uther Pendragon!"

It was warm in the great hall of Urien's stronghold, truly warm. The massive hearth was piled high with logs and a roaring blaze was going. Uther realized he had hardly remembered what it felt like not to be cold, and he savored the wave of heat coming from the fire. He still wore his armor, and his tunic and cloak were slashed and soaked with blood. He had a torn rag tied over a nasty gash on his arm, where a Pictish chieftan had scored a hit before Uther ran him through. The battle had raged all night, for the enemy on the northern side of the city had been warned and fought back fiercely. Once the two sides were engaged it was a confused melee, warrior against warrior, and by midday the field was covered with the fallen. All around the walls the dead and wounded lay in the bloodstained snow.

Urien had sent Caelin back into the city to bring orders for the infantry within to sally out and take the enemy in the rear, and once again the young warrior made his way past the foe and carried out his king's command. He and 500 infantry streamed out of the main gate, and the Picts, already exhausted and now beset on all sides, broke and ran, with Uther and Urien leading their mounted warriors in vengeful pursuit.

Across the frozen river they had chased the foe, slaying all they could reach, and then they charged into the force besieging Uxelodunum, sweeping all away. All save one band, which stood fast under their giant chieftan, and for a time looked as though they might become a rally point.

Uther, dismounted when his horse took a spear to the thigh, faced the Pictish champion in single combat. It was an epic battle, and for long they traded blows, each unable to gain the advantage. The Pict was the stronger, but Uther the faster, and their swords clanged loudly amid the din of battle. Finally, the Pict slashed Uther with the tip of his sword, opening a long, ragged gash in his arm. Uther stumbled as if he were about to fall, but then spun around and plunged the point of his sword through his adversary's back, shoving with all that remained of his strength. The Pict bellowed loudly and then looked confused for a moment as he stared down in bewilderment at the bloody sword protruding from his chest before it finally occurred to him to die.

Uther pushed the body of his enemy to the ground, letting it slide slowly off his blood-covered sword, and then he raised his weapon over his head and screamed a terrible war cry. Seeing their great chief slain, the rest of the Picts lost heart and fled in rout. Uther's men began a half-hearted pursuit, but they were at the end of their strength and soon returned to the field and sank to the ground in exhaustion. Uther stood in the center of the field, blood pumping out of his wound and dripping into the snow. Caelin rushed to his side, and tearing a section from his own tunic, he bound the wound the best he could. He then bade Uther take his horse that he might ride into Carlisle with King Urien as was his due.

As Uther mounted, a cheer arose from the assembled warriors, his and Urien's, and even Gorlois' men from Cornwall. All along his route back to Carlisle they chanted, "Uther, Uther, Uther!" He waved as he rode, but finally he could feel his strength fading, and once they were through the main gates he slumped forward and let the horse bear him into the stronghold.

Now, the warmth of the fire brought some feeling back to his frozen and exhausted body. Servants arrived, bearing flagons of hot wine and trays of food, and King Urien himself poured a cup and served it to Uther. "My thanks to you, Lord Uther and my loyalty and friendship for all time. You have saved my kingdom and people, and ever shall you and your brave warriors be welcome in Rheged."

"King Urien," Uther replied, "honored I am to count you as an ally. Much there is we must discuss, for little can you know of events in the south."

"I am most anxious to hear all you have to tell me. Yet a poor host, and worse friend, would I be if I did not offer you food and see your wounds properly tended."

"Indeed, I am hungry. I had quite forgotten food for the cold and the battle, but now the warmth of your hall restores my vitality, and I would gladly accept your hospitality. Let us sit and eat and talk of things, for the wound will wait until supper is finished. Caelin has done a credible job of bandaging, and I am sure it shall hold for now." They sat together and ate, for Urien's servants had brought large plates heaped with bread and salted meats and cheeses.

"Alas, I fear my larder is rather bare. I wish that I had more to offer than this poor fare."

Uther smiled. "After a fortnight on the winter trail, such as you have set before me is a feast worthy of an emperor." He took his knife and skewered a large hunk of salt pork, dumping it on the plate in front of him and sawing off a slice.

After Uther had filled his plate, Urien took a hunk of bread and a large slice of cheese. "I have given orders that all of your men be fed and their wounds tended. Your warriors shall all sleep indoors tonight, for I cannot imagine the ordeal you all suffered in marching to our aid in such weather. We had been rationing our firewood, but now with the siege broken, there shall be no hearth unlit tonight."

Uther washed down the slice of pork with a hearty gulp of wine. "You have my thanks, Urien, for our march was hard indeed, and the losses we bore today were bitter. Other tidings I bear, and these also are dark, for my brothers are all slain, and my father lies in Caer Guricon, close to death."

Urien looked up from his plate with a start. "All of your brothers dead? And old Constantine dying? How did things come to such a pass?"

"My brothers were all killed in the field. Indeed, Constans fell leading a relief force north to aid you last summer. I fear there were spies in his host, for they were ambushed on the march and my brother slain. I would have you know that my father did not ignore your need, and that he did try to send forces to your aid."

"Never did I doubt your father, yet I could not divine why

no help had come. For almost a year I looked to the south each
dawn and dusk, waiting, praying to see the relieving army marching to our aid. When I saw the torches of your forces charging
down the hillside it was as if the fires of hell had come forth to
swallow the enemy."

Urien looked down at the table silently for a moment. "Sorry
I am about your father, yet not surprised. For at the council I
thought he was troubled by some ill, though he fought mightily
to hide it. But your brothers...all three of them. These are evil
tidings. Such loss you have suffered. I would offer my condo-
lences and my respect to the fallen."

"I thank you for your kind words. Yet we must purpose
ourselves to the task that lies ahead, for many battles remain
before us, I fear. Time enough to mourn the dead when the
fight is won."

"You shall be king of Powys. All my life I have been destined for the throne. Since boyhood I have been trained to be
king, and every waking moment was tasked to that purpose until
the thought of wearing the crown was hateful. Yet such was
the calling of my birth. But you, my friend, find the kingship
falling to you unexpected. Many burdens does the crown carry,
as you will no doubt come to see. As you have indeed already
come to know."

"Fate does not ask our council." Uther's tone was matter-
of-fact. "King I shall be, whether I will it or no. But if I am to
be king, then I shall be also high king, for such was my father's
right, and by succession, mine. This land must be united. No
more can we waste our strength fighting among ourselves while
invaders and usurpers gain power."

"I was prepared to accept your father as high king." Urien's
eyes bored into Uther's as he spoke. "In you I perceive a strength
such as I have never seen in another. I, Urien, King of Rheged,
will be the first to accept you as High King of Britannia. And
at your side I shall fight this war - north, south, east, west, wherever the enemy may be. Wherever you command me to go, I
shall go. Let it be victory or death."

"Honored I am to accept your fealty and your friendship. I

shall have great need of warriors and honorable friends such as you."

When they had supped, Urien sent for his sister, Andra, and bade her stitch up Uther's wound. Andra came into the hall, clad in a simple yellow dress. She was beautiful, with long dark hair and shimmering blue eyes, and she bowed before Uther, smiling sweetly as she sat beside him and slowly unwound the blood-crusted bandage from his arm. Uther winced slightly as Andra pulled the wound together and began stitching. Urien was thinking also of matches, for his sister would make an ideal wife for Uther. But no thought did Uther give to a wife, or indeed to any woman save one, and she was far away and not his.

Uther remained at Carlisle for a month after the battle, for his men had suffered greatly and needed rest. Many days the heralds had spent tallying the fallen, and no record has survived with reliable numbers of those slain at the battle, now called Gwen Ystrad. Yet it is said that a generation of Picts fell, and fewer than one in five ever returned to their lands in the north. Those few that did brought with them tales of the terrible warrior king, Uther Pendragon. For days the fires smoldered as the victors burned the bodies of the dead invaders. It was a decade or more before the northerners again troubled the Britons living to the south, and never again did they do so in the same numbers.

Uther had lost a third of his men, though of these, many were wounded and would heal to fight again. Urien's forces suffered greater losses, for they had endured nearly a year of siege, and many had succumbed to pestilence and disease or died defending the walls. Barely 600 men remained under arms in Carlisle, and in Uxelodunum, only seventy of the original five hundred defenders marched out of the relieved fortress.

In the weeks following the battle, Urien was strengthened by the arrival of the contingents of those lords who had been unable to reach Carlisle before it was cut off and besieged. Predominantly from the remote western regions of the kingdom, together they fielded over 700 men, mostly mounted men at arms.

One evening, about a month after the battle, Uther came to Urien, for they had much to discuss. His wound was nearly healed, for Andra had been very attentive. Uther became fond of the girl, but his heart belonged to his lost love, then and always, and he made certain not to give Urien's sister hope of more than his gratitude and friendship.

"Urien, my friend." Uther spoke as he walked into the throne room. "I would speak with you if I may."

"Indeed, you may speak with me anytime, for already do I regard you as my high king, and the war leader of the alliance. What may I do for you?"

"I would charge you with a dangerous task, for I must soon return to Powys. If we have not yet been attacked there, we soon shall be, and I can waste no more time now. Yet still must I find out what has happened to King Lot, for there has been no word from Luthien in many months.

"I will leave you a thousand of my men to augment your forces. Carlisle will be safe from attack for the near future, and I believe you can leave it lightly held. I would bid you take an army north and east and find out what has happened in Luthien. I know that Rheged and Luthien have ever had disputes, but now we are all allied, and it stains the honor of all if any of us is left to face the enemy alone."

"Such feuds of old shall not trouble us." Urien spoke with obvious sincereity. "I am committed to help you unite Britannia under your high kingship. I shall do as you bid, now and always. Five hundred men shall garrison Carlisle along with what remains of the town watch, and the rest shall march to Luthien."

"I am grateful for your loyalty. If I have allies such as you then I do not doubt for our victory."

The two of them sat, discussing strategy for Urien's march to Luthien when a servant entered the room and bowed to them both. "King Urien, a messenger has arrived from Caer Guricon and craves admittance to see Lord Uther. He says his business is urgent."

Urien glanced at Uther, then back to the servant. "Send him in immediately, Emlyn."

The servant bowed again and hurried out into the corridor, returning a moment later with a tall warrior clad in armor and the blue and silver livery of Caer Guricon's house guard. The visitor bowed to Urien and then knelt before Uther, awaiting permission to speak.

Uther knew the visitor, for he was one of the captains of Caer Guricon. "Speak, Grigor, for you have traveled long to see me. Who dispatched you?"

"Merlin bade me come to you, sire, for he sends me with grave tidings. You father, God bless his soul, is dead."

Urien's face showed his grief, but Uther sat impassively, and he replied without emotion. "Thank you, Grigor, for bringing me this news. Have you other messages from Merlin?"

"Yes, my king," replied the still-kneeling warrior. He handed Uther a worn leather pouch full of parchments.

Uther reached out and took the satchel, and noticing that the messenger was still kneeling he motioned for him to stand. "Rise, Grigor, for you and I have bled together in battle. I would not have you wear holes in the knees of your pants."

Grigor rose and, reaching into a sack he had slung over his shoulder he pulled a small package, wrapped carefully in silken cloth. He handed it reverently to Uther. "He sent this as well, sire."

Uther took the bundle, and removed the silk coverings. In his hands he held the crown of Powys, solid gold, with five silver dragons perched along the top. The dragon's eyes were sparkling red gems, and along the bottom there was detailed scrollwork, listing the names of the kings of Powys. At the end of the list, freshly engraved, was written, Uther I. Uther found himself amused that his name was already on the crown. He thought to himself, you waste no time, do you Merlin? Indeed, he thought, Merlin is wise as always, for we have no time to waste.

"I thank you again, Grigor. You shall join our forces here, for I have need of loyal and true captains. Soon we will march back to Caer Guricon, for though we have won a victory here, it is but a brief respite, and the forces moving against us are still stronger then we."

"We shall march into hell itself, sire, if you lead us there." Grigor looked at Uther with great reverence. No enemy shall stand in our wake."

Uther's granite expression yielded to a tiny smile. "Your loyalty is greatly valued, Grigor. But now I command you to rest, for your journey was long, and I suspect you slept little on your way. Go now, and eat and sleep, and we shall speak again later.

Urien commanded his servant to make quarters ready for Grigor and to have the kitchens prepare a supper for the new arrival. Bowing again, the servant bade Grigor to follow, and the two of them walked out into the corridor, leaving Urien and Uther alone to speak long into the night.

Uther stood before the assembled army, for he had ordered all his captains to form their men in the plain north of Carlisle. On his head was the crown of Powys, and though it perched well upon him, he found it carried a weight far greater than that of just the gold and silver from which it was forged. For though he had already acted as king for many months, the priceless treasure he wore was a constant reminder of the burdens that were now his, and would always be until he closed his eyes for the final time.

As he stepped out onto the battlement over the main gate and looked down on the warriors assembled below, some in the front saw the crown on his head. Understanding the significance, they began to shout, "Hail Uther, king!" It began among a small group of the men from Powys, but soon the entire army chanted his name, and men from Rheged and Cornwall joined his own soldiers in celebrating his kingship.

He held out his arms to quiet them, but the tumult continued, and it was many minutes before he was able to speak. Finally he spoke, his voice loud and strong. "King Constantine is dead. May God bless his immortal soul."

The wave of noise from the troops rose again, not quite as loudly, as many of the troops shouted blessings for Constantine.

Uther waited for the shouting to subside and then continued. "My father began a great undertaking before he died, bringing together this mighty alliance, and we are going to see this war through to its victorious finish!"

Again Uther had to pause, for the shouts from the army were deafening. "This is not just Powys' fight, nor is it only Rheged's or Cornwall's, for all Britannia faces the same peril. Alone, none of us can stand, but united we will drive the invaders into the sea and punish those of our countrymen who have treacherously allied with the barbarians!"

The cries rose again, thousands of men cheering and shouting the same thing again and again. "Hail the high king, Uther!"

"Soon we will march. Some of you will go south with me, others north and east with King Urien, but we will still be together, brothers in arms, united against the foe! Our enemies have erred grievously, for they have placed their confidence in their numbers, not reckoning the true strength of free Britons fighting for their homes!"

He held his fist high in the air as he spoke, and his deep, booming voice carried over the assembled host. The warriors were driven nearly to a frenzy, screaming, banging their swords on their shields, and raising their arms in the air. Those who held banners or standards waved them frantically, and others grabbed torches and timbers from the fires to hold aloft.

Uther continued, his hands raised high in the air. "I ask naught of you than to fight alongside me, my brothers, for never shall I rest until our foes are beaten and driven before our arms. We will not fear, we will not hesitate, we will not negotiate! To hell we will send all who have despoiled our land and slain our comrades! To hell our blades shall dispatch them in thousands. To hell, where they all belong!"

The tumult continued as Uther disappeared below the battlements, and when a moment later he walked out of the open main gate, the cheering became even louder, with warriors screaming, pushing, trying to touch his cloak or just get closer as he walked among them. For an hour he strode through the ranks, clasping hands with barons and stopping to ask the names of the lowliest peasant levies. When he was done, the army - Gorlois' and Urien's men as well as the Powys levies - was his. The faltering morale from early defeats and the hard march north was forgotten, and in its place was the spirit of an army aching to follow its commander into any fight. Uther looked around as he walked from cluster to cluster of adoring soldiers and thought to himself, they are ready.

A woman's scream echoed through the halls of Tintagel Castle, then another, louder one. Outside, a late summer storm raged, and the howling winds whipped the torrential rains around the crenellated tower. Inside, behind the battened windows and great stone walls, there was excitement and activity, for a queen was about to give birth.

Igraine was lying on the richly made bed, her legs spread wide as the midwife spoke to her in calm, soothing tones. "The baby is almost here, my queen." She spoke softly, and gently rubbed Igraine's sweat-covered brow with a wet cloth. "Now you must push again."

Igraine breathed deeply and struggled, screaming at the agony. The midwife spoke again, this time excitedly. "The baby is coming. One more great push, my queen, and it shall be done." Igraine's magnificent copper-colored hair was a disheveled mess and her face was drenched with sweat. She clenched her fists and strained again, and then, just as she thought she could push no more, she heard the cries of the baby and the joyful mutterings of the midwife and her ladies.

"You have a healthy daughter, my queen." The midwife smiled happily. She took the child over to a basin of warm water and washed her gently before swaddling her in soft cloth. She walked back to Igraine, carrying the newborn bundled in clean white cloth, and handed the child into the waiting arms of the new mother. Igraine took her daughter into her arms and held her tightly. He face was plump and pink, and she had wisps of soft red hair, but it was her eyes that Igraine noticed first, for she had seen that steely gray color before.

Igraine was exhausted and pale, her bed clothes soaked with

sweat. Her ladies cleaned her up and brought her fresh bed coverings, while the midwife took the child and placed her in a small basket, covered in silken blankets.

It was perhaps an hour later when King Gorlois strode into the room, taking a cursory glance at the child, now sleeping in the basket beside Igraine. "Pleased we are, lady, that you have come through the birth well, though we had rather hoped for a son."

She looked up at her husband and spoke, her voice tone-less and without emotion. "Thank you, my lord. I am sorry that I did not give you a son and heir." His comment would have been hurtful if she truly cared what he thought, but she didn't. Gorlois did not smile exactly, but his dour expression softened slightly. "Worry not, my lady, for you yet shall give me an heir. Rest now." He turned and left the room as abruptly as he'd entered, without so much as another glance at the sleeping newborn.

Igraine sighed softly and thought about her life at Tintagel. So much had been taken from her, for she'd been forced to leave all she loved behind and journey to a strange land. Gorlois was a callous and cruel man, and little joy did she have in her marriage. She had done her duty in marrying him and accepted her obligations as his wife and queen, but she didn't love the course and thoughtless brute. She didn't even like him. She lived her life caught in a trap, a gilded one with many comforts, but a trap and a cage nonetheless.

She was achingly alone, for Gorlois would permit none of her former ladies to attend her at Tintagel, and though he'd pro-vided her with a retinue befitting a queen, no friend among them did she have. She saw little of her husband, and that only when he came to her bedchamber, though even then he mounted her like a bull and was done and gone in a few moments. It was noth-ing like her night with Uther. She smiled sadly as she thought of that brief moment of her life…and of Uther Pendragon.

Ah, Uther my love, she thought, where are you now? Do you suffer as I do? Are you safe at Caer Guricon, or do you struggle and bleed on the battlefield far from my aid and comfort? God keep you safe, my love, wherever fate may lead you. I do not think I could bear it if you were hurt or slain. Though I know you cannot come home to me, I beg God to spare you that you come home to whatever joys you may find in this life.

She turned and looked at her sleeping daughter and smiled warmly. "Anna, I shall name you, little one, for such was called Uther's mother. Your grandmother."

Chapter Six
The Field of Blood

478 AD
Canterbury, Capital of the Kingdom of Kent

"Since Uther Pendragon has returned our fortunes have taken an ill turn. When we set our bargain, Vortigern, I trusted to your words and plans. The conquest was to be a quick one, yet now we find ourselves pushed back and uncertain...and my brother Horsa slain in your son's defeat at the hands of Leodegrance and Merlin. Seven kingdoms are allied to Powys, and though our early battles were victories, and they looked ripe to fall, none have we yet taken. Too much faith did you place in the Picts, and by their failure the north has been lost, freeing Uther's warriors to face us, and three more victories has he since won. We are driven back everywhere."

Vortigern sat impassively and listened to the giant Germanic warrior king rant, for he was a vital ally, especially now. Six and a half feet stood Hengist, and as broad and strong as he was tall. Blue eyed, with long blond hair braided down his back, he wore a simple brown tunic belted over leather pants and boots. On his head was a crown, simply cast from bronze and adorned with semi-precious stones in a variety of colors. What a poor excuse for a king, Vortigern thought to himself. He looks like a barbarian pulled from the forest and crowned with a cheap child's toy. Which, of course, is exactly what he is. But he is still useful.

"Hengist, my friend, we have suffered setbacks, it is true, but we are still stronger than our foes." Vortigern spoke calmly, seeking to ease his ally's concerns. "Uther Pendragon is a problem, for his leadership has greatly exceeded my expectations. Indeed, of late he seems like a force of nature, emotionless and impervious to suffering, either his or of those who serve him. He is in some way possessed by a force we do not understand.

But we will prevail nonetheless."

He looked at Hengist, staring into the barbarian's blue eyes. "Many years it took me the gain control over Constantine's valet, and to make him the manner of the king's death. Yet despite the poison that should have taken him quickly, Constantine lived for many months more and looked even to regain his vigor for a time. Merlin, I fear, was the source of that last burst of strength, though in the end even he was unable to save the king. I feared for a time that Constantine's wily wizard had discovered my plot, but in the end he was fooled just as they all were." His lips tensed slightly as he spoke of Merlin, betraying fear of the mysterious old wanderer, but Hengist wasn't perceptive enough to discern it.

"Constantine Pendragon, I perceived, was the only man capable of forging such an alliance as we now face, and by Merlin's cursed interference he lived long enough to do so. Still would this coalition have faltered, but unlooked for was his youngest son's force of will, for the kings now follow Uther unquestioningly…and with greater obedience than ever they offered his father, for they not only respect him, they fear him as well."

Vortigern looked silently at the pewter cup in front of him, still half full of the harsh red wine he favored. He was an old man, older even than Constantine had been, though through his knowledge of the ancient arts he had slowed his decline somewhat. He was of middling height, and though once of powerful build, he had become thinner and frailer with age. His hair was silvery gray and his eyes dark brown, and he was clad in extremely fine red silken robes.

"We must attack soon, Hengist, for Uther's strength grows with each victory. Indeed, more than his strength, for quickly is Uther Pendragon becoming a legend. We can defeat warriors, we can defeat kings, but men are wont to perform extraordinary deeds when he whom they follow ceases to be a man and crosses into mythical stature. I daresay, an assassin may prove more useful than a score of armies, for the alliance would collapse without Uther, and indeed, his mystique would work then for us. All of the seven kings and their warriors would plunge into despair were their invincible warrior king to die, poisoned by his soup."

Vortigern paused and drank from his cup. "Merlin I would also have slain if such can be managed, for he has thwarted me too many times. For though Uther is the tool he uses against us now, and Constantine before him, it is Merlin who is the true enemy and architect of that which stands between us and dominion over Britannia."

Hengist shifted uncomfortably on his feet, with the barbarian's fear of the mystical. "Who can face a wizard and prevail? For any warrior can my men slay, even Uther Pendragon, but he who can summon sorcery is beyond the powers of men to confront."

Vortigern was amused by his companion's primitive superstitions. "Merlin is powerful and sly, yet he can be slain as any other man. Old he is, and wise, for he was aged already when I was a but a boy. But a man he is, and though long-lived, only a man. In him are the last vestiges of druidic power, yet these are waning, and with them his strength. And behind his skills and knowledge, he is mortal, even as you and I."

Hengist still looked nervous, as if they discussed something haunted and unspeakable. He opened his mouth to talk, but managed only a short grunt.

Vortigern wore an amused grin. "Worry not about Merlin, Hengist. Task yourself to rousing your men, that they might defeat Uther's army in the field. Concern yourself with cold steel and the hands that wield it, and leave the wizard you so fear to me."

Hengist was stung by Vortigern's taunt, and he flushed with anger. "I fear nothing." He slammed his fist onto the table and turned away.

Fool, Vortigern thought to himself. Do you remember nothing about how to handle these savages? "Hengist, you are a king and a trusted ally." His tone was coldly calculating, though his far less sophisticated companion did not perceive the manipulation. "Never would I doubt your courage or prowess in the field. I meant only that Merlin is an adversary more suited to my skills, while Uther and his army are best met with your veteran warriors."

Vortigern's words calmed Hengist's ruffled pride, and the blonde giant turned back to the table and sat down. "Forgive my anger, Vortigern. When we meet his army in the field, I shall personally take the head of Uther Pendragon and present it to you."

Such pointless bluster, Vortigern mused silently. Working with these barbarians is indeed trying. If you meet Uther Pendragon in battle, he thought, I fear it is your head that will fall, and that toy crown of yours will decorate the mantelpiece in Caer Guricon. "I depend on your valor, my friend." He stood up and placed a hand on Hengist's shoulder. "Though I have some hope that Uther Pendragon might die ere he reaches the field. Prepare your warriors, for soon we will march west and fight the final battle, whether he be alive to lead his host or no." He turned and began walking toward the large double door that led to the main corridor. He paused at the doorway and looked back at Hengist. "But now I have other tasks that await my attention. We shall speak again later." And with that, he disappeared into the corridor.

"Do you trust him, father?" A large blonde warrior spoke a moment later while walking in from the corridor leading to the kitchens. He was taller even than Hengist, and he had to duck to pass through the doorway without striking his head. He resembled Hengist greatly, for he was Octa, the king's eldest son and heir.

"Nay, my son." Vortigern thinks we are but stupid savages that he can use as he wills. Alliance has so far been to our advantage, but as high king he will never allow us to retain our rule in Kent, for he is a Christian, or at least all of his lords are. I know not what Vortigern worships in his heart. Perhaps only himself."

"I can have him seized now, father." Octa was brave, but young and impulsive. "He is within our castle and few of his own guards are present. We could be rid of him and the threat he poses."

Hengist frowned at Octa's reckless suggestion. "Don't be a fool, my son. You must think before you act. Still we must face Uther Pendragon and the kings of his alliance. A mighty warrior he is, and he will drive us into the sea if he may. No quarter does he give, nor does he compromise with foes. There can be no peace with this king; either he must be defeated and destroyed or we shall be. And he has able allies. Leodegrance, whose army slew your uncle, Horsa. Caradoc, the Visigothic prince. Urien, another warrior-king who cleared the north of Vortigern's allies after Uther broke the siege of his capital.

"The Britons allied with Vortigern are vital to us, for I fear we could not defeat King Uther without their numbers added to our own. And fighting alongside Uther is Merlin, who they say is a wizard of great power. No force have we to face the conjurings of a sorcerer. We must have Vortigern to deal with Merlin. Perhaps Vortigern's schemings will even work, and Uther and Merlin be slain in their stronghold by an assassin's blade." Hengist paused, and a wicked smile formed on his lips. "First we must face these foes. Then, once Uther's army is destroyed and Merlin defeated, shall we deal with Vortigern. Then all of Britannia shall be ours."

Vortigern walked through the corridors of the ancient stronghold that Hengist had claimed as his castle. Like most everything in Britannia that was strong and lasting, it had been built by the Romans. Indeed, some said that the original fort had been constructed by Caesar himself, when first the legions set foot upon the island.

He continued out into the courtyard and through the main gate, for he had set this meeting to take place where none of Hengist's men might listen. Alone he followed the winding trail that led down from the hilltop stronghold, and soon he was walking through the light woods in the valley below. In about ten minutes he came upon the large black rock that was his marker, and he turned left and followed a much rougher pathway through the trees and the sparse undergrowth. Finally, he could hear the sounds of a stream and a small waterfall ahead, and he knew he was close. At last, he thought, for my legs are leaden and they ache with pain. As he turned the corner he saw the meandering stream, fed by a four foot high waterfall, and standing on the bank waiting was a man who could have been a younger version of himself…his eldest son, Vortimer.

Vortimer held his hand up in greeting. "Hail, father. I have waited long for you. Were there problems?" Vortigern's son was clad in a black tunic over a chainmail shirt, and on his breast was emblazoned the red hawk, his father's device. His brown leather boots were covered with mud, and a large greatsword hung from his waist.

"Nay, my son. None other than bolstering Hengist's courage, for like all our lords, greatly does he fear King Uther."

"I do not trust these Saxons, father. I feel that only ill will come of alliance with them. And now we have made this pagan a king? Over a Britannic domain? Is this wise? Will it not hinder your relations with the other kings?"

Vortigern smiled. "Worry not, my son, for I trust our Germanic friends no more than you do. Indeed, a good deal less than you, I would say, for I have lived among them for some time, and I know their ways. Or rather, I trust them to behave as I expect, which is treacherously. But we need not worry about that now, for they cannot face Uther alone, and they are terrified of Merlin, whom their fears have made into the Devil himself. They will make no move against us until the armies of the alliance are destroyed and Uther Pendragon and Merlin are put to the sword. And before the Saxons can strike against us, I shall already have dealt with them. No pagan barbarian shall rule as a king in my Britannia." Vortigern's voice was confident, though it was clear he was also fatigued.

"But now, Vortimer, I have a task for you, for I would again make use of our friend in the court of Caer Guricon. Uther has likely maintained his father's staff, so perhaps we can poison the son as we did the father. Indeed, I would have both Uther and Merlin dealt with by these means if it can be arranged."

Vortimer looked surprised. "Huarwar will be too afraid, even if he is still the king's valet. And though he aided us against

King Constantine, it was only because he had no choice. Likely he worships Uther as much as all they seem to now. He will refuse."

"He will surely refuse." Vortigern spoke darkly, his tone malevolent. "Unless we motivate him as we did before. Still we hold his daughter, do we not? And was this not the means of securing his aid against Constantine, whom he was also unwilling to betray at first?"

"Yes, father, but we agreed to release her after he aided us, and we did not do so. He will not trust us again."

"No, my son, we agreed to release her when House Pendragon had fallen and I ruled all of Britannia. That has not come to pass, because Uther has proven to be a worse threat than ever his father was. Now we will alter Huarwar's bargain, for our misfortune is his also. He must poison Uther and Merlin, though now we have no time for slow-acting potions. You will send him this," - he withdrew a small vial from the sleeve of his robe and handed it to Vortimer - "for it is deadly. Just a drop in each of their wine goblets and the deed shall be done."

Vortimer took the flask and looked at it thoughtfully. "Do you believe he will do it?"

"Indeed I do, my son. Because we will leave naught to chance. Last time we sent him his daughter's ring as proof we held her. Now, let us add to his fear and motivation. This time, along with this vial, shall you send the finger upon which the ring once rode."

Vortimer smiled coldly, for he enjoyed cruel work. "I shall attend to it personally."

"Huarwar's message is simple." Vortigern looked at his son as he spoke. "If Uther and Merlin die, poisoned by his hand, he shall be rewarded with much gold, and his daughter will be released to him at once. If he should fail us, then his precious child shall die, and in such torment as he cannot imagine."

"I will send the messenger at once, father. If all goes well, we shall be rid of Uther and Merlin within the fortnight."

Vortigern rubbed his hands together. "And without them this alliance shall wither, and we shall defeat them with ease. All of Britannia shall fall under my high kingship, to which you will one day succeed. Go now, and see this task done that we might complete our victory."

Vortimer bowed to Vortigern. "Fare thee well, father." He turned and followed a path heading north through the woods, and in a minute he was out of sight.

Vortigern remained for a few moments, staring at the water-fall and the crystal clear stream, but seeing neither. Lost he was, in old thoughts and memories. Constantine, he thought, you have cost me a lifetime of delay, but now finally my victory is at hand. The last of your line shall I now extinguish, and for all time my house shall rule Britannia.

Caer Guricon was an armed camp. As far as the eye could see from the battlements of the citadel, the hills and fields were covered with the tents of soldiers. They were arranged in rough clusters, with plain canvas shelters surrounding the colorful pavilions of the kings and barons. Uther looked out over this sea of armed might with grim satisfaction, for soon he would lead this great host east to destroy Vortigern and all who followed him.

Four battles he had fought since he drove the Picts from Carlisle. All had been victories, but they had been fought against ancillary forces and not Vortigern's main strength. Nevertheless, Uther's legend grew with each triumph, and fear spread in the ranks of the enemy. For Uther Pendragon took no prisoners, and all those who fell into his hands were put to the sword. Traitors he branded all Britons who fought for Vortigern and, if captured, they could count themselves fortunate for a quick execution. Those with less luck were burned or buried alive. The Saxons and other invaders he treated as animals, and if captured they were butchered in whatever manner was most convenient.

Uther was idolized by his soldiers, and they were fanatically devoted to him, though it was awe more than love he inspired. He was too cold, too grim, too unflinchingly merciless for most men to love. But he gave them victory, and he made them understand that they fought for their homes, their wives, their children. He gave them pride and forged a victorious army from factions that had long fought each other in pointless feuds and petty duels.

The kings too were under his spell, for they knew well that without his leadership they would be deposed or become little more than Vortigern's slaves. They feared him also, for in the whole host there was not a man so courageous as to face Uther Pendragon's wrath. Such was the force that held this unlikely confederation together. All knew that there was little that would enrage Uther as much as petty arguments between his kings and allies, and none would risk his anger.

The hero was an empty man though, and in his soul, beneath the iron will and the driving passion to win, was a deep apathy. Uther fought because the war must be won. He was high king because that was his right, and he would suffer no one to deny him, not because he craved power or prestige. The true source of his elemental strength was something few understood. All that mattered to him he had already sacrificed to forge this weapon, and he would not allow that loss to be in vain. Whatever further price he may pay, regardless of the cost to others, Uther Pendragon would achieve the victory his heart demanded.

He heard the footsteps behind them, and he recognized the sound of that light, shuffling stride. "Hello Merlin."

Merlin was the one who came closest to truly understanding Uther Pendragon. Long had they been friends - for all of Uther's life, in fact. Merlin knew the price Uther had paid, and though he did not at first understand just how deeply wounded the king was by his loss, he had come to realize...and to regret his role in that tragedy. Sadness he felt for Igraine as well as Uther, for while the king could vent his pain into war and victories, for her there was nothing but the walls of Tintagel and a cruel husband she despised. You played a role in that Merlin, he thought. You sacrificed that beautiful young girl without hesitation.

"What is this?" Uther was surprised by his friend's dreamy silence. "Is it possible that Merlin has naught to say? Never did I think I would see the day."

Uther's quip brought Merlin from his deep thoughts. "And

is it possible that the dread High King Uther, destroyer of armies and merciless warlord, makes a jest? I thought never to see such again."

Uther gave Merlin a rare smile. "Indeed my friend, I must. For everyone else is too afraid of you to dare a mock. I sometimes wonder who is it they fear more, you or me?" The two of them stood side by side looking out over the camps. "So what think you, Merlin, of this vast host we have assembled. Only once have I seen so many warriors gathered together, in Italia when Odoacer slew Orestes and took control of the Roman army. Now but a few years later I have such a force at my command. Fate is indeed mysterious, my friend, for who could have imagined this road?"

"I tell you truly that I foresaw a great destiny for you, and thus I told your father." Merlin looked at Uther and smiled. "Yet even my vision was not so strong as to see this sight. Well have you done, my friend. Your father would be proud of you." Uther's face turned sour at the mention of his father, and he looked away as if to end the discussion. But Merlin was undeterred. "I am and always have been your friend, Uther, and I shall speak truly to you whether it anger you or no. You must let go of this anger and bitterness to your father. Deeply hurt he was when you refused to see him before you departed for Carlisle. I know the pain you have suffered from losing Igraine, but Constantine did only what he felt he must do, as did I. Forgive."

Uther was silent, staring out over the landscape, his hand sliding absent-mindedly over the stone of the battlement. Finally, he spoke, and his tone was gentle and sad. "Nay, Merlin. I cannot forgive. I took up my father's crown, and I brought the alliance that was so important to him to fruition. His shade will have to be content with that, for no more can I give."

"I also played a role in your pain, Uther."

Uther looked at Merlin, his steely gray eyes boring into the older man. "Indeed, and never shall I forgive you for that act. Yet I do not believe you knew what pain your actions would cause, and when you did, at least you made an effort at amends. I am angry with you for what you have done, but also grateful for that night with Igraine, for I know you went to great effort and no small risk to arrange it." Uther put up his hand to cut off further comments. "Let us discuss this no further. What is done is done. Tomorrow we march to our destiny, but for now I would have some supper. Join me?"

Merlin was about to say something, but he stopped and smiled at Uther. "Yes, my friend. I am hungry, and I would enjoy that."

Uther turned and held out his arm, gesturing for Merlin to step first through the entryway into the castle. Closing the heavy oaken door behind them, Uther followed Merlin down the winding, circular stairs to the main level then down the corridor to the great hall. Laid out on the long wooden table were platters heaped with mutton and game fowl and other meats. As they sat, Huarwar walked into the room with a large silver pitcher and filled their goblets.

Merlin took his cup into his hand, and Uther speared a small game bird with his knife, dropping it onto his plate before picking up his own goblet. He was about to drink deeply when Merlin, after suddenly putting his own goblet down, leapt up and slapped the cup from Uther's hand.

Uther stilled his instinctive reaction at being struck. "Merlin, have you gone mad?"

"Nay, my friend." Merlin's reply was breathless. "More than wine could I smell in my goblet. Essence of thorn apple. Though it has been many years since I have sensed that slight fragrance. Deadly poison, my dear friend. Too impatient to face you in the field, someone has struck at us in the heart of your stronghold, seeking to win the victory without a battle."

Uther looked at his counselor in stunned surprise, and was about to speak when Merlin noticed Huarwar lurking behind the doorway. At Merlin's glance the valet turned and started to run. "It was Huarwar."

Uther jumped to his feat. "Guards, bring me Huarwar, now! I want him alive." He turned back to Merlin. "And now you have saved my life by your uncanny senses. My thanks to you."

"And saved my own, as well, for it seems we were both targets of this assassination. Huarwar may be the tool employed, but there is no doubt that Vortigern is the puppet master. Nonetheless, I am surprised. Long has Huarwar served this house, and with great dedication. I would not have looked his way seeking a traitor. And thus, of course, did Vortigern also divine, for who better as an assassin than one whose loyalty was unquestioned."

It was but a moment before three guards dragged the terrified valet before the king. He was limping and bleeding from the mouth where two teeth were missing. The men at arms threw him to the floor in front of Uther and stood behind him with swords drawn.

"He is unarmed, sire."

Uther looked down on the prone, whimpering form of the valet. He was shocked, for the man had served his father for many years, and he could not imagine what had driven him to treachery. He was about to speak when Kelven, the captain of the guard came rushing into the hall.

He knelt just inside the entryway. "My lord Uther, I have just heard of this treachery. That such an act should occur under my guard. I am shamed my lord and deeply sorry. If you wish to dismiss me I understand."

Uther ignored the prostrate Huarwar for a minute and looked over at his captain. "Kelven, you have served this house for many years. Indeed, it was you who first taught me to wield my sword." He walked over and put his hand on the Kelven's shoulder. "Ever shall you be part of the Pendragon, my friend, for we would be diminished without you. This treachery went unnoticed by all. Indeed, it is only by Merlin's skills that we were spared. Now rise, captain, and we shall deal with this matter."

The king turned and walked back to the table, followed closely by Kelven. Uther's expression was emotionless as he looked down at the cowering servant, but there was murder on the captain's face. "Huarwar, why this treachery? Always have you been well-treated by my family."

The valet looked up at the king, tears streaming down his cheeks, but though he struggled hard he could not bring words to his lips. After a moment he looked away, unable to return

Uther's gaze any longer. Uther spoke again. "Huarwar, your life is forfeit for this act. Would you meet God with such a monstrous sin burdening your soul?" The valet remained silent, hunched over, staring at the polished stone floor. He made no sound but that of his piteous sobbing.

"Huarwar!" The voice was Merlin's, but there was an authority and coldness in it no one present had ever heard. Such was the power of that voice that even Uther was taken aback, and he said nothing and only watched his friend as he faced the treacherous valet.

"Stand, now and face your deed," said Merlin, and in his tone was the iciness of death. Huarwar looked up at him dully, his face smeared with blood and tears, and slowly he rose as Merlin commanded.

Merlin turned toward the guard captain, handing him a small bottle filled with a yellow liquid. "He is to drink this, Kelven. See that he takes it all and that none is spilled."

The captain motioned to the guards and two of them grabbed Huarwar's arms and held him fast, while the third pulled his head back and pried his mouth open. Kelven walked over, pulling a small stopper out of the bottle and pushing the vial into the valet's mouth. Huarwar choked and struggled, but he was held fast by the guards, and Kelven made sure every drop of the viscous fluid found its way down the prisoner's throat.

"Now, Huarwar." Merlin's voice dripped with ungraspable menace. "You will tell us all you know about this treachery. Who bade you commit this deed?"

Huarwar's face was utterly blank, as if his mind were wiped clean. He answered in a soulless monotone. "Vortimer, son of Vortigern commanded me to poison King Uther and the counselor Merlin." There was no emotion in his voice.

Merlin remained impassive, but Uther began to stiffen with rage. He remained silent, though, and allowed Merlin to continue.

"Why did you accept his command? Did he offer you gold?"

"Nay, my lord." He spoke in same lifeless voice. "He holds my daughter captive, for his raiders captured her as her party rode to her wedding in the north."

"And he threatened her?"

"Yes, my lord. The first time he sent me her ring to prove she was captive, but this time they severed her finger and sent it to me. I was ordered to poison the king and Merlin, or they would torture and kill her."

"The first time?" Merlin's voice was harsh, demanding. "What do you mean the first time?"

"When they commanded me to poison King Constantine. Many months did I put the drops in his wine goblet, though I was not always able to do so. That potion was different than this one. Long did it take, for they wished all to believe the king was ill and failing."

The room was silent, for everyone present was stunned by this news. Kelven's face was twisted in anger, and his body shook with the desire to break the neck of the treacherous servant. Uther was calmer, yet colder, his expression resolute and feral, as if ready to calmly cut Huarwar's throat without a word.

But it was Merlin whose expression was grimmest, for he slipped from his questioning deep into his own musings. Constantine, he thought darkly, blind must I have been, for I did not see in your ills this treachery. Indeed, had I been less blind you might still be alive. Forgive me, friend, for I too am old, and my powers fail me.

Huarwar stood unmoving, still looking forward as if in a trance. It was Uther who finally broke the silence. "Long has treachery worked against us in this fight." He looked at Huarwar, though the valet was still staring blankly at Merlin. "No more need I hear from this traitor. Take him away."

Uther watched the guards drag the valet's limp body into the corridor and out of sight. "Tomorrow we march, and all shall be redressed. The final battle is soon at hand, and we shall repay our enemy in full for his perfidies. God grant the Britons freedom and my soldiers victory. And for me..." He paused briefly. "For me I ask only vengeance."

Caer Guricon was a large town, its wattle and daub buildings surrounded in some places by an old stone wall, but in most with a wooden stockade built by Constantine after he gained the throne. The town was built all around a steep hillside, and at the peak was Uther's stronghold, built on the remains of an old legionary fortress. This day buzzards flew low over the battlements, for hanging in a cage from the rampart was Huarwar, not quite dead, but soon a meal for the scavengers.

At dawn, the great gates swung open, and out marched an army. Part of an army, for the rest was forming in the fields all around the town. First through the gate, mounted on a massive horse as black as obsidian, was Uther Pendragon, King of Powys and High King of Britannia, his raiment as dark as his hellish steed.

Alongside Uther rode Merlin, clad as always in his plain gray robes and riding a white horse that contrasted strongly with that of the king. Next came Uther's nobles and leaders - Kelven, captain of the guard of Caer Guricon, carrying the flapping blue and silver colors of the Pendragon; Caradoc, Visigothic noble and Uther's close friend; Elisedd, one of the great barons of Powys, and father of the king's lost love, Igraine. They were followed by all the lords and barons of the realm.

Next rode the lesser nobles and the men at arms, each contingent carrying both the banner of their own lord and that of the king. Finally, four abreast came the foot soldiers, commoners mostly, their spears and battleaxes held aloft as they marched. When the last supply wagon and laden mule passed through and the gate closed, Uther was already nearly a mile away, approaching the old east-west Roman road.

But the warriors of Powys were only a portion of Uther's strength, for after they marched down the road, the armies of the other kings formed up from their many camps and followed. First, the warriors of Cameliard, led by Leodegrance himself, his red banner flying high next to Uther's blue flag.

Next came Gareth, Marshal of Cornwall, leading the nobles and levies of Gorlois, their yellow and green pennants whipping wildly in the early morning wind.

Following them were the combined forces of Rheged and

Luthien, for King Lot had been trapped in his stronghold, grievously wounded, when Urien rescued him. Many old feuds were settled that day, and Urien now led the combined armies of the northern kingdoms to follow Uther wherever that road may lead.

Next came King Rience of Gwynned, who was a troublesome member of the alliance and frequently argued with the others. But Uther spoke with him privately one day, and he became pliable and cooperative. None but the two kings ever knew what Uther Pendragon said that day to his unruly ally.

Pellinore, leading the men of the Isles came next, and following his forces, the army of young King Vortiporius. There was bad blood between Pellinore and Vortiporius, but neither would dare defy King Uther, so they put aside their disputes and regarded each other with cool respect.

When the last of Vortiporius' levies from Dyfed marched down the road through the woods and out of sight of Caer Guricon, Uther was two hours and four miles distant, riding down the road heading east.

Twelve thousands marched with Uther Pendragon, all of the assembled might of the free Britons, for the final battle was near at hand, and great were the forces arrayed against them. Grimly they marched, for all knew what they faced and what was at stake. Their morale was strong despite the strength of the force arrayed against them, for they followed Uther Pendragon, the great warrior king. Death incarnate they imagined him, and it was said he'd killed over 100 men himself in this war.

Over the past twelve months, Uther had fought four battles, and though each was a complete victory, none was decisive. Only a tithe of the enemy's strength did he face in each, and while he instilled in them fear of his skill and ruthlessness, still they had under arms force greater than his. Finally, Uther had resolved to march east and one by one assault the strongholds of Vortigern's minions until he compelled them to meet him in the open field.

Now they marched to Barwick, capital of the kingdom of Elmet, the northernmost of Vortigern's remaining client states.

He proposed to take the stronghold of Masgwid, the king of Elmet, and burn the city to the ground. "I will make the east howl," he had said, "for they have joined with the invaders and are the blackest traitors." No force could dare face Uther except Vortigern's combined armies, so the usurper would either have to give battle, or see his allies destroyed one by one. For none could stand alone against Uther Pendragon and his warriors.

For ten days the army marched, through blazing heat and driving rains, and on the eleventh they camped on the outskirts of Barwick. They would attack at dawn. No siege would there be, declared Uther to all his host. They would assault the walls and not fall back until the town was theirs. At dawn the attack would begin. They would sup that night in Masgwid's castle or not a man would return. Such was the decree of Uther Pendragon.

Vortigern paced angrily before his allies and nobles. "Barwick! Taken in one day. One day! And Masgwid burned alive by that madman! Now east he marches, to Eboracum, so as to destroy the Kingdom of Deira as well as Elmet."

The usurper had raged all morning, for he had only just learned that his assassination plot had failed, and that Uther had marched the very next day, intent upon revenge. It was Vortimer who had told him. "Father, I fear that Huarwar has been caught and that Uther and Merlin yet live."

Vortigern had raged at the news. "That incompetent fool! He shall find that failing me has its consequences. His daughter - give her to the Saxons. I trust they will not be overly troubled that she has only nine fingers. They are to take her and pass her from one to another while she yet lives, and then her body is to be delivered to Uther's camp. Let them see what awaits their women and families when we have defeated them!"

Now, mere hours later a single messenger arrived from Barwick, and that one only because Uther allowed him to travel south with tidings. To add insult to injury, the courier had been branded with a dragon on each cheek. So angry was Vortigern that he slashed the envoy's throat himself then ordered his vassal kings and lords to assemble.

Now they stood before him, and he continued his rant. "Are you all afraid of Uther Pendragon? You had better be, for he comes for you...all of you. Best you rally your men and prepare to fight like demons. We are going to march and face this young conqueror, and you do not want to lose that battle. Do any of you think you can throw yourselves on Uther's mercy? Ha! For he has no mercy. King Masgwid, old and infirm, he had dragged screaming from his great hall and burned at the stake. If you go to King Uther you go to your own pyre, for he has sworn to slay all who have opposed him."

He looked at the uncertain faces of the kings and nobles standing around him. They were gathered in the great hall of his stronghold in Venta Belgarum, for Vortigern had summoned his allies and vassals together for a council of war. Uther's aggressiveness and the failure of his assassination plot had forced his hand. He disliked gambling all on one large battle, but he saw no other option. His forces would still outnumber his enemies, though Uther's destruction of the Picts, and now Masgwid, had narrowed the margin. He'd been forced to rely too heavily on the Saxons, and he knew this would make them difficult to handle after the victory was won. That, however, was tomorrow's problem. Today he had to face Uther Pendragon.

"You will assemble your levies here at Venta Belgarum, and the combined army shall march north. We shall take no chance at being set upon individually and destroyed by Uther's forces. Our march will put us between Uther and Powys, and he will be compelled to offer battle."

You will compel him to do exactly what he wants to do, thought Vortigern somberly. You have surrendered the initiative to this boy, and yet there is nothing else to be done. "Your forces are to be ready to march in seven days, for on the eighth we depart. A fortnight's journey shall bring us to battle, and then Uther Pendragon and his army will be destroyed."

Dawn came clear and cold to the fields around Verulamium, for fall had come early, and the night had seen the first frost.

The rays of early morning sun quickly warmed the day, which looked to be fair and pleasant. The old town, lying off to the west, was empty, for it had been abandoned a lifetime ago when the legions departed. Its stone walls and theater still stood, save for the gaping wounds where great chunks of building material had been excavated from the old structures. The city loomed ghostly and foreboding in the morning fog. To the north was a gentle ridge, and behind that a deep wood. Along the rise was formed an army, and in the center of that force, amid the flags and pennants of the host, flew the great blue and silver banner of the Pendragon.

No sound came from the assembled multitude, for they had been commanded to remain silent. Like shades they stood in their formations and watched, for in the valley below another army was hastily forming. The host of Vortigern had been caught unawares, for they had not thought to encounter Uther's army this far south. But the high king had foreseen their plan, and he had marched his men relentlessly that they might force battle sooner than the foe expected.

Uther sat upon his great black warhorse and watched the enemy warriors form themselves into hastily-organized lines. Tactics dictated that he should charge at once, and engage them while half their numbers were still marching onto the field. But Uther did not seek victory, he sought annihilation. He would wait until all of the enemy's troops were committed, for he was resolved that the opposing army be destroyed on this field.

In the valley there was much commotion, as lords shouted orders to their warriors, forcing them into a ragged line as quickly as possible. On the plain behind the newly assembled formation was Vortigern, mounted on a large brown stallion, a mail shirt over his usual red silk robes. "Curse Uther Pendragon," His voice was bitter. "How did he move so quickly? Not for half a fortnight did we expect battle."

But Uther had Leodegrance's huntsmen, the same company that had convinced Catigern they were a host of Visigoths, and he had them deployed to watch Vortigern's movements. When the great army began to march north, slowly and in disorder,

riders were sent immediately to King Uther. The king acted at
once, leaving a small force screening Eboracum and marching
south with great haste, driving his troops to make 25 miles a
day. By such efforts, they reached the field in a week. The army
facing his was disordered and caught by surprise, but they were
more than half again his number. Twenty thousands of warriors did Vortigern bring to Verulamium, and his lines extended
past Uther's on both flanks.

Uther's strategy was simple. In the center he positioned his
best heavy cavalry, for he would lead their charge himself and
split the enemy army in two. The horsemen were in the woods,
out of sight of Vortigern's men, and in front of them was the
lightest of his foot, mostly peasant levies from the west, armed
with javelins and shields.

To each side he deployed his heavy infantry, spearmen to
the left, opposite the best ground for an enemy cavalry attack,
and his own axemen on the right. On each flank was a large
company of horse, mostly lighter-armed levies from the northern borderlands. Leodegrance commanded the foot on the left,
while Caradoc led those on the right. The other kings were with
Uther, leading their men at arms as part of the great mounted
force.

Uther rode along the entire frontage of the army, shouting
to his troops and bidding them fight more fiercely than ever
they had. "Today we win this war." He shouted his exhorta-
tions and swinging his sword wildly as he rode before the cheering multitudes. "After this victory you shall all return to your
homes, to your wives, to your children." His words cut at him
as he uttered them, for he would return only to loneliness and
an empty castle. But now was the time for battle, and his own
pain he ignored.

"Free men of Britannia, never has a king commanded more
courageous and noble soldiers. I bid you fight like no men have
ever fought! Fight for your families. Fight for Britannia! Fight
for your high king! For I shall lead you in this battle, and I
swear I shall not leave the field other than in victory! If it not
be victory then you can leave my broken body a meal for the

buzzards."

All of this he repeated as he rode down the line, and the warriors worked themselves into a screaming frenzy, thrusting spears and axes and swords high into the air and shouting again and again, "Hail King Uther!"

Their foes had no such encouragement, for Vortigern could not inspire men in the field as Uther Pendragon. Indeed, his vassals and allied kings were hard pressed to get their men into line in time, for the massive army was a disorganized mob. The miserable levies and hastily assembled men at arms looked across the field at their shouting foes and their morale was leaden.

Vortigern's army was deployed conventionally, with the heavy cavalry on each flank, but they were still forming up to charge when the sounds of horns blared from the center of Uther's army, and the king galloped down the hillside with two thousands of heavily armored men at arms thundering behind him.

The earth shook from their charge, and the waiting infantry saw their doom approaching. They wavered, rallied for a moment at the urging of their captains, and then broke. Uther's horse plunged into their ranks as they fled, slashing and slaying wildly. With javelin and sword the men at arms massacred the routing foot, and soon the ground was littered with bodies and the surviving infantry from the center was in headlong flight.

Once they had broken the center infantry formations, another horn blew, and the horsemen rallied and split into two groups, one led by Uther and the other by Urien. They rode behind the remaining infantry lines toward Vortigern's cavalry forces on each flank.

Vortigern was stunned, for never had he seen mounted troops break off so abruptly from pursuing a broken enemy and reform to charge another target. But Uther's men obeyed his every command, not only out of respect but because none would risk his terrible wrath. Fear of Uther Pendragon overcame even bloodlust, for he had declared that any who ignored the blasts of the horns would be hanged, and none doubted his word.

Vortigern's men at arms hastily turned to face the threat from the rear and, with some disorder, they were able to meet the oncoming charges. Uther's men had morale and the disorganization of their foe in their favor, while Vortigern's fresher troops had numbers. On each flank, horse met horse in tumultuous melees, and for long they fought before the smaller cavalry forces Uther had posted on his flanks charged and struck the enemy men at arms in the rear. Beset on all sides, Vortigern's horsemen fell back in disarray, with Uther's exhausted men pursuing.

Throughout the melee, Uther Pendragon fought like a madman, and by the time Vortigern's cavalry were retreating he had slain at least twenty. On the other flank, Urien fought fiercely as well, and if his tally didn't equal Uther's, it was impressive nonetheless.

For another hour the cavalry forces fought, Vortigern's troops giving ground steadily. When the rout finally began, it happened quickly. First small groups of horsemen turned and fled, dropping their weapons and galloping away as quickly as they exhausted mounts could carry them. The panic spread rapidly, and within a few minutes, most of the survivors were in flight, and the few who stood were quickly overwhelmed. Pursuit wasn't an option this time, because the victor's mounts were exhausted and needed rest before they could charge again. Uther led a small force of the less-fatigued lightly armed cavalry behind the enemy army to aid Urien, but by the time they arrived the enemy had been put to flight on that flank as well.

While the horsemen were engaged, the infantry clashed all along the battle line. Uther's men charged down the hillside and slammed into the enemy foot, and the two sides were soon locked in a desperate struggle. On the right, Uther's forces steadily pushed back their more numerous adversaries, and losses were heavy on both sides. But on the left, Hengist's Saxons stood firm, positioned on a small hillside from which they repulsed the repeated charges of the infantry of Cornwall and Cameliard.

The giant Germanic king stood in the forefront of his men

and laid low all who came near him. Five times did they send the free Britons retreating down the hillside. For hours they stood firm, while all over the field their cause was being lost. Finally, Uther himself led the victorious infantry from the right around to assail the Saxons from behind, while Leodegrance rallied the defeated infantry and led them in one more charge.

Facing enemies both to the front and rear, Hengist formed his men into a circular formation and, using the hillside to great advantage, held out against the overwhelming assaults until late in the day. Finally, exhausted and no longer able to hold, Hengist led the best of his men as they cut their way through the encircling forces and fled the field. All along the hillside, scattered groups broke free and ran, while hundreds of others were cut down trying to flee.

The Saxons had been the last organized resistance remaining, and with their flight, Uther's victorious army stood alone on the field. The Battle of Verulamium was over.

Chapter Seven
The Vengeance of Uther Pendragon

478 AD
The Field of Verulamium

Uther stood grimly on the hard-fought hill where Hengist's men had made their last stand, and he watched the red sun setting slowly over the field of battle. Before him was a scene that could have been a vision of Hell. Nearly as far as the eye could see, the hillsides and plains were covered with the dead and wounded. The dead, at least, were at peace, but thousands yet remained alive, bleeding and broken on the field, and their moans chilled even Uther's soul. Horses, too, had been killed and maimed in hundreds, and the sounds of the wounded animals was louder and more piteous still than that of the men. And in the skies, the carrion birds screeched wildly, for never had such a feast been presented to them.

His men wandered over the field, gathering their wounded and dispatching the poor, terrified horses as quickly as they could reach them. They were all fatigued, and the task was overwhelming. Uther's body burned with exhaustion, for he had fought all day like a demon, and it had been long since he'd slept. Still he could not take his eyes off the bloody field. The wind had picked up, and the tattered banners rippled eerily in the fading light.

This is victory, Uther thought darkly. It is for this we fought so hard and sacrificed so much. These thousands have died that I might be high king instead of Vortigern. Was it worth it? Will the thousands of souls I have sent this day to petition before God speak my praises? Does it matter so much after all who rules?

It was indeed victory, for though Hengist and Vortigern

escaped the field, their armies were shattered, and many of their allied Britannic monarchs had fallen. There was work still to be done, but the issue was no longer in doubt. Uther Pendragon was high king of Britannia, and there were none with the strength to challenge his rule. It was Leodegrance's voice that woke Uther from his trance. "So we have prevailed, my old friend." He spoke softly, his voice hoarse, showing his fatigue. "And you are high king. Long may you rule." He bowed before Uther then walked up to stand beside him.

Uther turned and smiled grimly at his friend. Leodegrance wore a bloody makeshift bandage, for a Saxon sword had slashed open his shoulder, a wound messier than it was dangerous. With him stood Caradoc and Merlin. Caradoc too, was stained with blood from head to toe, though little of it was his own. He had fought with great passion and skill, and he'd slain ten foes that day. He looked at Uther and laughed softly. "It is quite a journey I embarked upon when I swore myself to your service. Though I am not a native of this land, I am proud to hail you as my king. And my friend."

Uther nodded to Caradoc, though still he was silent, for he knew not what to say. Blood flowed slowly from his arm where a javelin had pierced him, though he hardly seemed to notice the wound.

"Let me tend to that." It was Merlin who spoke, and he retrieved a small wooden box from his robe. He removed the top to reveal a foul-smelling black salve, which he then smeared on Uther's arm while the others made faces at the stench.

"Gods, Merlin," said Leodegrance, "from what rotten carcass did you harvest that evil concoction?"

"My concern is not the delicacy of your nostrils, my friend, but rather the effectiveness of my remedies. I daresay we have greater need of kings than to watch them die needlessly from festering wounds. Indeed, you are next, for that filthy wrapping covering the gash on your shoulder is far from adequate."

"Mercy, Merlin. For they shall mistake me for last year's compost when I enter the camp."

"It is better than this year's corpse."

The taunting exchange finally dragged words from Uther. "I beg you, no more. Allow Merlin to finish spreading this hideous ointment, for no chance is there he will relent."

They all laughed, even Merlin, and then were silent while both wounds were treated and wrapped in swaths of fresh linen.

"It shall soon be dark. Uther looked grim, his face stern and resolute. "We have yet have hard business this day."

"Still mean you to slay the prisoners?" Leodegrance fidgeted uncomfortably.

"Such was my declaration." There was no compassion in Uther's voice, no emotion at all. "For we shall set an example for all time to any Britons who would take the part of an invader against their own brethren. What we do here shall be remembered for a century. Though I loved battle once, I have had my fill of war. I would have the legacy of this conflict give pause to any who might conspire in the future. Perhaps today's harsh measures shall forestall tomorrow's war."

He could see hesitation still on their faces, and he continued, his tone darker, more ominous. "You are my closest friends, but I need neither your counsel nor approval in this, only your obedience. Will my orders be obeyed, or must I see this done myself?"

Chastised, Leodegrance bowed. "Now as always, I shall obey your commands." He turned stiffly to go and give the orders, with Caradoc following close behind.

"I see you remain behind, Merlin. There was a grim smile on Uther's lips. "No surprise should this be, for I can scare everyone but you, old friend. You disapprove, no doubt."

Merlin looked at Uther, his expression uncertain. "It is not my place to approve or disapprove of your commands. I, too, am aware that harsh methods are ofttimes needed. Yet, I would have you rule with justice and not fear if such be possible."

Uther laughed bitterly. "Men forget justice, Merlin. They speak of it with great longing, but they value it not unless it serves their needs. They cease to regard it as just when it goes against their desires. My father was a just king who held back from enforcing his rights to the high kingship. His diplomacy, bribery really, forged this alliance, but only my victory has held it together. These kings fight because we win battles, and because they know that if they betray me I shall seek them out wherever they may run and destroy them utterly. Thus is the true basis of their loyalty. They fear me. If they value me otherwise, it is as a leader our enemies also fear."

Merlin looked sadly at Uther. "Are you sure you do not strike out at the world to ease your own pain, my old friend?" His tone was gentle, sympathetic.

"There is no easing for my pain, Merlin. I shall bear it to my grave. These prisoners for whom you weep, these lords and bar-ons and warriors, they are the cause of my pain. I hate my father for what he did, yet I also recognize that he had little choice. But these traitors, they are the root cause, not only of my heart-break, but of the pain of thousands of wives and children, those of the many warriors who shall not return home. Now they must pay the price of their perfidy. If they wish forgiveness they may seek it from God, for they shall not have it from me."

"But surely there is also a place for mercy, Uther."

"Is there?" His tone was bitter. "Is there indeed? For whom? For Huarwar, who rewarded my father's loyalty and charity with treachery and murder and nearly took both you and I as well? Had he succeeded, all of Britannia is like to have been sold to slavery. For Vortigern, the architect of this calamity, who tortures young girls to recruit his assassins? Nay, Merlin, for men believe what they want, though life seeks to teach them otherwise. They find truth in whatever cause serves their base needs at each moment, and I do not believe most of them capa-ble of more. My justice will be soon forgotten, and my mercy but a passing remembrance. Yet the fear shall remain."

"Long indeed have I lived, my dear friend, and little trust do I place in men's goodness. Yet also I have seen that some worthiness there is, often in unlooked for places. You must rule as you see fit, but I beseech you not to discount the good in all men because of the hurts you have endured."

Uther said no more, but he looked thoughtfully at Merlin and nodded an assent he did not feel. He then took his leave of the counselor, for he wished to be alone for a time. He pulled his cloak up over his head that he might not be recognized, and he strode down the hillside to wander the field.

Before long a new sound was added to the wails of the wounded, for Uther's orders were being carried out, and from the pens where the prisoners had been confined there came terrible cries. Uther's warriors moved in from all sides, grimly putting the defenseless captives to the sword. His warriors were tough fighters all, and hard men, but they disliked this work. Butchering unarmed captives was not to their liking, yet they were bound to carry out the king's commands, and they did so with expediency. They surrounded the makeshift camp where the enemy warriors had been herded and moved inexorably forward, tightening the ring and slaughtering the prisoners like so many cattle.

Kelven commanded the force tasked with the job, and though he liked it no better than they, he pushed his men forward ruthlessly until not a prisoner was left alive. Whenever a man slowed or stopped in the work, Kelven would be there, slapping him with the flat of his sword and shoving him back to the task. When they had finished he dismissed the men and walked slowly toward the woods where, once he was out of sight of the field, he fell to his knees behind a great oak and wept.

Throughout the host there was no elation, no shouts of celebration, just a grim satisfaction that they had prevailed. Though the victory was theirs, it was tempered by the losses they had borne, for fully a third of their number had fallen. They slept that night where they were, on the field among the dead and dying, for they were too exhausted to move, or even to care.

Hengist ran quickly through the woods, surrounded by his most loyal warriors. For two days and nights they had fled without stop, for they sought the relative safety of the stronghold at Canterbury. Ten thousand men had Hengist led to Verulamium. There were fewer than a hundred with him now, though he was certain that several thousand had escaped from the field. Some were themselves also bound for Canterbury, while others had, no doubt, fled to the coast to seek any boats that might sail them home. Yet others had surrendered to Uther's men, but by the king's order, all of these had been slain. Still, Hengist was hopeful he could rally perhaps two thousands when he got back to his stronghold, for he had left a garrison of 700 there when he had marched out to join Vortigern.

The men still with Hengist were mostly his personal guards, and they were the best of his warriors. Many had light wounds; Hengist himself wore a bloodied bandage around his head. Those more seriously injured had fallen behind and were likely to be taken by Uther's men, which meant they were likely to die.

"Vortigern is the architect of this disaster." Hengist spat the words bitterly. "We have squandered our strength supporting his war, and now we must look to hold our last stronghold. At least we laid in supplies before we marched; we are well-provisioned to withstand a siege."

"How are we to hold, father?" Octa spoke with difficulty, breathless from running. "We have but a handful of warriors remaining. We cannot even man the walls."

"More will rally to us in Canterbury, for not all were slain. And forget not that we left a strong force behind. Those men are fresh and well-armed." The exhausted king tried to sound confident, but the doubt in his voice was obvious. "Nevertheless, we must try to make peace with Uther Pendragon, for we cannot hold Canterbury forever without relief. There is naught else for us to do, unless we would flee to the coast and take ship, and never shall I relinquish my kingdom."

"But father, what have we to offer to Uther? We have at best the strength to delay him, not defeat him. Indeed, we are not even strong enough to hold against him in our fortress if he is determined to take it."

Hengist stopped running and turned to face his son. "We will give him Vortigern. Indeed, we will rid him of all his enemies, and in so doing, become his friend."

Octa wiped the grime from his face as he considered his father's words. "Uther Pendragon is without mercy, without fatigue, without pity. He will not make peace with us. He will never accept us."

Hengist stood and stared into his son's eyes. "Indeed, were Uther alone then nothing we could offer would make the peace. But though he is the high king, and now basking in glory and triumph, he must also reckon with those who follow him. The kings, who long to return to their lands; the men, who have fought to exhaustion and seen so many of their number fall; the peasants facing starvation as lands lie fallow."

"So how shall we achieve this, father? How shall we deliver his enemies to him?" Octa was doubtful, but he saw no course of action other than what his father suggested.

"We must get word to Vortigern. To him and to all of his allied Britannic kings who yet live. All flee now in disarray. We must convince them to come to Canterbury."

"And how are we to do this, father? The army is scattered and in flight. All know the losses we have taken. We are in no better condition than they. Why would they come? They will flee to their strongholds and look to their own defenses."

"They cannot hope to hold their own castles against Uther now. Canterbury is a great fortress, vastly stronger than their own keeps. And we are the only ones who could hope for aid from across the sea. We will tell them we have made an alliance with King Clovis of the Franks, and that his army is even now sailing to our aid."

Octa looked doubtfully at his father. "Why would they believe this? We have said naught to them before of any effort to secure the aid of the Franks. And you know that such an alliance will never happen. Clovis is not our friend."

"They will believe, my son, because they are desperate. They cannot go to Uther, for he will surely put them to death. And they have not the strength to fight him off when he invades their lands. They will believe because they want to believe, because they need to. We shall tell them my brother Horsa has been in the court of Clovis for many months seeking this alliance. They know not that he was slain fighting Leodegrance, and it will seem right to them that I would send him to forge this alliance. We will offer them protection and guarantees to help them defend their lands. They will come."

"Perhaps you are right, Father. Indeed, it is true they have few options. We must convene this meeting before King Uther puts Canterbury under siege. How much time do you think we have?"

Hengist smiled grimly. "Uther considers us invaders, but he thinks of them as traitors. He will look to take their castles and lands before they can regroup and rebuild their strength. He will attack them first."

Octa looked skeptical. "Likely he could split his army and deal with them and us at the same time. He has many able commanders. If he should march both north and south we could be hard-pressed within days."

"Nay, my son. Uther's victory was total, but not without cost. His army has suffered grievously, and he will have to feed and supply his men before he can march on anyone. He knows he may have to conduct sieges to take his enemies' strongholds, and he will not want his forces divided. He feels he has little to fear from us if he first moves against his Britannic rivals. Indeed, such is but the truth, for what can we do given several months except rally what few men remain and lay in more supplies to feed us for some weeks? Except, perhaps, to deliver King Uther's enemies unto him."

Vortimer was troubled, and for long he rode in silence through the shade of the deep wood. Where once they had led an army, now they had but a few dozen ragged retainers. His father had accepted Hengist's invitation to gather at Canterbury to seek safety and meet with the emissaries of Clovis, King of the Franks. Vortimer did not see any choice, but in his gut he did not like any of it.

The army of Uther Pendragon ravaged the northern kingdoms, exacting a terrible price from the kings and lords who had supported Vortigern. All were stripped of their kingships, and any who were captured were condemned for high treason and hanged like common thieves. All those who remained now rushed to Canterbury, seeking the hope and protection offered by Hengist and his new Frankish allies.

Finally, he could hold his tongue no longer. "Father, I fear that naught but ill can come of this. I trusted Hengist not when we wielded great power and now, in our vulnerability, my faith is weaker still."

Vortigern did not answer his son at first, but instead kept riding silently for another moment. Finally, he turned to face Vortimer. His eyes, once icy and calculating, were wild and glittering with madness. "Hengist would not dare betray me, my son. He will not risk my wrath. With the Frankish army, we shall defeat Uther Pendragon and restore our position in Britannia."

He is mad, Vortimer thought. This last terrible defeat, following on the misfortunes that preceded it, has been his undoing. But what shall I do? "Father, the Franks have never been allied with Hengist. Does it not seem strange to you that they would intervene now, after our cause has so withered?"

The path narrowed as they rode deeper into the forest, and the party halted to reorder into single file to proceed. Vortigern did not reply to his son's question, but just quietly sat his horse as Vortimer organized the men-at-arms. When half the men had ridden forward, he motioned for his father to ride ahead, and he fell in behind, followed by the rest of their men.

He is past my reaching him, Vortimer thought grimly. I must be on my guard during this visit, for though I cannot divine what trickery he is planning, I do not trust Hengist. Nor do I believe that Clovis has allied with him. We should be planning to escape from King Uther, not trusting to fantasy alliances to salvage our cause.

For long they rode, and finally they camped a half day's journey from Canterbury. There was little talk, and silently they sat around their fires and ate. The men-at-arms were Vortigern's most loyal followers, and while they had not deserted their master, their morale was broken, and none expected but to meet their deaths in futile defense of their lord.

The air was thick with acrid smoke, as the army of Uther Pendragon prepared to break camp and march south. Before

them lay the stronghold of King Gavin writhing in its death
agony, wooden ramparts and towers still ablaze. Uther's army
had stormed the castle at dawn, taking it quickly and, as they
had done at every stronghold they had assailed, putting the
defenders to the sword. All save one, for the king himself had
been hanged like a common thief. He had begged for mercy,
but Uther was unmoved. "You chose this fate when you swore
yourself to the usurper." Thus was all he said to the crying old
man, and he turned his back and walked away.

Since their victory at Verulamium, Uther's men had marched
east and north, attacking the remnants of their enemies' forces
and, one by one, assaulting their strongholds. Some castles they
found abandoned, but even those that were staunchly defended
quickly fell.

Uther's will had hardened into iron, and he resolutely refused
to take any prisoners from those who had supported Vortigern,
the usurper. Even his grimmest veterans were weary of the rivers of blood that flowed everywhere they marched. But none
would dare resist his commands. Finally, Leodegrance bade him
show mercy to King Gavin, for he was aged and sick and swore
that he was truly repentant.

Uther stood unmoving, his gaze not even shifting in response
to his friend's entreaties. "I proclaimed that the lives of all who
joined with the usurper and the invaders would be forfeit, and so
it shall be." His tone conveyed unshakeable finality.

When Uther walked throughout the host a hush fell over
the assembled men. The soldiers held their high king in awe,
for he had led them from the brink of defeat to total victory
and the annihilation of their enemies. Their trains were rich
with the spoils of sacked castles and their purses bulged with
gold and silver. Though the men were levies of eight different
kingdoms, Uther had forged them into one terrible weapon, and
they looked to him as their leader.

The kings were joyful at the victories, but their discontent
was growing as they saw their warriors chanting Uther's name
before battle. Though they all hailed Uther as high king, they
were protective of their own powers and perquisites, and they

began to feel their own positions threatened by the stature of
King Uther. But none would dare challenge the high king's
authority, for they all feared his terrible wrath.

Now they would march south to Canterbury, Hengist's great
fortress. King Gavin's keep had been the last of the Britannic
monarch's strongholds to fall, though many of the lords themselves had fled, presumably to make a last stand with Vortigern
and Hengist.

The army moved silently and in good order, for they were all
veterans now, and Uther had maintained tight discipline throughout the ranks. They marched first through Repton, the village
adjoining Gavin's fortress, and the terrified peasants hid in cel-
lars and barns until they had passed. Uther's men had earlier
ransacked the town, pulling cowering soldiers from their hiding
places, but the villagers were left unmolested. The high king was
not making war on the peasants, only on the lords and men at
arms who had committed treason, and he would not tolerate any
indiscipline among his troops. He had not hesitated to hang his
own men on more than one occasion when they disobeyed his
command and raped or robbed among the townsfolk.

Uther had become unapproachable, for even his adoring soldiers feared him, and many a veteran man at arms quaked at the
king's very approach. Though Uther commanded the loyalty
of thousands, only four men still remained close companions
to the cold-blooded monarch. Merlin, his advisor and lifelong
friend, still counseled Uther, and he was the one most able to
influence the king's actions, though more through clever manipulation than persuasion. Perhaps most of all Uther's companions, Merlin understood the terrible resolution within the king,
both its cause, it usefulness…and its dangers.

Leodegrance found himself disapproving of many of his
old companion's actions, but his loyalty was steadfast. Though
he influenced Uther less than he once had, he swore there would
never be a day when he feared to approach his old friend. And
he knew in his heart that whatever road Uther chose, Leodegrance of Cameliard would follow.

Caradoc the Visigoth had served the high king faithfully, and he had fought like a lion in Uther's wars. His name was known and feared throughout Britannia, and it is said that even he had lost count of the men he'd slain. He was, in mind and spirit, Uther's man, and perhaps more than any other he seemed undeterred by the king's coldness. Unlike the others, Caradoc was not at all troubled by Uther's unrelenting brutality, and he calmly and grimly carried out the king's commands. Caradoc had personally hanged King Gavin, as he had several of the others.

Kelven, for many long years the captain of the guard of Caer Guricon, was born into the service of the Pendragon, as was his father was before him. His simple unquestioning loyalty impressed Uther, and his service was valued and appreciated. Among the entire host, Kelven alone could say that he had saved the high king from enemy swords, for only once had Uther seemed like to fall in battle, and it was the captain whose blade intervened. Though he had tired of war and bloodshed, his sword would serve House Pendragon as long as God gave him the strength to wield it.

The army marched far each day, for the men were hardened by long service in the field, and they had travelled only a few days before the scouts reported that they were but a few hours' journey from Canterbury. The sun was already low in the sky, so Uther ordered a halt, and the men began the business of making camp.

All knew that the morrow would bring the final confrontation. Only here, in Canterbury, were there still enemies in arms. Once these were defeated, the men would return home to castles and farms and villages. When this last battle was won the rivers of blood would cease, and peace and prosperity would return. Throughout the host, the men sat quietly and ate their evening meal, and when they were done they talked of the war and the battles they had seen.

When the war began, the armies of the different kings were separate forces. They marched and ate and camped among themselves. But now the men were forged together as one, and they were like brothers. Around many a campfire sat men wearing different heraldry - men who would have fought against each other but a few years before. Would their brotherhood last, or after they returned home would they again find themselves fighting each other to settle petty disputes between the kings?

Uther, who had recently been dining alone, invited his four friends to share his table. The meal was a simple one, but appealing. In the center of the table was a large game fowl, well roasted and surrounded with vegetables. In addition there was cheese and fruit, along with fresh bread and a large bowl of nuts. When his guests had taken their seats, Uther raised his goblet. "Welcome, my truest companions. It is a simple joy to share a meal with one's dearest friends. Alas, the sort of pleasure for which we have had little time these past months."

They all took their cups in hand and raised them in a toast before drinking. When they had finished, it was Merlin who spoke first. "Indeed, Uther, there have been far too few moments such as this. Our quest has been a difficult one, and in many ways yours has been the darkest road. Yet, here you stand on the brink of victory. On the verge of peace. Your father would be proud of you."

Uther smiled, something his companions had not seen in some time. "You mean he would be surprised, Merlin. My father was like to expect to find me brawling in an inn rather than leading the armies of Britannia."

"Nay, Uther." Merlin's voice was heavy with emotion. "Though you and your father often clashed, he knew well your worth."

"To my father, Constantine Pendragon. And my brave brothers, all slain by the treachery of these Britannic fiends you would have me spare." Uther was trying to be mirthful, but the bitterness and resentment was difficult to hide.

They all ignored the barb and raised their glasses. Leodegrance drained his goblet and placed it down on the table. "Tomorrow, my friends," he said. "Tomorrow victory shall be within our grasp." One of the servants refilled his cup, and he raised it high. "To victory. To peace."

All those assembled repeated his words. "To victory, to peace."

Uther forced another smile for the benefit of his friends, but his own thoughts were darker. Victory? Perhaps, he mused. But peace? Is such a thing even possible? Do I even care?

There was a long table set upon trestles in the great hall at Canterbury, and seated around it were all those lords and kings allied to Vortigern who yet lived. They were well-feasted, for Hengist had ordered a great banquet to be prepared for his guests even though the fortress was on a siege footing. There were roasts and game birds and every manner of delicacy, with copious amounts of ale and wine to wash it down.

The guests were sated, and most were more than a little drunk, but they were becoming impatient, for Hengist had promised them all emissaries from King Clovis of the Franks, and none had yet appeared. Vortigern himself spoke to calm them, for he had so given himself over to the hope offered by Hengist that he believed in it whole-heartedly.

Vortimer was less convinced, and as the night wore on with little but Hengist's excuses, his suspicions grew. He had drunk little, and he had all his wits about him. Finally, feigning illness, he left the hall to return to his chambers. Twice, as he made his way down the corridor, he thought he heard scraping sounds on the stone floors behind him, but each time he turned about to look the way was clear. At last, he reached his door and calmly entered the dimly-lit room. He was ready for trouble, but the chamber was empty. Cautiously, he closed the door behind him and retrieved his sword from where it was laying against the wall.

Thus, he was ready when the door began to slide open slowly and, as his would-be assassin entered, Vortimer ran him through without pause. The black clad figure reached out as if trying to grab the wall for support and slumped forward onto the floor of the chamber. Hastily, Vortimer dragged the body all the way into the room, closing and bolting the door behind him.

A trap, he thought grimly. I knew...in my heart I knew, and yet I have walked into it right beside my father. I must get aid. The men, they are camped in the courtyard. I must rally them to rescue father and the lords. Yanking his sword free of the body, he unbolted the door and slowly pried it open. The hall was deserted, and Vortimer slipped through the door, closing it tightly behind him. He made his way to the end of the corridor, where a stone circular stair rose the full height of the fortress. He ran down to the ground level as quickly as he could and rounded the corner to emerge into the courtyard...just as all hell broke loose.

From the stables and the other buildings surrounding the yard, armed and armored Saxon warriors ran toward the Britannic soldiers sitting around fires eating their evening meal. Their surprise was total, and few of Vortigern's men were able to draw weapons before their attackers were upon them. Vortimer shouted a bitter curse and charged into the melee.

"So, my friends, at last we come to the purpose of our gathering." Hengist stood at his place at the end of the table and addressed his guests. "For no doubt, many of you have wondered what plan we might devise to face the force of Uther Pendragon." He gestured to Vortigern, who was seated at his side, and bid the old man to rise and stand beside him.

"This is what we shall do!" From under the table he retrieved a long dagger, and with one stroke he thrust it so forcefully through Vortigern's back that the tip of the blade protruded from the old man's chest. Vortigern's head turned, and for a second he looked in disbelief at Hengist. Then he spasmed once, coughing up a mouthful of blood, and crumpled to the ground at his killer's feet.

Even as Hengist struck his blow, Saxon warriors poured into the room from every entry, axes and swords swinging wildly as they fell upon the unarmed Britannic lords. The melee was brutal, for men facing death will fight savagely, though drunk and unarmed. The table was overturned with a loud crash, and all around the hall, with chairs and dinner knives and silver goblets...and even with bare hands...the victims fought futilely against their attackers. But their effort was in vain, and surprise and superior arms quickly put an end to things. When it was done, every Britannic lord in the great hall of Canterbury was dead.

Hengist looked over the room, now a blood-soaked wreck. His voice was firm, though his hands shook and his heart beat rapidly. "Collect their heads. We will deliver these to King Uther when he arrives and make our peace. These men were the last of his enemies, and by our hands they have been defeated."

In the courtyard, and in the fields around the stronghold, Hengist's men streamed from hidden spots and attacked the retinues of the lords, which were camped all about the walls. Some of the defenders were able to arm themselves, and the battles raged for a time on the hillsides around Canterbury. The Britons were incensed at the treachery and fought for their lives with elemental savagery. But they were outnumbered and over-matched and, while they made the Saxons pay a price, they were soon wiped out.

Hengist's plan had been a complete success. Vortigern and his allies had been taken by surprise, and they were no more. Now he had to deal with Uther Pendragon.

It was late morning as the army of Uther Pendragon emerged from the forest path and began to surround Canterbury. In the van rode the high king himself, with his veteran horsemen from Powys and the best of the heavy cavalry of the other contin-gents. They were followed by the forces of each of the kings. First were the levies from Powys, and behind them the troops of King Leodegrance of Cameliard. Next was King Urien, lead-ing the men of Rheged, veterans hardened in the brutal early battles against the Picts. Then came King Rience, whom no one liked or trusted, leading the forces of Gwynned. King Pellinore marched next in the procession, and behind his warriors of the Isles came Vortiporius and the contingent from Dyfed. The men from Cornwall followed, and in the last position was King Lot, mostly healed and returned to the field, with the soldiers of Luthien.

The army had conducted many sieges and assaults, and they quickly took up their positions around Hengist's stronghold. Uther had declared that, once again, no quarter would be given, so they did not bother with heralds or messengers. But there was surprise among the host as the gates of Canterbury opened, and an embassy emerged, flying before them a flag of truce.

At first, Uther would not hear their entreaties, for he was set in his decision that none would be spared among those warriors in Canterbury. But Merlin prevailed, and the king agreed to admit the ambassadors. He would not ride out to meet them nor appoint his own emissaries to do so. If they would speak to him, they would come to his tent and trust to his honor regarding their temporary safety.

Uther sat upon an oaken seat at the end of his tent, with ten of his greatest warriors arrayed around him. Among those present were Leodegrance, Urien, Caradoc, and Merlin, and these all stood silently along the side of the tent, watching the proceedings.

Hengist had sent two of his closest advisors, and these were accompanied by six warriors, carrying three large wooden chests. One of Hengist's ambassadors waved for the soldiers to set down the boxes then he turned and bowed to King Uther. He was tall and broad, with long hair and a beard, which had once been blond, but were now mostly gray. "The most honorable greetings to the High King Uther. I am Aric, and I am come to treat with your majesty. My master, King Hengist wishes me to express his deepest respects to you, great king, and his most profound regrets that we have fought as enemies in this war."

Uther did not move or even glance over at the visitors. He sat impassive, like a statue hewn from marble, and his response was icy. "We need not have fought against each other had your master remained in his homeland. But he chose to invade this nation, and once here to proclaim his allegiance to a foul usurper. For this his condemnation is decreed, as is such for all who have followed him. You may now leave us, so that you may prepare to meet your doom in such a way as seems fitting to you."

Uther waved his hand in dismissal, but Aric bowed his head and again spoke. "King Uther, I beseech thee to receive these gifts, which my master has sent to..."

"I desire no tribute from your master. The time for such

niceties is long past. I bid thee one last time, go now while still I am willing to allow it." Uther turned his head and glared at the emissaries with a gaze so withering even his own men quaked at the sight of it.

But Aric remained steadfast, though his voice was wavering and his hands shook. He waved for the warriors to open the chests, and he reached into one and pulled out a small bundle. "Behold, High King of Britannia, the head of your enemy, Vortigern. This is the gift of my master, as are these..." - he pointed to the other chests - "...which contain the heads of all of the lords of Britannia who had sworn loyalty to the usurper."

There were gasps of shock throughout the room, though of them all, only Merlin had actually seen Vortigern before. Uther glanced at his advisor, who acknowledged the king's unspoken question with a small nod. This was indeed the head of Vortigern.

Aric stood expectantly, awaiting Uther's reaction. When it came, he was utterly unprepared for its ferocity. The king leapt to his feet, yelling with a level of cold hostility beyond anything the emissaries had ever experienced. "What thinks your chieftan?" - Uther would not grant Hengist the title of king, even just in speaking - "That treachery wipes away treachery? These lords and kings were marked to die, but by the lawful judgment of the high king, not by the deceits and trickery of a barbarian warlord."

Uther walked toward Aric until he stood but a few feet from the Saxon, who cowered before the will and onslaught of the king. The men at arms moved to follow Uther and to place themselves between him and the enemy warriors, but he waved them back forcefully. He stared directly at Aric and continued his withering speech. "Could Hengist truly believe I would treat with a heathen invader because he slew these men? He has but added to his crimes, for though Vortigern was my enemy, Hengist was sworn to his service. Your master is a betrayer and a traitor, and he is fit only to be devoured by the crows. Go now and be gone, for this is my last mercy. Go to your chief and tell him to prepare, for his end is upon him."

Uther gestured to the warriors along the back of the tent, and they moved forward, drawing their swords. Aric and his companions bowed low and hurried out of the tent. Once outside, they ran back toward the fortress, seeking the relative safety of the walls before the king changed his mind and slew them at once. Uther turned to face his advisors, his face contorted with rage. "Assemble the troops. We attack at once."

All along the walls of Canterbury, the scaling ladders of Uther's men were raised, and warriors climbed quickly to the battlements. Atop the walls, the defenders pushed down ladders and dropped rocks on the climbing soldiers, but the ferocity of the attack had unnerved them, and their fragile morale was quickly broken.

Near the main gate, Uther Pendragon himself, ignoring the pleas of his advisors and men, climbed one of the ladders and was the first to reach the top. On the battlement he fought like a man possessed, throwing three Saxons over the edge and felling two more with deadly sword strokes. Behind him came Caradoc and next Kelven, and once atop the battlements, these three great warriors slew all who came against them, while their comrades poured up the ladders and into the fortress.

A similar scene took place a few hundred yards down the wall, where Leodegrance and Urien led their men in a ferocious charge, taking one of the towers and opening the secondary gate. The armies of Cameliard and Rheged poured through the captured entry and into the main courtyard. In the slowly fading light they slaughtered all who stood before them.

Throughout the corridors and towers of the massive stronghold, men battled viciously in small groups. The defenders tried to flee, but they were everywhere pursued by Uther's men, and the orders of the high king had been clear. The Saxons fought with the desperation of doomed men, but they were overwhelmed, and by nightfall every defender in the keep was slain, save those barricaded in the last tower.

Atop that tower, surrounded by his last few guards, was Hengist, self-proclaimed king of Kent. Once the leader of 10,000 veteran warriors, the Saxon chief was now trapped in the last bastion of his stronghold with barely a score of men. His plan to negotiate had failed utterly, and in his final moments he was at a loss to understand. Uther Pendragon was the most coldly relentless force he had ever encountered. In his last desperation he muttered softly to himself. "What drives him with such brutal resolve?"

Hengist leaned out the window and looked down to the base of the tower. The attackers had battered down the door, and Uther's men were pouring inside. His mind raced, but he could see no way to escape his doom. Octa was not in the room. He must have fallen, Hengist thought, fighting on the battlements. I will be with you soon, my son. He girded himself and drew the greatsword from his scabbard. He wore a mail shirt, but no helm, for on his head was the crown of Kent. He would die as a king.

The men in the room, scarcely two dozen, waited silently, weapons drawn. Within a few minutes they could hear fighting outside, and then the sounds of something heavy banging against the great oaken door. Finally, the door burst off its hinges and fell to the floor inside the room. There was a loud thud as the attackers dropped the stone column they had used as a ram, followed by shouting from both sides as Uther's men stormed into the room and the melee was joined.

The doorway was narrow and in the confined space of the room it was some time before the attackers' numbers began to tell. The Saxons fought with the ferocity of men with naught to lose, and they made the Britons pay dearly for the victory. In the center of the room fought Hengist, and he had struck down half a dozen enemies. Finally, Eldol, one of Uther Pendragon's champions, strode up to the Saxon chief. The two engaged in a great battle, as all around them more warriors poured into the room. Hengist's men were losing their desperate fight. Other Britons had rushed to take Hengist from behind, but Eldol called them off, for he was determined that the Saxon leader would be his tribute to his sovereign. At last, when there remained but a handful of defenders standing, Eldol's broadsword found its mark. Hengist, chieftan of the Saxons and would-be king of Kent, fell to the floor, mortally wounded.

When Uther entered the room a few moments later there was not a live Saxon left. His men began to cheer, first in the room where the last defenders had fallen, then in the stairwell of the tower. Soon the entire army was chanting Uther's name. Amid the growing din, the high king praised Eldol for slaying Hengist, and proclaimed him a lord of Powys.

Then he strode down the stairs, past the shouting soldiers and out into the courtyard, waving as he walked, acknowledging the acclaim of the army. This is what it must have been like for my grandfather, he thought, when his army proclaimed him emperor. Yet Uther felt no joy beyond the grim satisfaction that he had completed his task. Now he faced the true burden of the high kingship, for he must maintain the loyalty of the kings when they were no longer faced with mortal peril from outside. This, he suspected, would prove more difficult, and he hoped the firmness he had displayed in the war would stay the hands of would-be traitors.

The men had gathered and lit bunches of straw or sticks, and the seething, joyful mass turned into a torchlit procession that followed Uther out through the gates and back to camp. Though the king himself soon retired to his tent, the lords and men sang and drank well into the night. The war was over.

The victory at Canterbury had been complete. Indeed, only two warriors escaped from the fortress. Octa had been knocked from the wall early in the battle, and while the fight raged he was lying unconscious, half buried in straw. When he finally woke, the battle was almost over, and he could see it was lost. Let me die in arms, he thought, as he prepared to run toward his father's tower, even then being assaulted. But he did not charge out as he willed himself to do. Whether it was good sense or cowardice or the desire to live to gain revenge one day, none could ever know. He slipped quietly into the keep and down the stairs to the hidden passage that led out of the fortress and into the woods. Though Hengist did not know it when he breathed his last breath, his dynasty lived on.

The other survivor had escaped before Uther's men even reached the fortress. Vortimer had plunged into the melee in the courtyard the previous night, joining his father' ambushed men. Though he fought well, he was soon overmatched and knocked to the ground, and his last recollection was a sharp pain in his head. When he awoke he was in the forest, slung over the shoulder of Wendel, one of his father's most loyal soldiers. A giant, almost seven feet tall, Wendel was wounded multiple times and covered in blood. Yet still he had managed to escape the keep and carry Vortimer to safety before he finally fell to the ground. Vortimer crawled over to aid his benefactor, but the big man's wounds were obviously mortal, and just a few moments later, he died. Vortimer sat long next to his body, and there was but one thought in his mind. Revenge. Against Hengist and his traitorous race. And against Uther Pendragon.

Uther returned to Caer Guricon amid tumultuous celebration, but though he played his role, in his heart he was joyless. War, at least, had given him a purpose, and now he had returned to an empty castle and endless days to ponder his loss. Certainly there were warriors and advisors and servants in Caer Guricon, but Uther's father and brothers were dead, and the woman he loved was far away, married to another. It was to a life of duty and loneliness the last of the Pendragon had returned.

The great army had dispersed, and men who had fought and bled together bade each other tearful farewells, for many were like never to see each other again. In the villages and castle halls the victorious warriors were welcomed with quiet, joyful celebrations. Their cheer, though strong, was restrained by the losses they had borne, for they had fought in a dozen battles and countless skirmishes and sieges. They had battled Picts and Saxons and Britons from many kingdoms, and they had beaten all. But they paid dearly for their victories. Barely half those who had marched away to follow Uther Pendragon returned home, and those who survived came back to withered farms and fallow fields. Their comrades lay buried in graves across Britannia, and the homecoming, though joyful, was also bitter for the many empty chairs.

They had fought to unite Britannia under one high king, and they had done so. Now, they wondered, would their indomitable war leader rule justly? Would the land recover and prosperity return?

Chapter Eight
Igraine

488 AD
Caer Guricon, Capital of the Kingdom of Powys

Uther Pendragon had been high king of Britannia for a decade, and the country was restored to prosperity. For years now, the harvests had been bountiful, and the storehouses were bursting with grain. The shortages from the war years had been made up, and the famine and pestilence that had ravaged the land were increasingly distant memories. The dead had been buried, and fresh pain of loss had given way to fond memory of fallen heroes.

Uther's warriors rode throughout the kingdom, enforcing the king's laws and driving Saxon raiding parties back into the sea. For ten years the land had seen a level of peace and prosperity unknown since the legions had departed. Some of the kings might have resented the loss of independence, but none dared challenge Uther, for all knew he was quick to anger and totally without mercy to any who opposed him. That much they had seen during the war, when he had made good on his oath to slay all who had fought with Vortigern.

Fresh from victory, Uther had traveled widely throughout Britannia, visiting all the kingdoms and accepting the fealty of the kings. But as the years passed he became more reclusive, until finally he rarely left the castle at Caer Guricon.

Throughout the land there was one great concern - the high king had no heir. He had been offered many daughters and sisters of kings, but he would take no wife. The entreaties of his closest friends and advisors were to no avail, for Uther was a stubborn man, and once his mind was set, none could change it. Thus was there a pall hanging over the prosperity, for few could doubt that if Uther died without an heir, the kings would again be fighting among themselves for position, and the land would once more bleed. The high king was young, it is true, but as the years went by and still he would not marry, the worries became greater.

The usually grim atmosphere of Caer Guricon was replaced with mirth, for Merlin had returned after an absence of five years, and Uther joyfully welcomed his friend and advisor back. Merlin had always come and gone with little predictability and even less explanation, but he had been away long this time, and Uther had missed him greatly.

They sat together well into the night before the fire in the great hall, talking as they had in years past. Merlin was one of the few people who knew why Uther refused to take a wife. He also understood just how obstinate the king could be, so he approached the issue with great caution. "My friend, we have spoken of many trivial matters, but we must discuss the important issue. You have terrorized everyone else so they will not dare mention it, but you know as well as I do that you must have an heir. Indeed, all you fought for, all your sacrifices, would be in vain were the high kingship to fail. Would you have the thousands who died to have done so in vain? Would you consign thousands more to die in future strife?"

Uther shifted uncomfortably in his seat. "I wondered when you would raise the issue, for it seems to be the only matter concerning anyone."

Merlin took his cup from the small table and drank deeply of the warm spiced wine. "You did not take my head off, which suggests to me that you too understand the problem. Uther, my friend, I more than anyone know the cause of your sadness, but you chose this path to save Britannia. Would you see all that was bought with that heartbreak, yours and Igraine's, vanish at your death?"

Uther was staring into the fire as he listened, for he was deep in thought. "What is the limit of sacrifice, Merlin? Was not my blood enough? Was not my soul enough? For surely I shall have a reckoning with God for all I have done. Is one woman so much to ask?"

Merlin sat still, his eyes aching with compassion for his

friend. "But it cannot be, Uther, for she is married to another. Even the high king cannot undo this. No one can ever replace Igraine for you. I know this, and I would not try to tell you otherwise. But a king must have an heir. You must take a wife."

Uther looked back at the fire and was silent for a long while, absent-mindedly fingering the small ring he wore on a chain around his neck. Merlin took another drink, putting his cup gently back on the table as he sat quietly, enjoying the warmth from the hearth. Though he had lived many lifetimes of normal men, time was at last catching up with him, and he felt the cold more now that he had before.

Finally, Uther turned to face Merlin and spoke harshly. "I have thought long on this, my friend. I will have Igraine. I will take her from Gorlois. I am high king, and I shall have as I command."

Merlin was silent, for he was surprised by Uther's words, and he could hear the madness in the king's voice. Tread carefully here, he thought to himself.

Uther was surprised by Merlin's silence. "What? No reasoned argument against my plan? No urging me to caution? No list of dire consequences?"

Merlin held his hands out near the fire. "There will be consequences, Uther. Surely you see that?"

Uther's face twisted into an angry grimace. "Then damn the consequences. I have waited long enough, and Igraine has languished too many years in Cornwall, wife to a man she doesn't love."

"You risk all you have fought for." Merlin's voice was measured. "All your men have died for."

"And why must that be so? Think you my nobles and warriors would deny me the bride of my choosing? They have little love for Gorlois. Indeed, some of them almost rebelled when I made him king of Cornwall."

"They will fear, Uther. For if you would steal a king's wife, then what might you not do? They do not like Gorlois, but they will think that next time it will be them. They accept you as high king, but still they are protective of their positions. They will not support you if they fear you will undermine their own power. You will face constant rebellion and treachery."

Merlin moved uncomfortably in his chair, shifting his gaze from the fire to Uther. "Remember, Igraine has been married to Gorlois for more than twelve years. Even if you were to wrest her away, she could give you naught but a bastard, and such an heir would not be accepted by the kings. How do you propose to end the marriage? No bishop will annul a union that has lasted so long and produced children."

Uther sat unmoving in his chair and looked at Merlin with frozen eyes. "That is simple, Merlin. I propose to kill Gorlois."

The queen of Cornwall sat in her room in Tintagel Castle sewing with her daughters. Anna was eleven and the image of her mother...except for her gray eyes. Morgan was seven, and though she had much of her mother's beauty, she also had Gorlois' large nose and thin brown hair. Igraine herself was still as beautiful as ever, though there was a pervasive sadness about her, and her eyes, which once sparkled like gemstones, were dull and lifeless.

She looked out the window at the waves crashing on the rocks. She loved the sea; it was the only thing she enjoyed about living at Tintagel. Many days she would sit and watch the sun set over the ocean, and in the light dancing over the rippling water she would often see images, ghosts from the past. Her beloved father, killed at the Battle of Verulamium - God, was that ten years ago already? Her mother, gone so long, but still in her thoughts. And Uther Pendragon, the love of her life, torn from her by political forces that overshadowed their desires, though he had loved her as deeply as she him. Of that, at least, she was certain.

I wonder if you have forgotten about me, my love, she thought wistfully. Part of her truly hoped he had, for she found no salve for her hurts in his pain. Yet she also clung to him, and she drew comfort from the thought that he may still long for her as she did for him. She had heard Gorlois and his advisors speaking several times, discussing Uther's refusal to marry.

Does he refuse to take a wife, she wondered, because he still belongs to me in his heart?

Her life with Gorlois had never been a happy one, but in recent years things had become worse. He was angry because she had failed to give him a son, and he was cruel when he even bothered to notice her. It was a relief that in recent years she only rarely had to put up with him sweating and grunting on top of her, for she couldn't stand the sight of him. She was lonely - desperately, achingly alone, for other than her daughters she had no one. She was not allowed to leave Tintagel Castle without Gorlois' permission, and this he rarely gave. Occasionally, he allowed her to ride through the countryside surrounding the keep, but otherwise her days were spent willing the hours to pass. Her father had taught her to read, but her husband did not believe in a literate woman, and he denied her even a bible, stating, "You shall seek your salvation through the sermons of the priests and not by reading that which you cannot possibly understand, despite your father's foolish indulgences."

Though she loved both of her daughters, she couldn't help but share a special closeness with Anna for, unknown to all but Igraine, she was the child of Uther Pendragon, conceived during the one night the two had shared. All the while she carried the baby, Igraine wondered who was the father, but when first she held the child and saw those steely gray eyes she knew. She had looked many times into those eyes, and they had looked into hers with love and compassion. She was thrilled that God had given her Uther's baby, though at first she had been terrified that Gorlois would know. He will kill us both, she had thought many times that first year. But the newly-crowned king of Cornwall had little interest in his daughters, and he rarely came to see them. Her fears had been for naught; Gorlois never suspected.

Anna was a willful child, but sweet and very intelligent. Igraine saw much of her father in her, and she loved her all the more for it, though it often made her more difficult to raise. She had Uther's intransigence, and her stubbornness often strained Igraine's patience.

Morgan, too, was smart, but it saddened Igraine that she was also cruel and manipulative. Though she loved her daughter greatly, she could see there was a darkness in the child that she could not understand. Though Gorlois ignored her as much as he did Igraine and Anna, Morgan was very fond of her father, and she came to blame her mother for the infrequency of his visits.

Igraine tried to teach her daughters to read and write, but without books or parchment it was impossible. She would tell them stories she remembered from her childhood, tales of Rome, and legends even older, for Igraine's lineage went far back, to the shadowy past and the Celtic kings and queens who had ruled Britannia for centuries before the legions arrived.

In the years after the war, Merlin had visited Tintagel several times, and though he purported to have matters to discuss with Gorlois, Igraine suspected he was truly there to see how she fared. Whether he had come on his own or at the behest of Uther she could not know, though whatever brought him to visit, she was grateful. Merlin had always been kind to her, and he was greatly troubled at the sacrifice she had been forced to make and guilty about his part in it. But it had been many years since she had last seen him, so even that occasional contact with her past had been lost. Everything Igraine cared about except her daughters had been taken from her, and she knew that even her babies would one day be lost, for Gorlois would barter them off as brides to whatever allies he deemed most crucial. Then Igraine would truly be alone with her despair.

The room had become dark. A storm was coming in off the sea, and the sun had fallen behind the approaching clouds. She rose and lit a small splint of wood in the fireplace and used it to light the candles in the room. In the flickering candlelight she checked on the work her daughters had done and then, placing her own fabric aside, she sat near the window and looked out, watching the dark clouds roll in over the sea and thinking of times and people long gone.

Uther and Merlin walked through the deep woods north of Caer Guricon, and while the entire household thought they were out hunting, their true purpose was to speak privately. For Merlin had silenced Uther the evening before, bidding him not repeat what he had said until they were sure they were alone.

The day was dark and ominous, but so far the rain had held off. Uther carried a bow and had a quiver of arrows strung across his back, and Merlin held two javelins. They had briefly spotted a stag earlier, but otherwise their half-hearted attempts at hunting had been fruitless.

"I know you better than to think I can change your mind, no matter how rash and foolish is your plan." Merlin was the only person alive who would dare call Uther Pendragon foolish. "But I beg you, take care in how you resolve to proceed. If you are determined to pursue this course we must create a pretext. We must spread rumors that Gorlois is plotting against you."

Uther turned to face Merlin and let out a deep breath. "I know of no plots."

"No." Merlin sighed softly. "In fact, Gorlois, to my surprise, has honored every commitment he has made. I suspect he initially planned treachery, but then he became too fearful to challenge you. But we must not have the others believe that you repaid his loyalty by murdering him because you coveted his wife - the wife you yourself gave him."

Uther had a puzzled look on his face. "You would have us lie and falsely accuse him?"

Merlin's face bore an expression of dark amusement. "Come to terms with what you intend, Uther. You resolve to murder a man so you may steal his wife, yet you hesitate at lying and plotting? This is an evil plan no matter how we proceed; only ill shall come of it. But if you insist on taking this course we must use every tool to limit the damage."

Uther considered Merlin's words, and he pondered how far he would go to make Igraine his. "I will do whatever I must, Merlin."

"Then we must be creative and play our parts well, for failure is like to destroy all you have wrought."

"The others have never liked Gorlois." Uther spoke plainly, though there was a small hitch in his voice. Deep down, he knew he was trying to justify his intended actions. "Indeed, many resisted recognizing his kingship, for they believe he is of inferior lineage. They will incline to believe his treachery. I need your help, Merlin, but with it or no, I am resolved to take Igraine. Will you aid me, old friend?"

Merlin was silent for a brief moment. He could see the madness in his friend, and he knew Uther was beyond listening to reason. He would proceed no matter what Merlin did, and without his help all would know that Uther had slain one of the kings because he lusted after his wife. Within a year, the kingdoms would again be at war.

Merlin looked glumly at Uther. "I will help you, but I beg you to reconsider, though I know it to be futile." Merlin wasn't at all certain that the fraud they intended to perpetrate would succeed, but he resolved he must try. When it was clear Uther was not going to respond, Merlin continued. "We must carefully create the accusation and send a summons to Tintagel commanding Gorlois to appear to answer the charges. Likely he will refuse, outraged at the false accusation. This shall be your justification to invade Cornwall."

"And if he does surrender himself? Have you one of you potions that will make him confess publicly?"

Merlin frowned and when he spoke his tone was dark and ominous. "It is black art you seek now, my friend, and such is never without a price."

Uther exhaled sharply, an annoyed look on his face. "Spare me your riddles, Merlin. Have you what I need?"

Merlin sighed and answered simply. "Yes."

"Good." Uther snapped his response, and he trod forward, as if his interest in the hunt had been momentarily renewed.

Merlin followed behind his friend, silent but deep in thought and very troubled. I am losing you, Uther, he thought sadly. You are going down a dark road, and I fear you will allow none to deter you. Always shall you be my friend, yet now must I look to what will follow you. An heir now is more important than ever. I will help you free Igraine, but the cost is like to be more than you now comprehend. Forgive me, my friend.

The heralds rode forth from Caer Guricon, bound for Tintagel Castle and the strongholds of the other kings of Britannia.
The monarchs were ordered to make themselves ready to travel
to Caer Guricon, for King Gorlois was accused of conspiring
with Vortigern's son, Vortimer, and the Saxons to seize the high
kingship.

The proclamation was signed by Uther Pendragon, but it
had been written, every word of it, by Merlin. It is with deep
sadness that High King Uther must call the assembled kings
of Britannia to hear evidence and pass judgment on Gorlois,
King of Cornwall on charges of high treason. So it began, and
it went on in excruciating detail to list a series of offenses that,
if proven, would warrant deposition and execution. The document was beautifully worded and carefully constructed, and vir-
tually every word was a fabrication.

The proclamation was greeted with surprise by most, for ten
years had passed without any unrest in the land, and conspiracy
was now unlooked for. But few of the kings thought well of
Gorlois and, indeed, many of them were secretly pleased at the
prospect of his downfall. All responded with messages of support and promises to do as King Uther bade them. Gorlois
would be tried by his fellow kings, and his guilt would be proven
or disproven.

In Tintagel the parchment was received with shock and
anger, for Gorlois had, in fact, done nothing at all. Though he
despised Uther Pendragon, he had been totally loyal both during and after the war. In truth, he would have betrayed Uther if
he'd had the opportunity, but the high king was strong, and fear
had stayed Gorlois' hand all these years. A lengthy response was
hastily drafted, expressing outrage at the accusations and declar-
ing Gorlois' innocence. It was sent by courier to Caer Guricon
and to every court in Britannia.

Merlin, no stranger to complex manipulations, urged Uther
to bide his time and repeat his demand that Gorlois present
himself. Indeed, he had been so ordered in the first proclamation, and he was therefore in violation of the high king's edict.

But while he had not come to Caer Guricon as he was commanded to do, he had responded to the summons respectfully and in great detail.

"Patience will help to put the other kings at ease, Uther" Merlin was beseeching his old friend. "If you move too swiftly it will create unease and suspicion."

But Uther Pendragon was not a man to heed counsels of caution, and having decided on his course of action, he was determined to proceed without delay. "Igraine has been a prisoner in that hateful castle for far too long. It is long past time I finish this. I will march on Cornwall and take Tintagel Castle."

They sat in the great hall at Caer Guricon, as they had so many times before. Long into the night they spoke, but try as he might, Merlin could not sway Uther. Next to them sat plates of food, picked at but largely uneaten, and a flagon of ale, still full, now stale and flat. Servants would have cleared the plates and refreshed the ale, but Uther had angrily ordered them out hours earlier. They cowered in the kitchen, uneasy at not serving the king but too scared to risk his temper again.

Uther loved Merlin above all other men, and he thought of him as a father and a friend, an advisor and a confidante. Though no force on Earth would sway him from his intended path, still he sat and listened to Merlin's arguments, when he would have sent anyone else fleeing angry taunts and thrown pewter. When the old man finally gave up and ceased his debates, Uther slowly rose, his joints stiff and slow from long hours in his chair. "Merlin, my oldest friend and ally, I know that you do not agree with me in this, but I must do what I must do. Give me your aid in this endeavor, as you have in all other things, for though I will still proceed without it if need be, I am grateful for your cunning and support."

Merlin looked sadly back into the fire and softly sighed. "You shall have my support, Uther, as you always have. And always shall."

"Thank you, old friend." The king turned away, the sound of his boots echoing on the hard granite floor as we walked toward the corridor that led to his chamber.

Merlin sat unmoving. His eyes, unseen at that moment by any other, betrayed a deep sadness as they stared into the flames. Indeed, my friend, he thought, I shall support you, though you do not imagine the form that shall take. Resolved you are to seek your doom, and no power I have can stop that. If you are to take this step then Igraine becomes vital, for an heir is like to be the only way to save your house.

Merlin could see what lay ahead, and he knew the part he must play. Many kings had he served, yet he had loved none as he did Uther Pendragon. Long he sat alone in the hall, thinking of days past and feeling the weight of his many years, until the shafts of dawn light pierced the clerestory windows and brightened the darkness. Finally, achingly, he rose and made his way slowly to his chamber.

Though he had retired very late, Uther Pendragon rose early and stormed around the castle issuing one command after another. "Bring me Kelven and Eldol at once." The servants and soldiers hurried to obey the king's orders, and all of Caer Guricon was in an uproar. Servants brought breakfast into the great hall, but Uther ignored the food, taking only a cup half-filled with ale as he bellowed orders to his assembled advisors.

"Where are Kelven and El..." Uther stifled his question as his two captains came rushing into the hall, hurriedly bowing before the king. Uther motioned for the two to sit, then pointed toward empty chairs. "Come, my friends. Break the fast with me, for we have much to plan." Uther tore off a small piece of bread from a large loaf and motioned again, this time for his companions to eat. "We will be marching for Cornwall. Gorlois has disobeyed my command, so I will take Tintagel Castle by storm and enforce my justice."

Kelven had a somber look on his face, and he sat quietly, not eating anything. Eldol had taken some fruit and a small piece of salted pork. He looked concerned, though not as glum at Kelven. Uther saw his captain's concern. "Speak freely, Kelven. Never shall I be so complacent as to ignore the thoughts of my great war captain."

Kelven was hesitant. He had known Uther since the king was a baby, but he was still uncomfortable disagreeing with his sovereign. "My king…Tintagel is one of the strongest fortresses in all Britannia. We must prepare much for such a siege, and build up a great store of supplies. It will take long to call in all the levies and rally the kings."

Uther looked over and motioned toward Eldol, who quickly swallowed a piece of salt pork he'd just shoved in his mouth. "My king, I must agree with Kelven. Tintagel is hardly approachable by land. Without a fleet we will be forced to attack across the narrow causeway. It will be costly."

"And with a fleet? For I have dispatched an embassy to King Pellinore bidding him sail his ships to Cornwall and aid us. Tintagel shall receive no supply from the sea."

Kelven was unconvinced, but he knew Uther and understood that when the king set his mind to a thing nothing could deter him. "What are your commands, sire?"

"We leave in one week." Uther's voice was hard and determined, and he ignored the looks of shock on his captain's faces. "I want the levy assembled and ready to depart seven days from now."

Eldol glanced at Kelven, who had been in Uther's service longer, but the old captain shook his head briefly, warning him off. His mouth had opened, but he closed it without speaking. Finally it was Kelven who broke the silence. "Yes, my king. It will be done." He then stood and bowed before Uther. "I beg your leave to go, for Eldol and I have much work to do."

Uther nodded his assent, and after they had turned to leave he spoke softly so no one could hear. "I am coming, Igraine. This time no one shall hinder me."

The summer had been hot and long, and the army of Uther Pendragon marched slowly on dry, dusty roads. Though the king drove his men hard, they could make but 7 or 8 miles a day in the scorching heat, lest men and horses begin dying along the trail in even greater numbers. The force was small for, though Kelven and Eldol worked day and night, it had proved impos-

sible to assemble the entire levy of Powys in seven days, and no
detachments from the other kings had arrived by the time they
left Caer Guricon.

On the twelfth day of the march they met Leodegrance and
those warriors of Cameliard he could quickly assemble. But
even combined, they were barely 2,500 strong. Merlin rode
with Uther, and his spirit was leaden. Even if the other kings
responded to Uther's call, their troops would be many weeks
behind, and winter would be approaching before they could
arrive. He was sure that Urien, at least, would send forces, but
his troops had even greater distances to march.

Uther was untroubled, however. His rigid determination to
destroy Gorlois and free Igraine from her marriage had blinded
him to all fear and reason. Never a cautious man, he had become
driven and reckless, and he could not be persuaded to wait until
all his forces had assembled.

Gorlois had sent new messengers, repeating his claims of
innocence, but Uther would not receive them. Uther's lords and
men were loyal, but they wondered why the high king was so
driven to move on Gorlois before the army was ready. Surely,
even if the king of Cornwall was guilty of treason, there was no
immediate threat.

They entered Cornwall unopposed, and at last the heat
broke and autumn came, bringing with it torrential rains and
turning the dusty roads into impassable quagmires. Tintagel was
in the extreme west of the kingdom, many days march from the
borders, and Uther's forces continued their relentless advance.
Halfway between the frontier of Cornwall and Tintagel, they
came upon Gorlois' army blocking the road, formed for battle.

Before the defending troops there was an embassy, and they
rode toward Uther's army under flag of truce. They were led
by Hurrin, one of the highest-ranked lords of Cornwall, and
one of Gorlois' few real friends, and they were taken to a hastily
pitched tent wherein the high king of Britannia sat upon a camp
stool awaiting them. Tall and clad in spotless armor and livery,
Hurrin knelt before Uther, waiting for permission to speak. The
king, by contrast, wore armor soiled from the field and an old

and faded tunic bearing the Pendragon heraldry. Uther was a warrior, and he had little use for the finery of court. He looked at the visiting lord, his face impassive. "You may speak, Hurrin. I will hear your embassy."

The visitor hesitated for a moment. Uther's tone was icy, and though he had not raised his voice, Hurrin was intimidated nonetheless. "King Uther, I am here to assure you most profoundly that King Gorlois is, as ever, loyal to your majesty. I have been sent to plead this case and to reaffirm the loyalty of the king and all Cornwall to your high kingship."

Uther waited for Hurrin to complete his speech. He sat upon his stool unmoving, a graven image of solid, unyielding granite. His voice, when he spoke, projected utter finality. "You speak lies, Hurrin, or you are a fool. For your lord" - Uther deliberately avoided calling Gorlois a king - "was commanded to present himself at Caer Guricon. Instead of obeying, he sent ambassadors with more lies. And now, an army of Cornwall lies before me. What purpose has this? Think you 'tis loyalty to bar the march of your high king with armed warriors?" Uther was becoming angry, his voice rising like a gathering storm. "Your lord may be convicted from his own deeds, for it was treason to disobey my command to appear, apart from his former actions that prompted that by edict. And now, yet again, he proves himself a traitor for sending his army against his lawful liege." His voice had reached a crescendo, and all in the tent cringed at the unleashed fury of Uther Pendragon.

Uther rose, the stool tumbling behind him as he walked toward Hurrin. "Go now, and tell your lord that he has condemned himself. I shall hang him as the traitor he is even if I must dig him cowering from the ruins of Tintagel. Go to your army and see what men you can rally to attack the high king of Britannia, for no quarter shall be given to those who do." Uther was a force of nature, and it took all of Hurrin's resolve simply to stand before the king and endure the withering barrage. "Now, begone, before I strike you down as a traitor yourself. You have one hour to clear your rabble from the road. If you do not, I shall."

Hurrin bowed low and hurriedly retreated from the tent. His orders were to stand and fight if he could not negotiate a truce, but his courage was beginning to fail. Uther's rage had unnerved him, for Hurrin had fought in the war against Vortigern, and he had seen firsthand how Uther dealt with those he perceived as treacherous. Gorlois was his lawful sovereign, yet Uther Pendragon was high king to whom he also owed allegiance. He could not obey one without betraying the other. In despair he thought to himself, what can I do?

Hurrin walked into his tent, waving off all who tried to follow him. He had ridden back from Uther's camp, saying nothing to his entourage. He rode back at such a pace they could barely keep up with him, and now he had stormed into his tent, closing the flap behind him.

"I would speak with you, Hurrin." The voice was familiar and mysteriously compelling. The figure in the corner of the tent was unmoving, clad in a gray, hooded cloak.

"Who is there? Merlin? Is that you?"

The figure remained motionless, his face hidden by the drawn hood. "I am a friend. An advisor. That is all you need know. Remember that and ask no more. I have counsel to offer."

He is here without Uther's knowledge, thought Hurrin. Perhaps Merlin would offer him a solution to his dilemma. "I would hear your counsel if you would offer it." He motioned for the visitor to take a seat, but the robed figure remained unmoving.

"You are at a crossroads, Hurrin. Do you side with Gorlois or with Uther? And, having made your choice, will the other lords and men adhere to your decision?" The gray visitor paused to allow Hurrin to consider the situation. "You have taken the field with Uther Pendragon before. Do you believe you can best him in battle? If you stand for Gorlois on this field you will die. Your men will die, for Uther will show no mercy to those who defy his will. You know this to be true."

Hurrin stood silently, listening to Merlin's words, and he began to hope. Perhaps there is an escape from this pending doom.

"Gorlois is lost. No man can now save him from his fate. I would not see you and your men slaughtered, nor Uther lose brave warriors in pointless battle. And I would spare Cornwall from the wrath of the high king should he believe the whole kingdom to be disloyal. Yet neither would I counsel you to join Uther and march on Tintagel, for such would be dishonorable, and would breed dissension in your ranks."

Merlin paused once again, as he could see that Hurrin was paying heed to his words, and he wanted to give him time to consider. "If you would take my counsel, go you now, before Uther's deadline has passed, and declare to your lords and men that you cannot honorably war against either the king of Cornwall or the high king of Britannia. State that you will return to your own keep and you give leave to all to do what their hearts dictate. Those who would fight for Gorlois will be allowed to march to Tintagel Castle. Any who would join King Uther are free to do so. Those who feel as you do may depart and return to their homes with honor."

Hurrin stood silently for a moment, considering his options. "But, Mer.., sir, would not Uther be wrathful were I to leave the field and not support his cause?"

"Nay. You likely will not be in great favor, but you will not be punished, for the high king will recognize your act as an honorable one. Indeed, he will suspect the motives of those who would so easily abandon their king to join his standard."

Hurrin considered his options for another moment, but he knew he had no choice. "I thank you for your counsel. I shall do as you propose."

The gray-clad figure bowed slightly, and without a sound slipped out of the tent and was gone.

The army of Cornwall had broken up. The lines of battle disintegrated as men streamed back to camp. Tents were struck and possessions gathered, and men departed in various directions. Several hundred crossed the field, offering their services to Uther's army. Some were veterans of the old war who had fought closely alongside the high king, though others were simply opportunistic, choosing the side they thought would win. Another group formed up to march to Tintagel Castle to join the king of Cornwall. Mostly lords and retainers with especially close ties to Gorlois, they numbered perhaps five hundred in all.

The largest number, indeed two in three of those present, chose the same path as Hurrin, and they departed the field in every direction, bound for their keeps and homes and farms. Torn between loyalties and obligations, they would remain uncommitted.

The force bound for Tintagel marched briskly, intent on reaching the relative safety of the keep as quickly as possible. But the trail wound for many miles through a deep forest, and they were strung out and slowed by the narrowness of the path. Hidden from view in the dense undergrowth, a gray-robed man crouched down, speaking softly with a richly attired warrior. "Are your men ready, Caradoc?"

Caradoc, the son of a great Visigothic lord and, by Uther's hand, a king these past ten years, turned to face his companion. "They are ready, Merlin. But I am ill at ease undertaking this action without King Uther's leave. Are you sure this is wise?"

Merlin put his hand on Caradoc's shoulder. "You are a true friend to Uther, this I know. I trust you have no doubts about my own loyalty to the house of Pendragon."

Caradoc answered abruptly, afraid he had inadvertently insulted his companion. "No doubts, Merlin. Indeed, none could question your devotion. But to draw first blood in this affair without the high king's consent?"

I have to tell him more, thought Merlin. "Caradoc, we share a love of Uther, yet be both know he is not a cautious man. He marches on Gorlois ill-prepared, with only those levies he could gather quickly. I have, with words, dispersed the greater part of the army of Cornwall, yet still these hundreds remain pledged to Gorlois. Tintagel is one of the greatest fortresses in Britannia. We cannot allow it to become more strongly held than already it is. Uther would dash his army to pieces against its great bastions. We must make certain these warriors never reach their destination."

Caradoc exhaled loudly. He was still worried, but he could not escape the conclusion that Merlin was right. Uther Pendragon had taken him into his inner circle, rewarded him with trust and friendship, and finally given him a crown. He would do whatever he must to protect the high king. He would face Uther's legendary anger if needs be, but he would not allow his friend to face peril that he could reduce. "Very well, Merlin. I am with you."

It started in the rear of the marching force, warriors charging through the woods, smashing into the shocked men of Cornwall. The surprise was total, and many of the defenders were slain before they could mount a strong resistance. In other areas along the line they began to flee, but Caradoc had men waiting on the other side of the trail, and all who ran that way were slain.

On the path itself, some of the men of Cornwall managed to put up a stronger defense, and Caradoc's troops began to suffer losses as well. Near the front of the column a group of defenders had rallied around one giant warrior, and all about them lay the bodies of the attackers. It was Caradoc himself, and five other warriors, the last remaining of the ten who had accompanied him to Britannia, who charged in and overwhelmed the holdouts. When it was over, two of the brave Visigoths had fallen, and Caradoc himself had struck down the massive Cornish warrior.

Finally, the last of the defenders had been slain, and a grim quiet settled along the path. Caradoc's men gathered their wounded and counted their dead. They had lost fifty killed and ninety hurt from their total of six hundred. Around them, on the path and in the surrounding woods, lay five hundred of their enemies slain or dying. Merlin walked up to Caradoc, who was bleeding from a wound to the shoulder, the last blow of the giant of Cornwall. "Let me tend to that, lest it fester."

Caradoc seemed unconcerned about the injury, but he allowed Merlin to bind it. He winced when the old man sprinkled some yellow powder in the gash. "By god, Merlin, what is that? Powdered fire?"

Merlin smiled as he wrapped the shoulder in clean linen. "It will cleanse the wound and speed the healing. By the time battle is joined at Tintagel you will ready again for the fight."

Caradoc looked down at the ground silently for a few moments, then back at Merlin. "We shall soon meet with Uther, for he cannot be but a few miles east of here. Whether he shall embrace me or hang me I know not. But I would not have done other than I have."

Tintagel Castle rose above the sea, a dark monolith against the setting sun. Built by the Romans centuries earlier, it had been expanded and strengthened by Gorlois' line, the dukes of Cornwall. On three sides the sea crashed against the rocks below the great battlements, and on the land side were two great towers and a massive oaken gate.

Before that gate was arrayed the army of Uther Pendragon. Five times they had assailed the walls, and five times they had been thwarted by the nearly impregnable fortifications. Now the sounds of axes and tools could be heard all day as they felled trees and built siege engines of every manner. Four large ballistae they had already constructed, and even now these hurled great stones against the walls day and night.

They had suffered painful losses in the failed attacks, but reinforcements had arrived from Powys and Cameliard, and with these added to Caradoc's men, their numbers had swelled to 3,500. The defenders had also lost men, and fewer than 800 remained to man the walls.

Standing next to the largest of the ballistae, as the crew levered a large boulder into place, Leodegrance directed the siege operations. He was troubled over the entire affair and, indeed, he had thrice argued with Uther, beseeching his friend to pull back and seek a negotiated resolution. The last time the exchange had ended badly, with the first cross words the two had ever exchanged.

But Leodegrance's loyalty was absolute, and though he disapproved, he would help Uther with all his strength. Indeed, his close direction of the ballistae had been fruitful, and they were near to collapsing a section of the wall. They would continue to fire all night, and while the crews would be replaced, Leodegrance would remain. He had been two nights without sleep; this would be the third. But he was confident they could complete the breach by sunrise, and he would not be distracted. If he could not dissuade Uther from this course of action, he would see it done as quickly as possible.

The night was without a moon, and in the inky blackness, men in five boats rowed from the far side of the fortress. They had quietly filed out of a sally port on the seaward wall, carrying their small craft down to the water's edge. Uther had resolved to cut off Tintagel by sea, but King Pellinore's ships had not arrived, and the sallying force reached the shore undetected. One hundred strong, picked men all, they stealthily made their way toward the siege engines. One man in five carried a cask of oil, for it was their intent to burn the ballistae that had been so effective under Leodegrance's direction. They crept to within ten yards of the nearest ballista, and on a pre-planned signal, they threw their javelins at the crew.

Five men went down, and a few seconds later the attackers were on them, dispatching the wounded men and assailing those still standing. The defenders shouted the alarm, but already Gorlois' men had broken casks of oil on two of the great catapults, and a moment later both were engulfed in flames. The alarm roused Uther's men, and they had begun to rally. The raiders were soon fighting for their lives well short of the other two ballistae. They fought briefly, pushed back by the growing numbers of their adversaries. Finally, they fled back to their boats, their pursuers close behind. Two boats managed to escape, carrying fewer than half those who had sallied out. The sortie was over. It had been a partial success, but a costly one.

Uther's tent was on the far side of the camp, and by the time he arrived the battle was over. The two ballistae burned brightly, giant torches lighting the area where the fight had occurred, an area now littered with dead and wounded. As he approached, a great wail began to rise from the warriors around the stricken engines. A warrior staggered around from behind the great fire. "He is down. King Leodegrance is down. He is gravely wounded."

Uther ran to the man and grabbed him roughly on the shoulders. "Where is he? Where is Leodegrance?" His voice was harsh and urgent.

Before the dazed warrior could answer, Uther saw a small group of men clustered about a figure lying on the ground. Shoving the distraught man out of his way, he ran to the spot and saw the stricken king of Cameliard. A javelin had pierced his chest, and his tunic was soaked with blood.

Logan, one of his captains, knelt beside him. He saw Uther and looked up. "I bade him wear his cuirass, but he was too fatigued, and he would don naught but this soft leather." The man, a grizzled warrior who had fought many battles alongside Uther and Leodegrance, was choked with tears. "It is mortal, King Uther. King Leodegrance is dying."

Uther pushed everyone aside and knelt over his stricken friend. "Leo, it is Uther. Can you hear me?" His voice was broken and strained with emotion.

Leodegrance turned his head and looked up at Uther. His eyes were glistening and unfocused, and his lips were slick with blood. He struggled to speak, and when he did his words were bitter. "Curse this war of yours, for only ill shall come of it." He coughed and tried to spit the blood from his mouth, but it just dribbled down his cheek. "What has become of my friend, Uther Pendragon? Down what wrong path have you turned my old companion. God had judged me for following you. I pray he has mercy on you."

He let out a great breath and faded away. Uther commanded the unconscious king be borne to his tent, and he ordered his own healer sent to his friend's side, though he knew it was hopeless. Uther stood there long after Leodegrance had been carried away, and for a moment he was uncertain. I have been the cause of this, he thought. No man more just has ever lived than Leodegrance. It is my fault. Forgive me, my friend.

But soon his rage began to build. "Cursed Gorlois," he whispered, his voice dripping with hate. "Leodegrance is a better man than you or I. You shall not outlive him." He strode purposefully back toward the center of the camp. "Kelven! Eldol! Rouse the men. We take Tintagel Castle at dawn."

Merlin could hear the sounds of the army forming for the final assault, but he ignored it as he looked down at Leodegrance. Usually impassive and unreadable, his eyes betrayed great sadness. "This entire endeavor is evil, and I fear only more ill shall come of it." He stared at the wounded king. Soon the death struggle would begin.

For long Merlin stood there, having banished all others from the tent. Finally, he made a decision. "No. This is too much injustice. You are a man of untainted honor, perhaps the only one I have met in my long lifetime. I shall not allow you to die in this sorry affair."

Merlin breathed deeply, for what he intended to do was not easy, and it would drain him greatly. "Have I even the strength remaining to do this?" He whispered to himself, his voice barely audible. Slowly, he pulled back the cloth of Leodegrance's tunic , exposing the terrible wound. His men had broken the javelin, but they had not dared to remove the point from the king's chest. Indeed, thought Merlin, the blood loss will be enormous. I must be careful.

He reached into the pockets of his robe and pulled out two vials. One, which held a clear liquid, he placed against Leodegrance's lips, carefully pouring some into his mouth and raising his head so the fluid would slide down his throat. "This will slow your body, my friend. You will seem almost as if death has taken you, but you shall be only in restful slumber, and it shall greatly slow the bleeding."

He pulled the cork from the second vial, and almost immediately the room was filled with a pleasing scent, and the smell of blood and death was driven from the room. Merlin looked at the vial, which held but a few drops of thick, pink liquid, and he spoke softly to himself. "Many years has it been since I have seen the plant that bore this nectar, and I fear that these few droplets are all that remain in this world. I pray this be enough, for this worthy man deserves not this mean death."

Merlin grabbed the end of the javelin point and pulled hard. It resisted at first then came free, leaving a large hole in Leodegrance's chest. Blood welled up from the wound, though far less than would have normally. Merlin poured the droplets from the vial into the wound and then bound it tightly in clean cloth. Then he sat next to Leodegrance, his hand over the wound, and he began to chant softly, calling on the last traces of powers and forces that had all but passed from this world.

"Rouse yourselves men, for today we take Tintagel Castle. Therein lies a traitor, a foul creature who compounds his treason by sending assassins in the night to fell brave Leodegrance." Uther was mounted upon his great black steed, and he rode along the line as he spoke. "Let nothing stop you today. Many battles have we fought, brave warriors, and much glory have you reaped."

The men responded, for Uther was a great warrior and an inspiring leader. But the cheers were subdued, not what they had been ten years before when the mere site of Uther cause hysteria in the ranks. The old magic was gone, replaced with a grudging sense of duty. They knew they were here because of some treachery Gorlois had allegedly committed, but they didn't relish fighting against old allies who had stood with them in the war against Vortigern. They couldn't understand why they had been rushed here before they could properly prepare and rally all their numbers. They were loyal to Uther and would follow him where he commanded, but they were troubled. Something seemed somehow...wrong.

"Follow me now men, and we shall end this fight today! We shall enforce our justice and return to hearth and home, wife and family." With that Uther dismounted - horses were of little use in attacking a fortress - and, sword pointed forward, he ran toward the partial breach.

Their king's rally overcame their doubts and, with one massive shout, the army surged forward, following Uther to victory or death. The defenders stood upon the battlements, and when the attackers reached the base of the walls they hurled javelins and dropped stones and vats of oil upon them. The attackers placed their scaling ladders and climbed up, seeking to attain the battlements. Many were repulsed, their ladders overturned or oil poured on the men as they climbed. But in two places the troops reached the top, and the first men to seize the positions held fast while their comrades streamed up and over the crenellated walls.

At Leodegrance's breach, the wall had partially collapsed, and Uther was the first up and over, followed by Kelven and Eldol leading the pick of the men of Powys. They crashed into the defenders and the battle was joined. Uther fought as he had never done before, and around him lay the bodies of every enemy who dared approach. At first the defenders held, bolstered by the men on the walls above throwing down stones and javelins. But more and more of Uther's men poured through the gap, and soon the Cornish warriors were overwhelmed and driven back.

Along the wall to the south, Caradoc's men had taken the battlements and one of the towers, and they were even now streaming into the courtyard, pursuing the routed defenders. Tintagel Castle was doomed, with attackers pouring through the defenses at multiple locations.

Uther ran forward toward the main keep, Gorlois' residence. Four Cornish warriors burst out of the entrance and ran to the king. Kelven ran after him, with a group of Powys troops, but before he could get there, Uther had slain all four attackers and pushed his way inside. Kelven swore under his breath and raced to follow his king into Gorlois' last bastion.

"Get the girls ready. We must leave here now." Gorlois spoke harshly to his wife, and he slammed the door as he left the room without another word.

Igraine knew something had been happening for weeks now, and for the last few days it had been obvious the castle was under siege. But Gorlois had kept her locked in her room and would tell her nothing, becoming angry if she even asked. She still had bruises from the last time she had tried.

She did not want to leave, preferring to take her chances with an unknown enemy than to flee with her monster of a husband. But she knew Gorlois would never allow her to remain, and she would only earn another beating if she insisted. Besides, she would never take such a chance with her daughters.

She began packing a few items into a small leather bag. "Anna, Morgan. Come here, girls. We are going on a trip." She couldn't understand. If Cornwall were under attack by some invader, would not Uther as high king come to aid Gorlois? My God, she thought frantically, could some enemy have already defeated my beloved Uther? She couldn't imagine that was the case, for Uther was the greatest warrior in Britannia, and his victory in the last war had been total. But now she fretted for him and longed to know what was happening.

"Anna, Morgan. Come to me now." She opened the door to the room where the girls slept and peered inside. With a start she saw that the door leading into the corridor was ajar. Hurrying across the room she ran out into the hall. "Anna, Morgan. Where are you, girls?" Her voice was shrill with worry.

She heard the sounds of fighting and then Anna calling to her. "Mother, the men are fighting. Father is fighting. Morgan is there." Her oldest daughter came bounding up the stairs and ran to Igraine, who threw her arms around the girl.

"Go back to your room, Anna." Igraine let go of the girl, who stood there next to her mother without moving. "Now, Anna. Back to your room." Igraine ran to the end of the hall and down the circular stairs. The sounds of fighting were closer now. She almost tripped and fell, but caught herself in time.

Igraine rounded the turn and came out on the landing. She stopped with a gasp. Morgan was on the other side of the room, pressed against the wall, and in between there were dead and wounded men. In the center of the room was Gorlois with two of his men fighting with an enemy. A moment later she shrieked. They were fighting Uther.

As she was watching, Uther ducked and sliced the throat of one of Gorlois' warriors, leaving a spray of blood hanging in the air for an instant as the man fell to the floor. The other warrior moved to attack, but Uther sidestepped his swing, which impacted hard on the floor. He tried to recover his balance, but too late. Uther has shoved his blade under his shoulder and into the chest cavity.

Gorlois leaned forward to attack, but Uther pulled his blade out of his last victim and turned to face his enemy, just as Kelven and three warriors came running onto the landing from the stairs opposite Igraine. They moved toward Gorlois, but Uther waved them off. "Let us finish this, Gorlois."

The king of Cornwall stood motionless, paralyzed with fear. There was death in Uther's eyes, and Gorlois new there was no escape. His heart was pounding, and his mind was wild with panic, for he knew this was the end. But then Uther saw Igraine standing against the wall by the stairs and his eyes fixed upon her. Seeing his chance in Uther's distraction, Gorlois lunged forward with his sword.

"Sire!" It was Kelven's panicked cry that warned the king. Uther's gaze shifted just in time. He moved aside and Gorlois' blade pierced his shoulder rather than his chest. The cold steel drove through his jerkin and into the flesh. Without so much as a shout of pain, Uther turned to face Gorlois, his sword poised to strike. When the blow came, it was driven home with such force that Gorlois' blade was knocked from his grasp and his arm was broken.

The king of Cornwall sank to his knees, shouting in pain and shaking with fear. "No!" shrieked Morgan as Uther raised his blade one more time. The child ran from where she had stood against the wall, trying to reach her father. But the killing strike landed before she could reach him, and she got there in time for him to fall to the floor at her feet, his blood splattering on her dress.

Igraine ran to Morgan and took the screaming girl into her arms, but she looked up at Uther. There he stood, his arm covered in blood from the terrible shoulder wound. Igraine stood in shock, and she longed to run to his arms. His tunic was torn and she could see something hanging around his neck. It was a ring on a chain. A ring she recognized immediately. Her eyes filled with tears as she realized what had happened. She was a prisoner no more. Her true love had come for her.

"Igraine." Uther's voice was gentle, soothing. "Comfort the child. For we shall have all the time we have been denied. I am here for you, and never again shall we be parted."

Chapter Nine
The Death of a King

493 AD
Caer Guricon, Capital of the Kingdom of Powys

"Leodegrance, you old dog!" Uther was jubilant. "Far too long has it been, my friend. Far too long." He wore a cheerful grin as he walked across the room and embraced his friend.

"Did you think I would let the birth of my best friend's first son go unheralded? Indeed, I am here bearing gifts, for soon all of Britannia will be sending treasures, and I would be the first. My heartfelt congratulations to you. Long you waited for your Igraine, my friend, and greatly have you both paid in pain and anguish. Now that she is your queen, and your son sleeps in his royal nursery, tell me, are you truly happy?"

Uther smiled broadly. "Yes, my friend, I am happy now, for Igraine and my son are most important to me of all things. And friends, like you, Leo. I feared that I had lost your friendship over that whole Gorlois affair. Indeed, I feared we had lost you entirely to that dreadful wound."

Leodegrance frowned slightly. "I still disapprove of your actions, Uther. I will not lie and tell you otherwise. But I, more than anyone, know how long you hurt and how desperately you ached for Igraine. Gods, it was all you could speak about even years ago, when we traveled to Italia. Truly, what happened to the two of you was a tragedy. And, certainly, Gorlois was a pig and no great loss to the world." Leodegrance paused briefly, and his frown gave way to a look of sadness. "But still, it was a black deed."

"Indeed." Uther looked sadly at his friend. "And now they call me wife-stealer and worse. After the victory over Vortigern they spoke of me with reverence and respect. Now they mock me and call me names they think do not reach my ears, and plots fester in every dark corner. Merlin warned me thus, yet still would I do what I have done."

There was an uncomfortable silence. Finally, Leodegrance spoke. "Has there been any word of Merlin?"

Uther looked down at the ground, his mood somber. "I have heard naught from Merlin since the day Tintagel Castle fell. It can only have been he who healed your hurt, my friend, for your wound was mortal. I had the field of battle searched and searched again, for fear that he had gotten caught in the fighting and had fallen. But all for naught. He has just vanished."

Leodegrance frowned for a moment, then smiled and clapped his hand on Uther's back. "Enough of such talk, for this is a happy occasion and I have gifts to give. For you, my friend, I have brought apples. The apples from Cameliard's first harvest are the best in Britannia, and I recall a certain prince of Powys who was quite fond of them at one time."

Uther laughed heartily. "Yes, my friend, I am still quite fond of apples, particularly the early ones when they still have their snap. An apple should bite back. You have my thanks."

Leodegrance smiled. "For Igraine I have brought many gifts, for she is far prettier than you, Uther."

They both laughed again, and Uther filled two goblets from a large flagon, handing one to Leodegrance. Uther raised his cup. "To old friends." He paused, then continued somberly. "And to fallen brothers."

"To old friends and fallen brothers." Leodegrance drank deeply, then placed the empty goblet on the table. "For your son, I have brought but a single gift. Though I know others will bring wagons of treasure, I resolved to give something of greater meaning. Long has this been in my family, and it is said to have brought divine protection to any who have worn it. Many challenges will your son face, my dearest friend, and I would that he wore this amulet. May it protect him and give him strength through all his trials." He held up a small talisman of finely worked silver. It was excellent work, and ancient, but on it, newly inscribed, was the name, Arthur.

Uther was touched, for he recognized the amulet; Leodegrance's father had worn it every time he went into battle. "I am without words, Leo. This is a treasure of your house. 'Tis a greater gift than a wagon filled with gold and jewels." Uther warmly embraced his friend. "Let us go inside, for we have much to discuss."

"Indeed, Uther." Leodegrance was suddenly very serious. "There is unrest among the kings. They fear that what happened to Gorlois could happen to them. They whisper about Igraine and say she bewitched you and you slew Gorlois to steal his wife. There are plots against you, and I fear there is great danger."

Uther looked at his friend and smiled weakly. "Indeed, my friend. I know much of this. Alas, for I would have Merlin's counsel now." He put his hand on his friend's shoulder. "But we shall talk of such later. For now, let me be the gracious host to an old friend. Let us talk of Italia and our times on the road."

Uther sat alone in the great hall. It was very late, and he was troubled and deep in thought. The fire had almost burned down to the remnants of one last log. A cup of ale sat forgotten on the table next to the remains of two apples - the last of the batch Leodegrance had brought.

The king of Cameliard had stayed for a week, and the two of them had talked of many things. Uther was happy that they had renewed their friendship, for they had seen little of each other these past few years, and there had been tension between them. But Leodegrance had also confirmed what Uther already knew but did not want to believe. There was worse than dissension in the land; there were already plots against him. He knew not who was involved, nor did Leodegrance, for he was known to be one of Uther's closest friends, and he would not be included in any treasonous cabals.

Uther considered what to do. Should he take the field? Against whom? He knew not who was friend and who was foe. God, Uther thought, I am tired in body and soul. Indeed, he feared not for himself, for such was not in his makeup. But Igraine and Arthur...and Anna - for so many years he had known nothing of his daughter - they must be safe.

Uther stared into the fire, not noticing the shadowy figure walking silently into the hall. "I see you still sit up late in this room, my friend. Many have been the nights that you and I have held this vigil together."

Uther leapt to his feet with such force his chair fell over, clattering loudly on the stone floor. "Merlin!" He rushed across the room and embraced his old friend and counselor. "Gods, Merlin, it is good to see you. Where have you been, my old friend? I feared for your fate."

"As I have feared for yours, and indeed still do." Merlin's voice was odd. There was happiness at seeing Uther after so long a time, but also sadness and loss. "I have been where I have had to be, my friend. I am old, and I grow weak. My power wanes."

Uther motioned for Merlin to sit as he reached over and set his own chair right. "I would have your counsel now, my old friend. And your forgiveness as well."

Merlin sat and put out his hands to the warmth of the fading embers. "There is naught for me to forgive, Uther. I am now and always have been your friend. Your actions were unwise, yet I understand the pain and need that drove them. You are a man, Uther, yet I fear we all wanted you to be a mountain made of stone. What we craved was too much for any man, even the great Uther Pendragon."

The old man - for the first time, Uther thought, Merlin looked truly old - dragged his chair closer to the dying fire. Uther could see the weariness in his friend, like his own, but with the weight of lifetimes pressing upon it. "And your counsel, Merlin? Will you help me, as you did of old?"

Merlin looked at Uther and managed an anemic smile. "What I have to give is yours, good friend. But I fear this time I know not how to heal what has been damaged." The smile drained from his face, replaced by a look of grave sadness and pain. "It may be, Uther, that it will fall to your son to rule a united Britannia."

Merlin's words hit Uther like a thunderclap, for the counselor had stated what none other would dare say to the king. He was silent for a moment, shocked. When he finally spoke his voice was soft and sad. "Has it come to that, Merlin? Is there no hope for me to restore the peace and stability of the land?"

"I know not, Uther. The kings feared you before, but they believed you just, and so they respected the high kingship and obeyed you. Now they only fear you, and fear turns easily to hate. Indeed, perhaps it has already so turned." Merlin paused, trying to decide if he should finish what he was going to say.

Finally, he continued. "Uther, it is possible you could crush all of the kings of Britannia, for you are the greatest warrior this land has seen, and in addition to your men of Powys, Leodegrance, at least, is loyal. Indeed, I believe that Urien would follow you, also. But such a course will bathe this land in blood such as we have never seen. For the enemy is less open now, and you will have to root out disloyalty wherever it has taken hold. Many who are innocent will die with the guilty. Famine and pestilence will ravage the land until the dead outnumber the living. Farms will burn and castles will fall. Are you ready to take such a road? Are you willing to do whatever it takes to crush any who oppose you and rule as a tyrant?"

Uther sat quietly, looking down as he rubbed his calloused hands slowly together. Finally he spoke. "No. I will not go down that road. I have lost the stomach for so much blood and suffering. I will not be a tyrant, hated by subjects who live their lives in fear and loathing." He looked at Merlin, his steely gray eyes dull and lifeless. "I would meet God with at least part of my soul still mine. I fear that those thousands I have sent to His judgment before me do not speak well of my virtues. Perhaps, however, I may yet avoid the fires of hell."

Merlin's heart ached for his friend. No man had bled more or struggled harder than Uther Pendragon. "You are a good man, my friend. Though my relationship with your God is uncertain, I feel your reckoning will be less grievous than you fear. You have sometimes erred, as all men do, but your heart is true."

The two sat long together, neither speaking, until finally the last embers had faded to gray ash and the first rays of dawn peaked through the great clerestory windows. Finally, Uther put his hand on Merlin's arm. "My old friend, I must ask something of you." Uther paused, trying to find the words he wished to say. "I have never allowed fear to govern me, Merlin, and I shall not begin now. Nor shall I allow it to compel me to actions I do not wish to take. If I attempt to uncover conspiracies, it will only further inflame the kings, for my actions would need be heavy handed were I to succeed. Indeed, men do not easily confess to treason. I will enhance the defenses and preparedness of Caer Guricon, but that is all. If that is not enough, then so be it." Uther rose slowly, stiffly. "I am fatigued, my friend, and though I do not think sleep will come, I will try nonetheless."

Merlin paused, but still Uther did not ask anything. "Goodnight, Uther, I will do all that I can to aid you."

Uther stopped at the oaken door that led to the main stair. He turned and looked at his companion. "Merlin, this is what I ask of you. Promise, should some doom befall me, that you will keep my family safe. I will meet whatever fate God has designed for me, but I would know that Igraine and Arthur and the girls come to no harm. In the last resort, Leodegrance will always offer them sanctuary. And guide Arthur when he is old enough to seek his birthright. Help him as you have always helped me. Promise me you will see to it."

Uther spoke as a man already condemned, and though it saddened Merlin to see him thus, he knew that this was as things must be. Were Uther to try to assert himself by force of might, it is possible he would prevail, yet this success would be fleeting. Merlin wished he could come to any other conclusion, but he knew the truth - that Uther could not now hold Britannia together, not in any lasting way. He was like to pay a great price for a fleeting few years with the woman he loved. "Of course, Uther, I shall protect them all with my life. Though let us not speak as if you are already gone."

Uther smiled warmly. "Thank you, Merlin. It puts my mind at ease to know you will be here for them should I fall. Goodnight, my friend."

Merlin felt pangs of guilt. For many years he had manipulated lords and kings, striving to heal the land. But Uther was special to him. He was tired in every fiber of his being, worn from lifetimes of manipulation. He longed to help Uther, but he knew to do so would likely condemn the young child, Arthur. It is in him our hopes for the future now lie, he thought as he walked silently from the great hall.

In the weeks following Merlin's return there were two assassination attempts. Both were thwarted by Kelven and Eldol, who had tasked themselves to keep the king safe. Indeed, the two were tireless, and at any time of the day or night, at least one of them could be found walking the halls of Caer Guricon, watchfully protecting the king.

They both bade Uther to call in the levy and march to face his enemies, but the king would take no action. King Pellinore was rumored to be involved in the plots, as was King Lot. A messenger had arrived from Urien with assurances of loyalty, seeking permission to take the field against Lot. The ambassador had been sent home with Uther's gratitude, but without leave to initiate hostilities.

Kelven and Eldol begged Uther to take action, but the king would do nothing except place more guards on his family. Always now, there were 100 men on duty at Caer Guricon, and Uther's tireless captains did all they could to protect their sovereign.

The attackers crept to the base of the hill of Caer Guricon in the pitch blackness of a moonless night. It took some time, but they finally found the secret passage they'd been told about. It was open, again as they had been told. There were seventy of them, skilled fighters all, and they had come for Uther Pendragon.

While the assassins crept through the narrow tunnel leading into the heart of Caer Guricon, throughout the castle, the men of the garrison were, one by one, falling into unconsciousness. Indeed, all who had drunk from the well had become first dizzy, then overcome with fatigue.

Eldol felt the strength draining from his body, and he staggered from his post, seeking Kelven to warn him. Finally, he stumbled through the door of Kelven's chamber and fell to his hands and knees. "We are poisoned. The garrison is poisoned. The well, it..." With that, the great warrior who had slain Hengist fell at Kelven's feet in deep slumber.

Kelven grabbed his sword from where he had set it a few hours before when he'd retired. There was no time to don his armor or aid Eldol. He stormed from the room, raising the alarm and calling to any of the guards who were still able to respond.

Uther, who had become used to lying awake nights, had fallen into a rare sleep, but he was awakened by the banging on the door. "Sire, forgive the intrusion. It is Kelven. We are under attack. The garrison is poisoned. You must come with me."

Igraine was also roused, and she sat up next to Uther, who leapt from the bed and unbolted the door. "Enter, Kelven. Tell me what is happening."

Kelven bowed quickly before Uther, and glanced briefly at Igraine. "My apologies, my lady." He looked back at Uther. "Most of the garrison have been rendered helpless. I fear the well was poisoned. Eldol himself warned me before he too faded to slumber. There are but few men fit for battle. We must get you to safety."

Uther turned to Igraine. "Wake the children. We must get you to a safe place until we can retrieve things." Igraine nodded and jumped to her feet, quickly disappearing through the door that led to the children's rooms.

"What men do we have, Kelven?" Uther was strapping his sword to his waist, even as he spoke.

"I have naught but two guardsman in the corridor, sire, though doubtless there are others still fit. I will find them."

Uther thought for an instant. "Nay, first we must get my family to..."

They were interrupted by Igraine's screaming in the next room. "Uther, I cannot find Morgan. She is gone!" She came running into the room holidng Arthur, with Anna following close behind.

Uther swore under his breath. "Kelven, get my family out of the castle. Take your two warriors and protect them with your life."

"Sire, I cannot leave you." The captain was anguished at the thought of abandoning the king.

"Kelven, obey my commands. I rely upon you in this. I put all that is valuable to me into your hands. Do as I say." Uther turned to Igraine. "Go with Kelven. Take Anna and Arthur. I will find Morgan." He looked into her beautiful emerald eyes one last time and kissed her. Then, he was gone.

Kelven led Igraine and the children down the main stairs toward one of the secret passages leading to the woods. He had resolved to get them out of the castle and then, if he could find none of the Pendragon retainers, to steal horses and ride to Caerleon. The king's family would be safe with Leodegrance.

At the base of the stair they turned left toward a small passage that was normally blocked by a closed portcullis, however the gate was open, and out of it came warriors, one after another. The leader spoke, his voice harsh and thick. "It is the king's family. Take them!"

Kelven sprung forward, swinging his blade with terrible resolve. He slew the warrior closest to him and then was upon the leader, with whom he traded great blows. His two men rushed forward and, for a moment, the three fighters of Powys held off ten times their number. But first one, then the other of Kelven's warriors fell, and the guard captain stood alone. At least ten of the invaders lay dead at his feet, and he bled from many wounds. Yet still he fought. Behind him, Anna crouched in the corner, Arthur cradled in her arms, and Igraine stood in front of her children holding a sword taken from one of the dead warriors.

At last, surrounded and overwhelmed by the numbers of the enemy, Kelven, the great captain of Caer Guricon fell, pierced in a dozen places. He lay on the cold ground, feeling his blood pumping from his body, and in his mouth was the bitter taste of defeat. As he faded to darkness he gasped his last words.

"Forgive me, my king, for I have failed thee."

The enemy warriors glowered at Igraine and Anna. They had suffered greatly in the fight, and while their orders were to take these women prisoner, they thought first to have some fun, for both were exceedingly beautiful. The leader, bleeding from a wound Kelven had given him, stepped forward, and with a great swing of his sword, he knocked the blade from Igraine's hands. He reached a filthy hand to her, grabbing the material of her dress to tear it off when his body froze and an unnatural fear took him. "Hold!" The voice was deafening, and none could disobey the command. There was a blinding flash in the room, and that was the last thing Igraine saw until she awoke hours later.

Uther Pendragon finally found Morgan in the kitchens behind the great hall. She stood near the door to the stairs and in her hands she held a key. On the table next to her was a large flask, now empty.

"Morgan, what have you done?" Uther was relieved to find the girl, but confused as well. "What are you doing here?"

She looked up at him and smiled, and in that instant he could see the face of Gorlois. "I have avenged my father, King Uther." She spat the word "king," pronouncing it with mockery. "I poisoned the well and opened the passage. I have brought House Pendragon down."

At that moment Uther realized what had happened, but it was too late. Enemy warriors streamed into the room from all of the entrances, and Uther found himself surrounded and over-whelmed. He fought with a terrible ferocity, and for a moment it looked as if he might somehow defeat every enemy within reach. But he was wounded, first in the leg, then in the arm, and finally he was pierced through his chest by a great spear. Still he fought on, covered in his own blood, and two more foes he dispatched before the last of his strength was gone and he fell to the stone floor. His enemies were on him, stabbing again and again, making certain their work was done.

Uther felt the first stab, but no more. He was floating now, and images passed before him. Days of his youth, playing in the castle courtyard with his brothers, the first time he had seen Igraine as a woman. Igraine...his hazy thoughts drifted back to Igraine. Is she safe? Was Merlin able to keep his promise to me? Such was his final thought as he at last gave in to the growing darkness and saw no more. Uther Pendragon was dead.

Igraine awoke lying in the back of a covered wagon. For a moment she thought she was in bed with Uther at Caer Guricon, and that she had awakened from a nightmare. But Uther was nowhere to be seen, only Eldol, who sat grimly beside her with his sword drawn and sitting on his lap. Beside her slept Anna. Morgan sat quietly on the other side of the wagon, a small smile on her lips.

"Eldol, where is the king?"

The captain looked at the queen, and in that instant she knew. "King Uther is dead, my lady." Eldol was a grim warrior, who had slain many men, yet tears streamed down his face.

Igraine gasped for air, for her grief was overwhelming. "No, it cannot be so. We had so little time together, my love." She wept uncontrollably. "And Arthur? Where is Arthur?"

Eldol swallowed hard, for he could not bear to say what he must. "The boy is also slain, my lady, and Caer Guricon is taken and burned. The Pendragon have fallen. I take you and your daughters to Leodegrance."

Igraine wailed in agony and heartbreak, and she cursed the fact that she had survived. "How did we escape?" Her voice was agony itself.

"It was Merlin, my lady. He saved you and your daughters from the assassins and bade me take you to Caerleon, to Leodegrance."

Anna had awakened, and she too sobbed piteously and threw her arms around her mother. Morgan just sat quietly in the corner of the wagon, saying nothing. She suppressed her slight smile, and thought to herself, father, I have avenged you.

Merlin walked swiftly from the ruins of Caer Guricon, carrying young Arthur, wrapped in a scrap of cloth. Nowhere will you be safe, young king, for your father's enemies will assail you wherever you are. I must allow all to believe that you are dead, slain in this treacherous attack, or I fear I shall be unable to protect you. To the east I shall bear you, to an unimportant place where no one will think to look.

Igraine, poor Igraine, he thought. I must let you believe your son is dead. Truly have I been your bane, though unwittingly so. And again I must hurt you, though it is only to protect your son...and the future of Britannia. I pray that one day you may forgive me for all I have done.

He walked down to the riverbank where the kings and lords had camped so many years before for Constantine's great council. There he walked up a gentle hillside, at the center of which stood a large outcropping of rock. Merlin carefully laid young Arthur on the cool, grassy hill and took a large canvas sack from under his robe. From the wrappings he pulled a sword. Not just any sword, but the blade of Constantine, Uther's grandfather. The sword of a Roman emperor. The sword that Uther Pendragon had wielded in his wars.

Slowly he walked toward the top of the great rock, careful not to lose his footing on the damp, moss-covered stones. Aloft he held the great sword, and he spoke loudly in an ancient and forgotten tongue. "Let this sword serve none but he to whom it rightfully belongs."

As he spoke the words he turned the sword over and drove the point deep into the center of the rock. Sparks flew all around, but the stone yielded until the blade was stuck deep, held fast in the solid granite.

Merlin pulled on the sword, but though he strained with all his might, he could not budge it from where it was lodged. Satisfied, he gently took Arthur into his arms and walked slowly away. When he reached the edge of the forest he glanced back over his shoulder, speaking softly to himself. "Only a true Pendragon shall remove the sword from the stone." He looked at the young child he carried. "You, Arthur. You shall be king of all Britannia."

By Jay Allan

Marines (Crimson Worlds I)

The Cost of Victory (Crimson Worlds II)

A Little Rebellion (Crimson Worlds III)

The First Imperium (Crimson Worlds IV)
(March 2013)

The Line Must Hold (Crimson Worlds V)
(July 2013)

The Dragon's Banner (Pendragon I)